LITTLE BLACK LIES

"A psychological suspense story smartly narrated...Zoe has a quick wit that emerges in wickedly unexpected ways."
—*New York Times Book Review*

"The suspense keeps building throughout until the shocking ending. This is a riveting debut from a promising new author."
—*Booklist*

"Heartbreakingly vulnerable and laugh-out-loud funny...I am a forever-fan of the Zoe Goldman series and will read anything Sandra Block writes. You should too."
—Lisa Scottoline, *New York Times* bestselling author

"*Little Black Lies* is a darkly intriguing mystery with a feisty young doctor as its protagonist. Sandra Block pulls you in deep and doesn't let go."
—Meg Gardiner, Edgar Award–winning author

"*Little Black Lies* is a daring, original debut that explores the dark side of memory. In Zoe, Block has created a character who is complicated, smart, and sympathetic. I can't wait to see what Block has in store for Zoe next."
—Heather Gudenkauf, *New York Times* bestselling author

THE GIRL
WITHOUT A NAME

ALSO BY SANDRA BLOCK

Little Black Lies

THE GIRL
WITHOUT A NAME

Sandra Block

GRAND CENTRAL
PUBLISHING

NEW YORK   BOSTON

ANTHEM
Written by Leonard Cohen
© 1992 Sony/ATV Songs LLC. All rights administered by Sony/ATV Music Publishing LLC., 424 Church Street, Nashville, TN 37219. All rights reserved. Used by permission.

Grand Central Publishing
Hachette Book Group
1290 Avenue of the Americas
New York, NY 10104

HachetteBookGroup.com

Printed in the United States of America

RRD-C

First Edition: September 2015
10 9 8 7 6 5 4

Grand Central Publishing is a division of Hachette Book Group, Inc.
The Grand Central Publishing name and logo is a trademark of Hachette Book Group, Inc.

The Hachette Speakers Bureau provides a wide range of authors for speaking events. To find out more, go to www.hachettespeakersbureau.com or call (866) 376-6591.

The publisher is not responsible for websites (or their content) that are not owned by the publisher.

Library of Congress Cataloging-in-Publication Data
Block, Sandra.
 The girl without a name / Sandra Block. — First edition.
   pages ; cm
 Summary: "From Sandra Block, another gripping page-turner featuring Zoe Goldman, the protagonist from Little Black Lies!" —Provided by publisher.
  ISBN 978-1-4555-8377-5 (softcover) — ISBN 978-1-4789-5976-2 (audio download) — ISBN 978-1-4555-8378-2 (ebook) 1. Women psychiatrists—Fiction. 2. Psychological fiction. I. Title.
 PS3602.L64285G57 2015
  813'.6—dc23   2015023342

For Patrick

Chapter One

We call her Jane, because she can't tell us her name.

Can't or won't, I'm not sure. She lies in a hospital bed, a strangely old expression upon her teenaged face. We don't know her age either. Twelve, fourteen maybe. A navy-blue hospital blanket sits across her knees in a neat square like a picnic blanket. A picnic in a hospital room, with a stained white ceiling for a sky and faded blue tiles for grass.

Dr. Berringer lifts the patient's arm, and it stays up, like a human puppet. "What do you think?" he asks.

"Catatonia," I answer. "Waxy catatonia."

"Bingo, Dr. Goldman," he says, his voice encouraging, with just a hint of New Orleans, where he's from. His voice doesn't match his face. He looks like a Kennedy, with sandy, wind-blown hair as if he just walked off a sailboat and blue eyes with lashes so long he could be wearing mascara. He is, in a word, handsome. He is also, in a word, married, much to the disappointment of the entire female staff at the

1

Children's Hospital of Buffalo. Let's just say the nurses perk up when Dr. Tad Berringer hits the floor.

Jane's arm drifts back down, her eyes still focused on the wall.

"But *why* is she catatonic?" I ask.

"That's the million-dollar question, isn't it?"

Jane Doe is our mystery. A police officer brought her to our doorstep this morning like a stork dropping off a baby. A few days ago, she was found wandering the streets of Buffalo, dazed and filthy, clothes torn, but apparently unharmed. No signs of bruising or rape. But she wouldn't speak. They coddled her, gave her hot chocolate (which grew cold in the mug), brought in a soft-speaking social worker, and Jane sat and stared. So the police canvassed the neighborhood, finger-printed her, ran her image through Interpol, put up missing posters adorned with her unsmiling, staring face.

NAME: UNKNOWN. RACE: AFRICAN AMERICAN. DOB: UN-KNOWN.

No one claimed her. They brought her to Children's and ran some tests. The ER said there was nothing wrong with her physically. So they sent her up to the psych floor. So we can figure out who she is and what's wrong with her.

"Schizophrenia maybe?" I ask.

"Could be." His eyes crinkle in thought. "But we also have to rule out other, less obvious causes." He leans over the bed and shines a penlight into her eyes. Her pupils con-tract, then bloom. "You ever hear of the hammer syndrome, Zoe?"

"No," I say, jotting this onto the back of my sheet.

"It goes like this: When all you have is a hammer, everything looks like a nail."

I stop writing, and he drops the penlight into his black doctor bag, smiling at me. "What can we establish here?" he asks, more a statement than a question. "Our patient has catatonia; that's all we know. So let's start with that. What's the differential for catatonia?"

"Schizophrenia."

"Okay, that's one."

"Right." I wait for the list to scramble into my head. That's the one good thing about ADHD. Alongside the scattered, ridiculous thoughts that pop up relentlessly (and which you have to keep banging down like a never-ending game of whack-a-mole) sprout elegant, detailed lists. Such as differential diagnoses. Lately that hasn't been happening for me, though. I don't know if my Adderall is working too well or not well enough. My dopamine isn't cooperating in any case, which is inconvenient, seeing as I'm on probation. My brain grinds on in slow motion with no list anywhere in sight, so I plow through the old standby mnemonic for the differential diagnosis of any disease. Something medical students learn the first day they step on the wards: VITAMIN D. Vascular, infectious, traumatic, autoimmune, metabolic, iatrogenic, neoplastic, degenerative.

"Status epilepticus," I say.

"Excellent thought. Did we order an EEG?"

"I will," I say, writing it in her chart.

"What else?"

A list crawls into my brain by inches. "Encephalitis?"

"Okay. Does she have a fever?"

I pull off the vital sheet hooked on the bed frame, scanning the blue, scribbled numbers from this morning. Vitals normal. "No fever, but it's still possible. Her labs are pending."

"Get neurology to see her. They can decide on a lumbar puncture. She'll probably need it, though, if the EEG is negative."

"They said she didn't need an LP in the ER."

He doesn't look impressed. "Just means the on-call didn't feel like it."

"We could get an MRI," I suggest.

"Fine. What are you looking for there?"

"Less common causes for catatonia...stroke, lupus, Hallervorden-Spatz," I say, cheered as the differential diagnosis list starts to soar in. "That could show up on MRI. PET scan, too."

"Let's start with an MRI," he says, tamping down my over-enthusiasm. "Let Neurology decide on the PET." Jane blinks, grimaces, then stares again. I hand Dr. Berringer her chart, which he balances in his palm, adding a couple of lines under my note then signing it with a flourish. He hands it back to me. "Onward and upward?"

We exit the quiet oasis of Jane's room, emerging into the hallway awash with hospital noises: the overhead speaker calling out, food carts rattling by with the malodorous smell of breakfast that no one will eat, medical students scampering around the floor like lost bunnies. Dr. Berringer's phone rings, to the tune of "When the Saints Go Marching In," and he picks it up as we head down the hall.

"Hello?" There is squawking on the other end. "She just showed up today." He listens a minute while we walk. "I'm sorry. I don't know any more than y'all." This is met with more squawking on the other end. "Right. Listen, I'll tell you as soon as I know something. I promise." He hangs up with an eye roll, smiling at me. "Admissions wants her demographic info. Jane Doe, folks. That's all I got." He strides in front of me into the nurses' station. Dr. Berringer has a jogger's body, long and lean, verging on skinny. He is tall, taller than me even, and I'm over six feet. As he leans in the door frame, a nurse, roundish in her lavender scrubs, openly gapes at him. "Any other consults come in overnight?" he asks Jason, who is sitting at the little brown Formica table, poring through a chart.

Jason adjusts his bow tie. He must have a hundred bow ties with matching shirts. I've never seen him repeat a color. "Three," he says. "I have two, and Zoe's got the new girl."

"And one more I haven't seen yet," I add. "Just came in this morning."

"So let's round later. Around two?" Dr. Berringer asks.

"That's good for me," Jason answers. Jason is chief resident, so he's in charge of rounding. I was all but promised the job when Dr. A (the smartest in our threesome and also the one who saved my life) transferred into the neurovascular fellowship. But then I was put on probation, so that was the end of that. Jason calls me Probation Girl.

"All right. See y'all later," Dr. Berringer says with a wave. His teeth are white-bright, bleached maybe, in perfect rows like pieces of Chiclets gum. My brother, Scotty, accuses me of having a crush on Dr. Berringer, claiming that "every sentence you say has his name in it," but he's exaggerating. If anything, it's a minor crush. Minimal.

"You want to bed that guy so badly," Jason says as soon as he's out of earshot.

"Please. That is beyond ridiculous."

"Whatever you say," he mutters, leaning over to grab another chart from the rack.

I crack open Jane's chart and finish off the orders. Neurology consult. IV fluids because she's not eating. DVT precautions because she's not moving. "Anyway, you're one to talk."

He pauses to think. "Okay, empirically he's good-looking, I agree with you. But he's just so...white." He pronounces the word with some distaste. Jason, being Chinese American, can say this.

"What about Dominic? Last I looked, he was white, too." Dominic is a nurse at the hospital and Jason's on-again, off-again boyfriend. Mostly off-again.

"Yeah, but he's Italian. He could pass as Hispanic or something. He's not Mr. Ralph Lauren."

"Sure, well, as long as he could *pass* as something ethnic." I shove Jane's chart aside, leaning back in the stiff, metal chair. "So are you back to dating Dominic this week?"

"I don't know. That guy's so hot and cold," he complains. "I see him at the bars and he's all over me. Then we come to work and he flirts with girls. I'm, like, just pick a goddamn team and play for it."

"You should just dump his ass," I say.

"Yeah, probably. Hey, speaking of dumping, whatever

happened with that French dude? You ever hear any more from him?"

"Who, Jean Luc?"

"Yeah. That boy was smoking hot."

Jason is right on that one. Jean Luc *was* smoking hot. Hotter than I am, that's for sure. I've always been a solid six, maybe seven on a good hair day. Jean Luc was more like an eleven, or a twelve. Still is, I imagine. "Not in a while," I answer. "Still with Melanie," I mention, before he can ask. Melanie, the model-beautiful girlfriend he left me for.

"Oh well. All's well that ends well," Jason says, meaning Mike. And he's definitely right about that one.

Jason turns back to his progress note, and I stash Jane's chart back in the rack, ready to see my next patient. On the way down the hall, I pass by Jane's room and see Dr. Berringer standing by the bed, staring at her. He lays his hand on her head, tenderly. Like a father patting his child's head.

Or a priest bestowing a benediction.

Chapter Two

It takes me a second to place him. A massive man in a saggy, black, windowpane suit, with his belly protruding over his belt, his hair in a thinning brush cut. He leans over Jane's bed.

"Detective Adams," I say.

He spins around and sees me in the doorway. It takes a second for him to place me as well. "Dr. Goldman," he returns. "I see your wound healed nicely." He points to his neck, referring to the scar on my neck where my patient stabbed me. Detective Adams was the officer on the case at the time. "And how are you on this fine day?"

"Good," I say, pausing to consider, then repeat, "good." Overall it's true, and he probably doesn't want the full backstory anyway.

"Have you heard from…your patient?" he asks.

I can tell he's not exactly sure how to refer to her, my patient who tried to kill me. "No. I'm on the prison's do-not-call list." That was after she left a fourth breathy message on my machine, sobbing about how sorry she was and begging me to please, please, please come and visit her. I let the first three messages slide. But the last one unnerved me a bit; she started talking about my birth mother. My brother called the prison to block her calls the next day.

"Good. Good to hear." Then he turns to Jane. "So what do you think of this one?"

"I was just going to ask you that." I walk over and take Jane's pulse, thready under my fingers. Her wrist stays elevated, then droops down. Jane is still Jane. Staring, unchanged.

Dr. Berringer comes into the room. "Hello." He nods to us both, which tells me he's already met the detective. "Any news on Jane?"

The detective frowns. "Nothing. And believe me, we're out there. We got posters up. We canvassed the neighborhood a tenth time."

Jane stares on in the silence.

"Do you think it would be any different if it were a white girl lying in the bed?" I ask. "I mean, there'd be TV crews and everything. I swear it's like nobody gives a damn."

"We all give a damn, Zoe," Detective Adams replies, sounding more tired than angry.

"I know. I'm not saying that you don't." I soften my voice. "I don't even know what I'm saying."

The detective stuffs his notebook in his breast pocket, the black stitching pouched at the corner. A tan, oblong coffee stain peeks out on the cuff of his sleeve. "Any idea when she'll start talking again?"

"*If* she'll start talking again," Dr. Berringer says. "Early days yet. We're still waiting on the LP." He looks to me to confirm.

I nod. "Neurology agreed to do it. And we have a few other tests pending."

The detective takes one more good look at Jane and turns away with a sigh. "Pleasure as always," he says to Dr. Berringer, then looks at me with an almost fatherly smile, like he would have tipped his hat if he'd been wearing one. "Good to see you, Zoe. You look great."

"Thanks," I murmur with some embarrassment. The last time he saw me, I was anemic in a hospital bed, tethered to an IV and hazy from pain pills. I would think, comparatively, I look like a billion bucks. Detective Adams leaves the room with the careful, bowlegged walk of knees that have played too much football. Dr. Berringer and I stand in silence broken only by the sound of the IV bag dripping.

He leans an elbow down on the bed in the small white space beside the lumpy outline of Jane's leg. The bed lets out a mechanical moan, moving to accommodate the new weight. This drove me crazy when I was in a hospital bed after my patient tried to kill me.

"Jane, Jane, Jane," he says, his voice tender. "When are you gonna talk to us, girl?"

Jane blinks twice, in some indecipherable code, and stares off again.

Over the gaggle of neurology residents, I see Jane curled in the shape of a crescent moon, her cocoa skin taut over her vertebrae.

"Was she given a sedative?" I ask.

"No need," answers Mary, chief resident of the neurology group. The first-year resident holds the test tube of clear spinal fluid, the finest tremor jostling the liquid. "But we numbed her up good," she says. "All bones. One-two-three. Easy-peasy." Mary has an odd, clipped speech pattern. The first-year switches tubes, a few drops of spinal fluid hitting the sheets in the transfer, and fits the tube into the holder with a squeak. The whole setup reminds me of my fifth-grade chemistry set, pouring one clear tube into another and watching when, like magic, an inky purple blooms. I don't envy the resident, though. I don't go anywhere near needles if I can help it. Psychiatrists and blood, we don't mix.

"Be done here in a jiffy," Mary says, which is my cue to make haste. The first-year is labeling the tubes with stickers.

"And if she gets a headache?"

Mary looks up at me. She doesn't quite hit five feet, so it's a stretch. "Don't see her complaining about it. But if so, give us a buzz."

"Okay." I linger one more second over poor Jane, contorted on the bed with a three-way stopcock jutting out of her back. But there is no other way. If she has encephalitis, we have to find out. A positive spinal tap could be her saving grace.

I get back to the nurses' station with every intention of hitting the UpToDate review on catatonia, but first I decide to put my chin in my hand and rest my eyes for a second. I am just drifting off when I startle awake to the sound of Jason whistling "Jessie's Girl." The tune bores a hole directly into my brain. I was on call last night, and between three new-onset deliriums and one acute psychosis, sleep was not in the cards.

"Bad night?" Jason asks, writing out a note.

I yawn. "You could say that."

"I had a lo-o-o-ng night, too."

"I so don't want to hear about it."

"What about you? How's Mike?" Jason asks.

"Mike's good," I answer.

"Good good? Or he's-a-bastard-and-I'm-not-talking-about-it good?"

"Good good. But seeing as I've been here since yesterday," I grumble, "he didn't rock me all night long as you're implying Dominic did."

"Honey, I'm not *implying* anything."

Dr. Berringer appears in the doorway then, leaning one hand against the frame. His gold wedding ring glints in the sun. "Zoe, you look beat. Rough night, champ?"

This makes me think of a boxer dog we had when I was six years old, named Champ. My mom named him after some tearjerker boxing movie. Champ was forever sneaking into the laundry room and eating underwear, which is really all I remember about him. Until he was hit by a car a year later. So he's probably up in doggy heaven snacking on a roomful of undergarments.

"Zoe?"

We are halfway down the hallway, though I don't remember walking there. Night call and ADHD have never been a winning combination. "Sorry, I was just thinking."

He smiles. "Anything interesting?"

"Not really. I once had a dog named Champ."

He stares at me, bemused. "Congratulations. I once had a dog named Lacy." He pauses. "She was an Alsatian. Lacy the Alsatian." An orderly walks by us, whistling. (I swear it's "Jessie's Girl" but I'm probably having auditory hallucinations by now.) "All right, Jason, who do we got?"

"Let's start with Mr. Gonzalez."

"Okay, what's the bullet on that one?"

"A nineteen-year-old Hispanic male with the known diagnosis of schizophrenia, brought in by his wife with an acute exacerbation."

"Okeydokey. Let's go."

As we enter the patient's room, the body odor is so overpowering that I have to breathe out of my mouth. He weighs in at 403 pounds, his blanket a mountain around him. The lines on his neck are caked with dirt, and his fingernails are tan with nicotine. "Daisy deals with daily deals, dozens of daily deals." He pauses then, smiling, his eyes glittering with joy. "Don't dally. Don't dally. Daisy doesn't dawdle, does she?"

I have no answer to this. I don't know any Daisy or if she tends to dawdle.

"Mr. Gonzalez," Dr. Berringer says, standing next to the bed.

The patient looks up like the doctor is in on the joke.

"Name, game, same, game, shame. No shame in a name game. Can't tame the name game, said the same dame."

Dr. Berringer looks delighted. "Okay, what type of speech is this?" he asks, turning to Jason.

"This would be clanging speech," Jason answers.

"Clang-a-lang-a-ding-a-dang," the patient answers.

"Mr. Gonzalez, have you been taking your medications?" Dr. Berringer asks.

"Dead meds, Fred said, no meds to the dead dread head."

"Jason, get ahold of the wife. See what the pill bottles look like. I suspect our dear Fred hasn't been taking his meds."

"Will do," he says.

Dr. Berringer pats the patient's shoulder, and Mr. Gonzalez looks up at him with a convivial nod.

"See you tomorrow, Mr. Gonzalez."

"The day has a way of making me say," he answers as if this is his usual good-bye. We exit to the hall, able to breathe freely again.

"Wow, that was a good one," Dr. Berringer says, clearly a man who loves his job. "What are his meds again?"

As Jason reels them off, my eyes wander to the window. The sun glimmers off the cars in the parking lot, tiny boxes in rows. Dew outlines a rectangle on the window.

"Earth to Zoe," Dr. Berringer bellows with a good-natured grin.

"I'm sorry. What?"

"Top three in the differential diagnosis of mania, I was asking you."

"Mania. Right, yes." I swallow, pause, waiting for a list to lumber into my brain. "Hyperthyroidism."

"Good, that's one."

I wait. "Steroid usage?"

"Excellent. Another one?"

I try to think. The harder I think, the blanker my brain.

"Jason? Want to help her out here?"

Jason takes a sip of coffee that I actually want to steal from him. "ADHD," he says.

"That's right, Jason. ADHD. Can be a tricky one."

Alas, the bitter, bitter irony.

"All right," Dr. Berringer says. "Let's see what our Jane is up to."

Jane is unchanged, like she's stuck in a freeze frame. She sits staring on her throne, her toes sticking out of the blue T.E.D. stockings, which travel well above her thighs like a bad Pippi Longstocking costume. She blinks and twitches her nose like a bunny. Dr. Berringer lifts her arm up again, and again it stays there, a macabre party trick, until he gently pushes it back down.

"No change, huh?" he says, disappointed.

"No. But we did get some results at least," I answer, lifting her growing plastic chart out of the rack.

"Okay, what do we got?"

"MRI was normal."

"How about the LP?"

"Just done."

He folds his arms. "Any stains sent out?"

"A few things," I answer. "RPR, India ink, HSV, cytol-

15

ogy. That'll take probably a week, but I can keep bugging the lab."

"Yeah, do that, would you?" he says. "Tox screen was negative, right?"

"Negative," I confirm. We stand there watching her. "I was thinking, what about a trial of benzodiazepines?" I ask.

"Which one?"

"Ativan, or Valium maybe? There have been reports on both."

He drops his stethoscope into his bag. "What do you think, Jason?"

"I don't know. Maybe we should wait for the LP."

Dr. Berringer lifts his hands, his fingers interlaced with his pointer fingers straight up against his lips like he's shushing someone. We wait for his decision. "Jason's right. I'm going to say hold off on the benzos for now. Let's wait on the LP and see what a tincture of time does for our Jane. Jason, got anyone else?"

"Actually, the rest of mine have all been discharged," he answers.

"Okay, good. I'll catch up with you later then. Zoe, can I have a quick word? If you don't mind?"

"Of course." My stomach does a somersault. I've been asked for a "quick word" many times in my life, and it's never a good thing. First off, it's never quick, and it's certainly never someone wanting to take a little time out just to tell you what a damn good job you're doing.

He motions toward the family conference room. He shuts the door behind us. Photos of baby animals of every ilk (puppies, kittens, baby seals, lion cubs, etc.) hang crookedly in cheap metal frames. The room smells musty, like it was just vacuumed with a bag that needs a change. We sit down side by side at the long table, my heart prancing in my chest.

"Just let me say, you're not in trouble or anything," he starts. "I just want to check in with you. See what's going on."

"Okay," I say. There is a pause, but I'm unsure how much more to offer. Two psychiatrists reflectively listening to each other doesn't make for a sparkling tête-à-tête.

"*Is* there anything going on?" he asks.

"In terms of?"

"In terms of you. Your focus. You just don't seem... I don't know... all there lately. We all have off days. And you're post-call, I know. Maybe that's all this is. But if there's more, or if there's something I can help you out with, I want to know about it." He leans back in his wooden chair, twisting the ring on his finger.

"I have ADHD," I announce. I hadn't really planned on sharing, but my brain apparently had.

He nods slowly with a concerned smile. A possibly practiced concerned smile.

"It's been a bit of a problem lately. I'm working on it with... well, with my psychiatrist. I know I've been off lately, as you noticed. Just so you're aware. I'm aware of it." I sound like an ass. Any more *awares* and I'll be clanging.

He crosses his long legs and leans back farther in his chair, staring at the ceiling tiles. "I'm glad you told me, Zoe. I'm glad you were comfortable enough to do that."

I nod, not sure what to say to this canned psychiatrist line.

"Life throws you curveballs sometimes. I know your mom died recently, and that's been tough, I'm sure."

"Yes. It has."

"I know how you feel. When my mom died…" He looks down at the table and doesn't finish the sentence.

"It was hard?" I offer. I can't help it; I'm a psychiatrist.

"Yeah, it sure was." He looks back to me. "And it wasn't easy moving to Buffalo either. I'm a Southern boy like a fish out of water up here, even after three years. My wife is on her last nerve in this place. Or maybe just with me," he jokes, raising his eyebrows. "Anyway, these things happen, right?"

"Right." I'm not sure who is treating whom here, or maybe that's not the point.

It does make me wonder, though, how he did end up in Buffalo. When he was hired, the Children's Hospital press release called him the "wunderkind from the Big Easy." Not yet forty and he's got a publication list longer than my arm. Even Jason will admit he's "wicked-fucking-smart." So what brought him to the polar vortex then? He clears his throat, and I realize he may be waiting for an answer. But I'm not sure what the question was.

"So I guess what I'm saying is, we all have our troubles, Zoe." He leans in toward me. "And it sounds like you've had more than your share since you've been a resident."

I wonder if he's talking about the patient who stabbed me. I didn't think he knew about that. But he probably does. Everybody around here does. I forged my way past whispers and stares for months after it happened. But eventually people's everyday life, real life—messy with its fender benders, cheating spouses, overdue cable bills, all the other quotid-ian tragedies—intervened, turning even homicidal, psycho-pathic patients a bit less eventful. Which is to say, everyone eventually forgot about me. Though every once in a while, a hush still falls over the elevator when I step on.

"You ever of hear Leonard Cohen?" he asks, putting his elbows on his knees.

"No, I don't think so."

"Let me tell you. He's one of my favorite songwriters. A poet, really."

"Okay?"

"He has a song where he says: *There is a crack in everything. That's how the light gets in.*" He pauses to let this sink in. "Like no one's perfect; we all have our demons. But that's what makes us who we are." He stares off at the wall, where the sunlight glares on the veneer of light-brown, fake-knotted wooden paneling. He puts his hand on my shoulder and gives it a squeeze. An attagirl kind of squeeze. Like he might give to Mr. Gonzalez, which makes me sad in a way. I really don't want to be his patient.

"I'm doing okay, though," I say. "I just think my meds need some tinkering is all. I'll be right as rain soon enough." Right as rain. Something my mom used to say.

"I'm sure you will be," he answers, standing up. End of the quick word. As he opens the door, the pressurized silence of the room evaporates, the hospital sounds zooming back in. We walk out, and he glances at his gold watch.

"I've got an appointment in a bit."

I stop myself from asking for what.

"And you're post-call, so get yourself home already!" He gives me another shoulder squeeze. "And Zoe?"

"Yes." I hear my foot tapping against the tile and stop it.

"Don't forget." He puts his hand up to his heart in a fist. *"That's how the light gets in."*

I stand there as he walks away, trying to decide if that was corny or not.

Chapter Three

Okay, my dopamine needs a serious tune-up here."

Sam cradles his chin, naked pink now without his goatee. (He told me last session his wife thought it made him look old.) It does take ten years off him, but he looks incomplete somehow. Like his brown hair and his brown eyes lost a friend. He also looks less Freudian, though maybe that was intentional. "What do you mean?" he asks.

"I don't know. My brain is sluggish. Like I'm underwater."

He nods. "And why do you think that is?"

I finger the row of brass buttons on the leather chair. "I don't know. I assume it's my ADHD acting up. It just feels like I'm brain-dead."

He waits for me to say more. "Can you give me an example?"

I bend over to the coffee table. Sam always has some kind of toy to play with in the office, to put patients at ease. I'll have to remember that trick when I'm out in practice next year. Assuming I don't get a fellowship, which I can't afford anyway. His newest toy is a small box of sand with a minia-ture rake and three smooth, gray-brown stones. Some Zen thing. "So we have this patient with catatonia, right?" I say, raking away.

"Right."

"She's probably about twelve or thirteen."

"Probably?"

"The thing is, we don't actually know her exact identity yet. The police are still working on that one."

"Interesting."

"And Dr. Berringer asks me for the differential for catato-nia. Which should be simple...but it takes me forever."

"I see."

"Same for the differential for mania. My brain just failed."

"So you couldn't come up with it."

"Dr. Berringer actually called me on it. Took me aside and asked if anything was wrong."

"Hmm." He cradles his chin again. "That is a concern."

"And then for Jane—"

"Jane?"

"That's what we call our girl with catatonia. Jane, as in Jane Doe."

"Ah." He nods.

"I just feel like...I can't help this girl if I'm not firing on all cylinders." Which makes me wonder exactly how many "all cylinders" entails. Six? A dozen? I couldn't venture to guess. I rake tic-tac-toe lines in the sand. "So I'm thinking we need to go up on my Adderall."

Sam leans forward, resting his elbows on his large, glossy desk. "I can see how you might think that. But honestly, I'm not so sure."

"No?" I fill in some X's and O's. "We need to do something. I mean, I failed the RITE exam. The RITE exam, for God's sake. I haven't failed a test since, like, fourth grade." I still remember the "64%" in bright red, scarring the top of my math test. I thought my young life was over.

"Let's talk about that," he says.

I pause. "Well, it *was* a long time ago—"

"No, no, not the fourth-grade thing. The RITE exam. Could the fact that you just lost your mother have anything to do with failing the exam? Do you think?"

"Maybe," I admit. It was two weeks later after all. Which is why I was put on probation but not canned. "Extenuating circumstances" as per the letter from the Psychiatry chairman. And the glowing, though unexpected, recommendation from Dr. Grant didn't hurt either. Unexpected because I thought Dr. Grant hated me, but it turns out he was "just challenging me to live up to the potential of a Yale medical graduate." Rattling my cage, as it were. No worries about that one anymore. The Yale thing has certainly lost its luster by now. And I don't have Dr. Grant to kick around now anyway. Now I've got Dr. Berringer, the esteemed head of Child Psychiatry, for my child-psych rotation, yet another attending to disappoint.

Sam's hands climb up to play with his goatee, find it missing, and descend back onto his desk. "How are you doing with your mom's death?"

"Which mom?" I ask, a poor attempt at humor. My birth mother died when I was a child. I only found out the whole truth about what happened in the first year of residency, when I first started seeing Sam.

"Your adopted mom," he answers with a half smile.

My "real" real mom, the one who raised me. "I don't know. I still think about her all the time. Every single day. Sometimes I grab my phone to call her and then remember I can't."

"Very common," he says, nodding. "She's still more alive than gone for you right now."

"I guess." I catch my reflection in the wall mirror, a huge circle with a dark wooden ship-wheel frame. The room has an overdone nautical theme; he should shoot the decorator for going overboard. (Yeah, I know. Pun intended.) "What happened to the compass?" I ask, noticing it missing, a behemoth of a thing on his desk that always pointed true north even though it faced east. In its place is an anchor paperweight matching the anchor bookends. The paperweight is huge, granite, a plausible murder weapon in a *CSI* plot.

"I don't remember. Let's focus back on your mother, okay?"

"Sure, okay." I sit up on the couch. "I don't know what more to say. She's gone, I'm sad. That's all." I drop the rake, the handle resting on one of the stones. "It's been almost a year now. It just seems like I should be further along."

He takes off his glasses and toys with the temple. "Grief has its own pace unfortunately. There's no shortcut for that."

"Yeah, I know. But to be honest, right now I'm more concerned about my brain not functioning."

"Yes, I know you are. But that's the connection I'm trying to make here. I don't think the slowed cognition has anything to do with your ADHD. But I think it has everything to do with your mother's death."

"As in depression?"

"You could call it that. Or grief. They go hand in hand."

I catch my reflection again, half a nose in the nautical mirror. "Should we go up on the Lexapro then?"

"Let's see." He turns to his computer, scrolling to get my medication page. "We have room to increase it if you want. Do you think it's necessary?"

"It's more than necessary. It's mandatory. I'm on probation here. Whatever it takes to get these gray cells jogging again."

He pauses, then pulls out his drawer with a rumble and starts filling out a script.

"Don't you guys have e-script yet?"

"Next month. At least that's what they told me last month." We both smile. "Let's try fifteen milligrams. Watch for diarrhea."

I fold the script in half and drop it in my purse. A bit of hope. Gathering up my things, I run through my list of belongings, a rote routine of mine since an "ADHD Skills Course" my mom dragged me to in eighth grade. Purse, check. Phone in purse, check.

"Hey," Sam says, standing up. "You figured out next year yet?"

It's almost October, and most people are on top of their fellowship applications. But I'm not quite there yet. Maybe because my brain is in slo-mo. Or maybe because I really don't know what the hell I want to do. Mike's been hinting all summer that I might want to come up with some semblance of a plan. Finally he just stopped talking about it altogether.

"Give yourself some time," Sam says when I appear stuck on an answer. "You'll figure it out eventually."

"I guess."

"And Zoe," Sam continues. "Work on being kinder to yourself. The RITE, for instance. I know it upsets you, but think about it: Your mom just died, you didn't study. I don't know many people who would actually pass an exam in that situation." He stands up from his desk. "I don't even think they should have put you on probation, but that's just my opinion."

"Really?" The thought buoys me. Probation has been a tough label, a scarlet P upon my chest.

"Really," he says. "See you next week."

I pull open the door. Cue next patient: the skinny woman I spotted in the waiting room. Perfectly coiffed, makeup on the severe side, whipping through an *Oprah Magazine* like she was being timed. Anxiety, I'm thinking.

And in another year, someone will actually pay me to make that diagnosis.

Later that day, I know I should be studying for the RITE, but I'm hanging out with Mike instead, ambling through the wares at Oktoberfest.

End of September, but they're still calling it that. It doesn't even feel like fall. More like a gorgeous summer day, the air warm, almost sticky. Most of the attendees are wandering around in shorts, lugging Windbreakers they brought just in case. Mike is wearing a frayed polo shirt and cargo shorts. I take his hand and can tell he is pleasantly surprised. I'm not usually the PDA type, but he does look extra-adorable today. We pass by a corn stand, and Mike picks up an ear of dried Indian corn, spattered with shiny russet, black, and white-yellow beads. I try not to think about how many people have touched that same corn and the number of germs amassed on each kernel.

"How much?" he asks.

"One dollar each, five for the bunch," the man answers, wrinkling his forehead into three distinct lines.

Mike pulls out a five. "I was thinking Samantha might like it," he tells me.

"She's visiting?"

"Columbus Day."

"Yeah, she'll love it," I agree. He dotes on Samantha, his niece, which is wonderful of course. But it worries me a bit. I'm not really the having-children type, and we haven't quite gotten around to discussing that yet. We walk on to the next booth, lined with pumpkins with happy, rouge-cheeked, painted-on faces.

"How much for one of these?" I ask, pointing to one of the pumpkins.

"Five dollars," the woman answers.

"Okay." I'm getting out my wallet when a little figurine

catches my eye. A ceramic ghost and scarecrow sitting on a bale of hay, their arms around each other. A dizzy memory washes over me then, of Scotty in a white sheet with one eye-hole bigger than the other and me dressed as a scarecrow, the straw scratching my wrists. My mom is taking a picture (back when they still used film) while my dad pours the candy out into a big, blue bowl. "Come on, please! Hurry up!" we are begging them. "It'll be over soon!"

I turn the glazed piece in my hands. "This one?"

"Ten dollars," she answers.

"Is that for you?" Mike asks.

"No." I hand her the money. "For Jane."

"Your patient?"

"Uh-huh."

He pauses, cocking his head. "That's actually really nice."

"Gee, thanks. I have my moments."

As we walk on, I spy a cotton candy stand in the distance and enter a full-fledged debate with myself. Pros: I want cotton candy. Cons: sticky hands, uncomfortably full feeling. Pros: all those colors, so fluffy. Cons: no redeeming value whatsoever, pure sugar. I subtly change our trajectory toward the cotton candy.

"What do you think about her anyway?" I ask.

"About who?"

"Jane."

He answers with a head shake. "Way above my pay grade."

"Yeah, I guess. I just wish I knew who she was." I run my fingers over a bright multicolor wool sweater. Bulky golds,

28

eggplant, wine-red threads. Something Mike would never wear. "So I called you this morning. Where were you?"

His sneakers kick up some pebbles. "I don't know. When did you call?"

"Like, eight?" We walk past scarecrows made out of corn husks. "I figured you were at the gym."

"No." He crinkles his eyes, trying to remember. "Actually, I *did* get a call, but it was blocked. That was you?"

"Oh yeah, sorry. I forgot. I always block it now. Last week a patient got my number. He was giving me hourly reports on his mood."

Mike lets out a loud chortle, catching stares. His bearish laugh matches him perfectly, with his broad shoulders that could veer into padding if it weren't for the gym. "He was depressed, I take it?"

"More like OCD. He was just obsessed with his mood. He would give me ten-scale updates, with decimals. Like, 'I think I'm a 5.4 today, which is better than yesterday. Yesterday I was a 4.8.' He was getting into the hundredths place when I told him my number changed and he had to page me."

"Zoe, Zoe, Zoe. Always an entertaining viewpoint on life."

I decide to take this as a compliment. "How about you? What's your mood today?"

"Hmmm." He pretends to think. "8.2."

"Not an 8.3?"

"Maybe. Just talking to you puts me at a 9.4."

"That's called mood elevation. I charge good money for that."

"Right," he guffaws. "You're a resident. You're not charging good money for shit."

Finally we are nearing the cotton candy. "You want any? My treat. Guaranteed 9.5."

He gives me a look. "Seriously? I just finished breakfast."

"Your loss. One pink one, please." I plunk down two dollars and am rewarded with a cloud of pale-pink goodness. We pass more pumpkin faces. "Oh," I say with disappointment, looking ahead.

"What?"

"Candy apples. I love candy apples." I pluck off a wad of cotton candy. "Should have held out."

"Yes, that is tragic. Back to an 8.3?"

Laughing, I slug him, and we head to the next booth, by a clump of coneflowers that are past bloom, the centers rusted and petals scraggly and wilted. The scarecrow-ghost duo crinkles in my plastic bag.

A present for Jane, who doesn't know it's Oktoberfest. Who isn't going to be a ghost, a scarecrow, or even a princess this Halloween. Who is staring in a blank hospital room, not outside at this picture-perfect day with a bright blue sky and not a cloud in sight.

⟵

Arthur greets me with a full-frontal attack, socking me in the solar plexus, then latching on to my right thigh and humping me like it's the first night of his honeymoon.

Arthur is my dog, a psychotic labradoodle who came out on the shallow end of both gene pools. Let's just say he misses me *a lot* when I'm away. Arthur was supposed to be my brother's dog. Scotty brought him home from the SPCA when Mom was dying, without having fully researched whether or not his apartment allowed pets. So needless to say, he soon became my hand-me-down. Scotty babysits at least. He walks him on his lunch and sleeps over if Mike and I are both on call.

I shove Arthur off my thigh, and he whines, his eyebrows upturned in aggrievement. He then proceeds to tear mad circles around the family room, his tail slapping me with every lap. He's a year old now but doesn't seem to realize this. I've even considered slipping him some of my Adderall. After about ten laps, Arthur plops onto his back, tail still wagging.

I sort through the mail—"SPOOKTACULAR" orange-and-black fliers for zombie costumes, red-white-and-blue ads where someone is Satan and someone is the Messiah for the election, and bills (too many)—when I see the letter. The cream-colored rectangle stands out from the rest of the junk. Thick, expensive paper with flowery black handwriting. Not computer-generated handwriting, actual by-hand handwriting. Being the last kid invited to a birthday party, I have always been enamored with the prospect of the handwritten invitation. I turn it over, and my heart skips a beat. It's from Jean Luc.

I tear it open. Jean Luc was my first love. We dated in medical school at Yale, when he was a postdoc in chemistry. And it's true, what I told Jason: I haven't heard from him in a while, in nearly a year. After he dumped me for the magazine-quality Melanie, we kind of ran out of things to say. Last I heard, she was happily transplanted in Paris and the toast of the town in party planning. I overheard her berating some poor vendor in perfectly accented French when Jean Luc and I last spoke. She frightens me, actually.

I shake out the envelope, and a black-and-white card falls out, an overly dramatic picture of Jean Luc and Melanie. They gaze, eyes glued to each other and unsmiling, like they're in an edgy magazine ad.

Upcoming Nuptials
Jean Luc and Melanie
Saturday, April 15
Paris, France

So not a birthday invitation, a save-the-date card. My stomach turns queasy.

He's *marrying* her? Dropping the announcement on the counter, I throw off my satchel and slump onto my comfy red couch. Arthur whines again so I grab his overflowing kibble bowl and bring it into the family room with me. (He gets lonely. Yes, he's both oversexed and spoiled.) The sound of Arthur's contented crunching fills the room, which at once feels despairingly empty.

I grab my phone and debate. I could call Mike, but complaining about your ex-boyfriend to your current boyfriend doesn't seem like a wise plan. Not that he would even necessarily be jealous. Mike is unflappable, almost annoyingly so.

Jean Luc is getting married to a maleficent creature? Okay, so what's the issue? It's over. Time to move on.

He's an ER doc, pragmatic. Right lower quadrant pain doesn't mean you may have borderline tendencies stemming from a troubled relationship with your emotionally distant father. It means you have appendicitis. That'll be two milligrams of morphine, surgical consult, and possibly a CT of the abdomen. Not to say he's unkind; he is more than kind. I still think of him visiting in the nursing home, watching television with my mom, who was in the later stages of dementia, grinning away like he was having the time of his life. He is thoughtful; he just doesn't overthink things. Overthinking is my forte. Jean Luc was an overthinker, too, in a way. He just thought mainly about himself.

I decide to call Scotty.

"Yo, what's up?" I hear strains of Vivaldi's *Four Seasons* in the background and his coworker yelling out orders. He's at work at the coffee shop.

"Hi, how are you?"

"What do you want?"

"What do you mean, what do I want? Can't I just call you?"

"You never just call me, Zoe. So what do you want?"

Arthur starts whining now for his water bowl, so I grab that from the foyer and spill half of it on the way back to the family room. "I got this letter."

"Yeah?"

"Never mind."

"Come on, you got a letter. Go on."

"Well, it's from Jean Luc. He's getting married."

I hear the slam of a register. "So who gives a fuck, Zoe? He's an asshole."

My ever-empathetic brother. "Yeah, but—"

"And Mike's actually a decent guy. So fuck Frog-boy. He wasn't good enough for you anyway."

Which is, I guess, what I wanted to hear. Even if it was delivered with typical Scotty flair. The coffee grinder sounds in the distance. "Oh, one more thing," I say before he can hang up. "It's about this case."

He groans. "What about it?"

"Remember that facial recognition program you got working?"

Scotty cobbled together a bare-bones facial recognition program off shareware to help me find my birth mother a couple of years ago. He may be my pain-in-the-ass kid brother, but he's also, oddly enough, a computer guru. "Yeah? What about it?"

"You think we could use it to find Jane?"

"Who the fuck is Jane?"

"My patient. With catatonia."

This time the coffee grinder seems to grate directly into my ear. "How old did you say she was? Like, twelve?"

"Twelve, fourteen. I'm not sure. Young teenager anyway. Why? Does that make a difference?"

"Yeah, it does actually. You need to match her picture to her image on the Internet from exactly the right age. Give or take six months maybe. Otherwise it gets hinky." Another coffee order gets barked out. "Text me her picture. I'll try, but I can't promise anything." With that, he hangs up, and Arthur trots by me with something white sticking out of his mouth.

"Arthur!" Here he turns away from me with the errant concept that if he can't see me, then I can't see him. Arthur hasn't hit all the Piaget stages just yet. "What do you have?"

Of course, he doesn't answer. But he only fights halfheartedly as I yank the soggy card stock out of his mouth. *Upcoming Nuptials*. Now missing a corner and part of Melanie's head, which is just as well. Arthur waits with uncharacteristic patience for the card and then gets bored when his doggy brain processes the idea that this isn't happening, and he slumps down to the floor. I sit there, watching him engage in some ill-advised licking, as my mood plummets to a 2.4.

Chapter Four

I'm lifting up the bedsheet when I notice the scar.

On her left ankle, it's an odd scar. A misshapen circle the size of a nickel with a hint of soft brown keloid on the rim. A cut? A burn? I rub the scar, but she doesn't budge. She just keeps staring her dead-eyed stare. Dr. Berringer finally relented to giving her a teeny dose of Ativan. It's been a week; it doesn't seem to be doing much. I pull out my camera phone and snap a picture of her ankle. Maybe it could help Detective Adams identify her.

Back at the nurses' station, Jason sits with a pile of charts. He's wearing a lime-green bow tie and shirt.

"Hey, it's a Chinese leprechaun!" I say, grabbing a chair.

He gives me the finger.

"Aren't we touchy today?"

"I'm in a shitty mood."

"And I bet I can guess why."

"Yeah, Dominic dumped me again."

36

"Dominic's an asshole." I grab a chart. "Forgive my lack of empathy."

"No, you're right." He hits another chart on the stack. "By the way, guess who's back?"

"No idea."

"Tiffany."

"Tiffany?" She has been my patient five times now. She gets admitted biannually to the County for crystal meth psychosis. Then off to rehab, or jail, depending on the alignment of the stars. Last time, I thought I convinced her to stay in rehab. I guess I was wrong. "What's she doing at Children's? She's practically got a bed reserved at the County."

"Preggers," he says.

I let out a whistle. "No shit."

"Yup." Jason gets the smile he always gets when relaying a particularly salacious bit of gossip. "And the County wants no part of detoxing a twenty-four-weeker."

"I'll bet."

"Shaved off a chunk of her arm, too," Jason adds.

"Ooh, why?" Wincing, I grab the chart from him and start looking through it.

"She thought she had maggots." He pulls out an order sheet. "At least she's still alive."

"Yes, that is something."

"Hey," Dr. Berringer calls into the room. "Let's round later today, okay? I just want to see Jane real quick." Jason nods and turns back to his notes. "How is she?" he asks as we walk down the hall.

"No change," I answer.

"So the Ativan's not hitting her yet?"

"Guess not."

We enter the room, and she doesn't move. Her almond eyes are glassy, vacant. She blinks, crinkles her nose, blinks again. Dr. Berringer lifts his index finger, waves it slowly in front of her eyes. She doesn't track it.

"Maybe we could go up on the Ativan?" I ask. "I called the pharmacist. He said we have tons of room to move up on it. Two mgs q six if she's not getting too sedated." (Actually, the pharmacist said, "Half a milligram isn't going to do jack. You guys might as well give her sugar water," but I leave that bit out.)

Dr. Berringer nods. "Might as well. Let's start with one mg q twelve. If she's tolerating it, then we go up more."

"Not two mgs? That's what the pharmacist recommended."

"One mg, Zoe. Low and slow."

"Okay," I agree with reluctance. "Hey, and another thing I noticed." I point at her foot, lifting up the sheet, and he walks over to see. "See the scar? Isn't that weird?"

"Yeah, it is." He gets in closer, putting his nose right up to it. "A burn maybe?"

"It looks like a circle or something."

He runs his hand up and down the scar, like a clinician, but with tenderness still. "Yeah. Cigarette burn, I'm thinking."

"It's kind of big for that, isn't it?"

"Hard to say with the keloid." He shrugs. "That's how it looks to me."

I nod, putting the sheet back down. It billows in the air, then settles.

"Abuse isn't uncommon in these cases unfortunately." He picks up the Halloween figurine, the buddy ghost and scarecrow from her bed stand. It looks chintzy in his hands. "Who gave her this?"

"Oh, I did." I start filling out an order sheet with the new Ativan dose.

He places it back down, gently. "You're a sweet girl, Zoe."

I hold back a smile. No one's ever called me a sweet girl before. When I glance up from the sheet, he is looking at me, his eyes glowing blue. I drop my gaze back down to the chart.

Later that morning, I head off to see how Tiffany's doing.

How she's doing is not well. Skeletal, thinner than last time I saw her, her belly with just a suggestion of a bump. Her face is dotted with scars, her arm taped with a large white bandage with yellow oozing through the cotton. The bandage smells rank. Probably infected. I write for a surgical consult in case it needs debridement, then sit next to her on the wrinkled blanket.

"Tiffany?"

She stares out, silent. Like Jane. But if Tiffany is catatonic, at least we know why. She gazes out the window at the yellow-green grass, half dead from all this warm, dry weather.

I stand up from the bed, and Tiffany rocks with the motion. After another minute, I decide not much therapy will be achieved right now. But as I get up from the bed, she surprises me by talking.

"I know I let you down," she says. Her voice is low and quiet. Exhausted.

"No." I turn to her. "You didn't."

Her top lip trembles, but she doesn't cry. "I filled out an application."

I wait for more. "An application?"

"Yeah. To be a flight attendant, like we talked about."

I vaguely recall this conversation from the last admission. She revealed to me that it had always been her dream to be a flight attendant. I urged her to go for it. "Okay?"

"It took me a month. There was a lot to fill in." Her voice is flat, dead.

I take a seat in the chair by her desk and wait a long time until she speaks again.

"I never handed it in."

I lean back in the chair. "Why not?"

"Because I'm a loser." She says this without a trace of self-pity.

"I don't think that's true," I say, scooting toward her. "I think you've got a bad disease."

"Same difference." There is another long pause. "And now I'm killing my baby."

I don't have a response for that.

"Can I be alone now, please?"

"Sure." Standing up, I put a hand on her shoulder, and she

stares off, not seeming to notice. I'm in the hallway, unfolding my patient list, when my text quacks.

got your pic of the scar. Thanks for the tip, I'll check it out. It's Detective Adams.

weird, isn't it? I reply. What do u think it is?

prob cig burn. Let u know if I find out anything.

So it's on to the next patient on my list. Caden Jennings.

The door opens to a painfully skinny fourteen-year-old. He pats his knee twice, then smacks his face. Hard, not just a light tap, leaving a red palm mark over the swirl of gray-purple bruising from pummeling himself before.

"Caden," I say, walking toward him.

He jumps out of his chair and reaches out his long arm, hyperextending his elbow. He has the look of a teenaged Ichabod Crane, his chin glazed pink with acne. After he shakes my hand, he flings his arm backward like he just touched a hot stove. Then he spins around counterclockwise, twice, and plops back down in the metal chair, scraping the tile with the force of his body. The tile at his feet is chipped from years of that very chair scraping at that very desk. I take the seat next to him.

"Sorry," he says, gazing at the floor. "I can't help it."

"Don't worry. That's why you're here." I try to sound cheerful, walking my pen down the order sheet. "Has the neurologist seen you yet?"

"I'm not sure. The medical students, I think?"

"Short coats or long coats?"

"Short," he answers.

"Yeah. That would be the medical students."

"They seemed pretty clueless, actually," he says, his voice breaking like it hasn't decided on a range yet. Puberty hasn't been kind to our Caden.

"Yup. That would be the medical students."

He laughs, his shoulders relaxing an inch. As if in rebuke, his left hand crosses over and taps his knee twice, then clocks the side of his face again. I force myself not to wince.

"So tell me about the thoughts you've been having," I say.

He gives his chin a vigorous scratch and exhales. "It started with the number six." He lets out a quick "screee!" noise and shakes his head to one side, like he's trying to get water out of his ear. "I try to avoid them. Sixes. But they're, like, really hard to avoid. Especially in math."

"I can see how that would be."

"And there's one in my address, too. A...a...six." He shivers like the word tastes bad. "So my mom got mad when I scratched it off the mailbox. But"—he pats his knee and gives his face a slap—"I felt like, if I didn't do it, something really, really bad was going to happen. So it's almost like she should be thanking me, but I knew she wouldn't understand that."

"Right."

"And then I was getting in trouble in math because I would cross all the sixes out and try to do the problems without them. I mean, I don't see what the big deal is. I'm still getting the concepts. I'm actually very good at math."

"Well, that's good," I say, encouraging.

He looks down, quiet for a moment, then lets out a "scree!"

"You said it started with sixes," I remind him.

"Yeah, it started there but then it, like, moved. Then I had a problem with colors. Well, not all colors, just black and sometimes green."

"Sometimes green?"

"It depends on the shade, you know? Like, lime green is okay, but forest green or any kind of dark green is just very bad, very evil-like, you know?"

"Sure," I answer, though I'm not really sure. Clearly I have to bone up on Tourette's.

"And if I spend too much time around those colors, it's going to be a problem. So I just try to avoid them. But, you know, if a teacher is wearing a green sweater, they don't necessarily want to take it off, you know? But, like, I don't actually see why that's a major problem, you know? I mean, unless it's really cold or something."

We share a smile. He may have been making a joke, or not. He taps his knee, slaps his face, and then hangs his head in exhaustion. I'm exhausted just watching him.

"And of course kids are making fun of me, which seems to be the job of the kids in my grade." Here he *screes* twice. "They keep putting black paper in my locker or handing me notes with the number six on it, like, a hundred times."

"Jeez."

"Yeah, I couldn't go near my locker for, like, an entire day."

A memory pops up then, of finding a note in my locker in fifth grade. Written in grape-purple ink, because girls are always the ones to be so unnecessarily mean.

ZOE IS GAY, ANNOYING, OBNOXOUS [*sic*] AND UGLY.

SIGNED, THE ENTIRE 5TH GRADE CLASS

P.S. WE WOULDN'T CARE IF YOU DIED

The note burned, a shameful secret in my backpack, for an entire week before my mother caught me crying in my room and I showed it to her. She hugged me, smelling of heavy perfume. Chanel number something. She was going to a party with my dad that night, the sitter already on her way. "Zoe," she said, "not one of these kids is worth the hair on your pinkie toe." This made me burst out laughing, and every time I thought of the note thereafter, it was paired with the hair on my pinkie toe. I can feel tears threatening and swallow them back.

"Are you okay?" Caden asks. He stares at me with nary a tic.

"Oh. Yeah." I wipe at my eyes. "Allergies," I add, sniffling my nose for effect.

"Okay," he answers doubtfully, like he's wondering which one of us is the patient here.

Chapter Five

The girl is in a cave.

"Jane!" I follow her deeper into the cold, damp air. Her footsteps echo as she runs from me. "Jane!" My voice rings off the walls. The air is pitch black, darker than night. I can't see my hands. "I want to help you! Jane! Stop!"

All at once, the footsteps slow down, and I do, too. Sweat turns cold on my neck. Then the footsteps stop, so I stop and listen. I reach out my hands like a blind person.

"Jane?"

I hear us breathing. My breath is short from running. As I reach out again, I touch something. Fabric, a shirt? It's damp. Her breathing gets louder, and I feel hot air on my cheek. She is whispering something to me. I lean in closer and just make out the words.

"It wasn't a cigarette."

My heart clenches in my chest as I sit up, my eyes darting around the room. A moment of panic, disorientation. I'm in the laundry room of my old house, in the fire again. I'm trying to find my birth mom. No, I'm running in a cave.

Where am I?

Slowly the fear recedes as familiar forms take shape. The outline of my lamp, the spine of a book jutting out, my fuzzy blue robe thrown over a chair. I'm in my bedroom, not a fire, not a cave. Arthur whines, then nestles into the back of my knee. The dog has successfully maneuvered his way between me and Mike yet again. I consider waking Mike but remember he's got to be up at 4:30 a.m. for work, so I let him sleep.

My heart slows back down, and I take a deep breath, like Sam taught me to do. I haven't had nightmares in a while now, not since I was dreaming about my birth mother dying in the fire. I'm not used to it. I lie there with my brain buzzing for some time and finally glance over at the clock.

Three a.m.

Getting up, I'm about to hit the medicine cabinet for my Xanax when I remember I don't have Xanax anymore and lie back down. After what feels like another hour but is only twenty-three minutes, I reach over and grab my iPad. Arthur moves down to my feet and puts all forty-five pounds on them. I type "missing african american girls" in the search engine, which brings up pages of headshots. Fifty smiling girls. Like photos from an all-girls-school yearbook, but of missing, not graduating, girls. I scroll through them all, but there's no picture of Jane.

"Hey," Mike says, his voice rough with sleep. He is squinting his eyes, his face a ghostly white in the glow off the iPad. "What are you doing?"

"Sorry." I tilt down the screen. "I was just looking at something."

"At three in the morning?"

"I can't sleep. I had a nightmare."

"Oh." He frowns. "About the fire again?"

"No, actually. About Jane."

He rubs his eyes. "What are you looking at?"

"Don't worry. Go back to sleep."

"No." He yawns. "I'm okay." Mike is so perpetually sleep-deprived I've seen him catnap on his feet before. He moves toward me, and Arthur woofs.

"It's a website for missing people."

"Huh." He props up his pillow. "Wasn't Scotty doing that facial recognition thing?"

"Yeah, but he's slow." I show him the screen. The banner is in bold letters: BLACK AND MISSING, BUT NOT FORGOTTEN. We watch as the website rolls through a slide show of missing African Americans, each one with a blurb underneath. A young woman in a purple scarf, her hand leaning against a tree trunk. A teenager with baby-pink heart earrings. An eighth-grade boy in a gold graduation cap.

"It's all African Americans?" he asks.

"Yeah." I point to the mission statement at the bottom: "To bring equal coverage and resources to people of all races." They might not get *Dateline*, but at least they get this. We wait out the slide show. No Jane.

"Go to bed, Zoe. We'll figure it out in the morning."

On the bottom of the page, they give instructions on sending in a picture of your own "loved one." My fingers debate for an instant. Mike turns his back toward me and immediately starts snoring again. I linger on the submit button. It's not a good idea. Logically, I know this. It's a HIPAA violation and more, and if Dr. Berringer or Detective Adams ever got wind of it, that would be lights-out for Probation Girl.

As quietly as I can, I transfer the photo of Jane as well as her scar from my phone, write up a no-frills blurb without revealing any sensitive information (which isn't hard, since I don't know any), and hit send. Probation be damned. I have to find out who this girl is.

Lying back down, I stare at the ceiling for a while, the shadows morphing into faces. I turn to one side, then the other, then readjust my pillow. All insomnia tricks that don't work. Then, just in case, I reach my hand down, feeling around under the sheets to investigate whether Mike might be awake or possibly interested in being so.

"What are you doing?" he asks, sleep in his voice.

"Oh, nothing," I mutter, moving my hand. But he pulls my wrist back where it was, and it appears he is fully awake and, indeed, *very* interested. As I start stroking him, he reaches over to me, his warm hand spiraling in slow circles on my stomach, descending lower and lower, slower and slower, until he hits the bull's-eye. And I purr and relax, deciding insomnia isn't such a bad thing after all.

Chapter Six

A cardinal darts by the window, bouncing on a branch like a spring. I squint my eyes at the glare through the glass. "The Lexapro isn't helping."

"Hmm." Sam tugs at his chin, which I just notice has the finest five o'clock brown shadow.

"You're growing back your goatee?"

"Oh yeah," he admits, his face tingeing pink.

"I like it."

"Thanks," he says, giving it a quick scratch. "But back to what you were saying."

"Yes, I think it's not helping because it's not depression."

"You're saying it feels like ADHD."

"Yes. And I have carried the diagnosis since age six."

He folds his hands together. "How are the other things in your life?"

"Like what?"

"Anything going on with Mike, for instance?"

I slump down in the sofa chair. "No, not really. He's good." I fail to mention my ex's upcoming nuptials, though. I pick up the miniature rake, which makes a pleasant scraping noise in the sand. I rake rows of lines, bird tracks. "I had a nightmare last night. About Jane."

"Uh-huh?"

"Took me forever to get back to sleep. I almost wished I had some Xanax." Sam and I had both agreed to stop Xanax when I developed an overfondness of them for nightmares, anxiety, and any other minor ill.

"I don't think it's the best idea, do you?" he asks.

I cross my legs. "No, probably not."

"With your family history and all." By this he means my *biological* family history, strewn with meth addicts and heroin fiends, not to mention garden-variety alcoholics.

"It's just this patient really gets to me for some reason."

"Jane?" he asks. "Or does she have a name yet?"

"No, still Jane. And I can't shake the feeling that there's something huge, right in front of my face. Some way to help her that I'm missing."

"You started the benzos?"

"Ativan."

"And it didn't help?"

"Not yet."

"Maybe you just need to push the dose?"

"We are," I say. "Too slow for my liking. But then, I've never been the paragon of patience."

He laughs, then clears his throat. Not to offend or anything. A flash of red sweeps by the window, and then there

50

are two cardinals sitting on the branch. The blood-red male and the duller, gray-red female. On a date maybe, or I suppose they could be just friends.

"You can only do so much, Zoe," he says. "They don't give us magic wands."

"I know." I trace spirals in the sand. "But I just feel like, I don't know, I need to help her. I mean, I want to help all my patients, of course. But this one's different."

"I see." He looks at me. "Any idea why this patient may be affecting you more than others?" He waits a moment but I have no answer. "Do you see any connection maybe, between yourself and her?"

"Connection?" I ponder this as deeply as my dopamine-depleted brain allows. "Well, she's my patient." Even I know this is a lame attempt, more evidence that all my neurons are not firing at full throttle.

He nods to be encouraging, then starts twiddling his thumbs. This is Sam's tell. He twiddles when he's waiting for me to make a breakthrough. After two years now, I can read the guy. He's old-school psychiatry, all Socratic method and waiting for me to hit my own breakthroughs. Though sometimes I wish he'd just stop playing the psychiatrist from *Ordinary People* and tell me already. "Anything strike you about her identity maybe?"

"Her identity?"

"Yes."

I stare at him in confusion. "What about her identity? She *has* no identity."

"Right."

I shrug my shoulders. "And?"

"And?" he repeats, drawing me out.

"And so what?"

"A little girl who doesn't know her identity? Sound familiar?"

My mouth opens. Of course. He's referring to my own identity crisis. In my first year of psychiatry, when I discovered the truth about my birth mother and my adopted mother. My poor mom, in the final throes of dementia, lying rail-thin on a nursing home bed, smelling of urine and not sure who she was, let alone who I was. My mom, who lost her own identity before she died.

He glances up quickly at the clock above my head. "Okay, Zoe. How about this? Let's wait another week. See if the Lexapro increase does anything. It can take some time. And if not, we can go up on the Adderall." He pauses. "But it's not a bottomless pit. At some point, the cardiovascular risks outweigh the benefits."

"I understand."

Sam stands up and pulls out his phone, and I pull out mine, like we're facing off for an iPhone duel. "I'm off next week for Yom Kippur," he says.

"Oh, right, glad you reminded me." I type this into my calendar. "What temple do you belong to?" I've never seen him at Beth Zion, my temple. I forgot to ask Scotty if he's coming this year. It'll be our first Yom Kippur without Mom, though she wasn't exactly compos mentis for the last one.

"Beth Zedek," he answers.

"Oh well, la-di-da. Conservative...a *real* Jew."

He laughs, thin wrinkle lines fanning out from his eyes, which I've never noticed before. "*L'shana tova*, Zoe," he says.

"*L'shana tova*," I answer back, hoping it will indeed be a happy new year.

"I feel like she's trying to tell me something through the dream."

"Yeah, that you're fucking crazy," Scotty answers. He leans back in the chair and yawns.

I am sitting in my favorite eggplant-covered settee by the fireplace, though it's superfluous in this Indian summer weather. I drain the last of my iced cappuccino, rattling the bronzed ice cubes. Scotty works here at the Coffee Spot, my home away from home since I came back to Buffalo. He started the job after flunking out of the University at Buffalo. I used to wonder how on earth anyone could fail out of college. Now I'm more forgiving on the matter.

Eddie, his coworker, walks by and gives me a wave with the dishrag, then scurries back to the front to take care of a customer. Eddie is a paradox of sorts: fit from yoga, tattooed, and ponytailed, but bumbling and diffident to the point of monosyllabic. I take another sip of my iced cappuccino, forgetting I've drained it, and put the cup down.

"So, nothing?"

"Not nothing. One hit." He hands me her picture, printed

off the computer. "It's just she happens to be an exchange student from Nigeria."

"In Houston, no less." I examine the picture, which is off a website from her high school. She's a freshman.

"So I gotta doubt she's your girl."

I fold the paper in quarters. "It's worth a phone call anyway."

"Whatever."

"What do you mean, whatever?"

"Do you possibly recognize a pattern here?" Scotty scratches under his Sabres cap. "This bizarre need to become obsessed with your patients?"

"It's called doing my job."

"Yeah, sure," he snorts. "Remember that fucking psychopathic lady? That ended well."

"*She* was obsessed with *me*," I argue, while he glances ahead at the melting numbers on the Dali clock to check the time left in his break. "Speaking of obsession, how is the great hunt for the Treasury bonds going?"

When Mom was spiraling into her dementia, she mentioned that Dad might have stashed away some Treasury bonds and she might have forgotten where they were. *Might* being the operative word here, because there *might* not have actually been any such bonds to begin with. But she became obsessed with finding them, and now Scotty's convinced there's gobs and gobs of money out there, just laid to waste.

"Crappy," he says. "I haven't found shit."

I shake my ice cubes. "Maybe that's because they don't actually exist."

"Yeah, so you've told me a million times."

"I'm consistent."

He takes a sip of his own iced cappuccino. "You know, Zoe, I know you think I'm a fucking idiot, et cetera, et cetera, and maybe the whole thing's one big circle jerk, and maybe she was just demented and delusional and whatever psycho-babble shit you want to call her, but I promised her on her fucking deathbed I would look for the bonds, and I'm looking for the bonds. All right?"

"All right, jeez." I break out my RITE review book.

Scotty pulls his straw in and out of the drink with an annoying squeak, not responding. I agree that it would be nice if there were money lying around. I'd be able to do a fellowship instead of hitting the streets to pay off my loans. It would be nice if we had world peace and an end to world hunger. It would also be nice if Mom were still alive. There are a lot of things that would be nice.

Scotty tosses his drink in the garbage with a well-practiced wrist flip, garners his two points, then gets up. "Back to work."

"Hey, before you go. Just take a quick look at this." I hold the phone up for him to see, and he bends down.

"Zoe, man, that's fucking disgusting."

"What? It's just a scar."

He shakes his head without answering and heads to the counter, grabbing an apron. I glance down at my RITE review book, but before making the commitment to open the thing, decide to check in on the Black and Missing website first. No comments under Jane's picture, just "Thank you. We received your picture and will do our best to help find your loved one." Deciding I'm all out of excuses, I open my review book. Question number one:

> A 21-year-old female college student is brought in by her boyfriend after increasingly confused and agitated behavior. Soon after, she is described as appearing fully awake but unresponsive. She is diagnosed correctly by the first-year resident as catatonic. Catatonia is characterized by which of the following?

Of course, the question is on catatonia. Apparently, God is making jokes now.

> a) a "waxy" state, where the body can be manipulated into various postures which the patient maintains
> b) excessive grimacing or blinking
> c) hyperkinetic state, with large-amplitude, purposeless movements
> d) all of the above

Unfortunately for Jane, the answer is d: all of the above. But that still doesn't answer the real question, the question that won't be in my review book: Who is she, and what is she doing here?

"Hi, Zoe."

I look up to see Dr. Berringer standing there.

"Oh, hi." I stand up, too.

"This is my wife, Trudy," he says. She takes my hand like

a queen. Trudy Berringer is pretty, if in a manufactured way. Boob-job, fake-blond, tanning-booth pretty. She has "former debutante" written all over her.

"You come here a lot?" he asks. His eyes look gray against his sweater.

"Oh, yeah, well, my brother works here." I point over to him, and Scotty gives a polite wave from afar.

"We were just walking by," he says, and Trudy nods her agreement. "Nice place," he comments, taking it in. We all stand there staring at each other. It strikes me that we really have nothing to talk about. I can't exactly ask about Jane in the middle of the coffeehouse. Nor can I reveal that, oh, by the way, I posted her picture on a missing persons website and unfortunately got no hits yet. "Well, we're going to grab something." He points up to the register.

"Right, right. I'll see you later."

"Nice to meet you," Trudy says.

I sit back down on my settee and open my book while Eddie takes their order. Number two:

Which of the following is true regarding post-traumatic stress disorder (PTSD)?
a) nightmares are often a troubling phenomenon
b) intrusive thoughts are a key feature
c) just witnessing a traumatic event may be a sufficient cause
d) hyperarousal state may be seen in these cases
e) all of the above

I circle *e*, then steal a glance over at the Berringer couple. They're sitting in the corner in the glare of a sunny window, sipping coffees. Both are watching the traffic from opposite sides of the table, not speaking. Vivaldi's *Four Seasons* starts playing. (Scotty threw out the Wagner after I complained about it enough, and now they play this ad nauseam. Management decision, he told me.) I look over at Tad and Trudy again.

Maybe it's just that you run out of things to say after years together. Maybe it's just companionable silence. Maybe, as a psychiatrist-in-training, I'm making too much of nonverbal clues. But as they sit there, staring past each other, I could swear they look unhappy.

Chapter Seven

The week flies by, and it's Yom Kippur already. Scotty and I walk out of the temple into a misty rain. This morning it was gray and muggy out, impossible weather to dress for. Clothes start out sweaty, then get soaked from a downpour an hour later. I can't wait to get into my jeans and out of my "temple clothes"—my pin-striped gray suit, which is a hair tight in the waist (likely due to a dry-cleaning issue), and scratched-up flats. I feel like a women's basketball coach in that suit, clapping up and down the sidelines and wishing she had her sweats on. As we walk down the street toward his car, rain starts falling in a lazy, light spray, deciding whether or not to come down in earnest. The type of rain that makes you consider but decide against an umbrella, a decision you'll regret in a half hour.

"So what did you think of the service?" Scotty asks.

"Fine. A little heavy on the music." Our rabbi is a big believer in music. My mom once cracked that his guitar was surgically attached to his hip. (She was the queen of one-liners before her brain started shrinking.) Not that I'm antimusic, but I can do without five musical versions of every prayer. If I wanted to sit in temple for three hours, I would have been conservative.

Scotty folds a rectangle of gum up like an accordion and pops it in his mouth, the same way he's eaten gum since he was six.

"You going in to work today?"

"No, I'm being a good Jew. You?"

"Yeah, unfortunately. Eddie's got the flu so I have to cover."

The rain has made its decision to go full bore now, pelting us and sending rivulets down the side of the street. Water rolls off my raincoat and onto my skirt, and Scotty's strategically gelled hair now lies flat on his head like a bowl cut. Our leisurely stroll becomes an all-out run until finally, we reach Scotty's car, a tiny silver hybrid. Being tall like me, he has to fold his body in half to get in. I lumber in on the other side.

"So I'm dropping you home?" he asks. The rain thuds against the windshield.

"Yup."

"Hey," he says, looking into the rearview mirror and wiping moisture off his forehead, "did you get a chance to get any of those pictures together?"

"Oh, right," I say, stalling. "Not yet."

Scotty's been asking me to gather pictures of Mom for a Web memorial he's doing. I'm not exactly sure what a Web memorial is—something like a website of Mom's life.

It's under construction but he showed me the home page, a photo of Mom from a party, her head back and laughing, unaware of the camera. She is beautiful in that picture, the essence of herself, a joyful, loving, self-assured woman. The complete opposite of who she was before she died. There were tabs running down the left side in categories: Vacations; Parties; Zoe; Scotty; Mom and Dad. An entire life shrunk down into a website, as if that were even possible.

We drive home, a sports station squawking about the Bills, with each caller enumerating the ways each player sucks, and Scotty pulls into my driveway. "Is Mike there?"

"No, he's working. You want to come in?" I ask.

"Nah. I got to get changed and back to work. Thanks anyway."

"Okay, see you later." I race in and let Arthur out of his crate. He immediately assumes the position, lying down rather promiscuously on his back, his tongue out and tail wagging. I can't claim to be as happy. Though getting out of my soaked temple-wear and into my lovely, dry jeans is a good start.

Now that I'm home, though, I have no idea what to do with myself. Yom Kippur means no schedule and no work, filling a Type A-er like me with dispiriting ennui. And anything I might want to do surely constitutes sinning. I can't study for the RITE or read up on further treatments for catatonia because that would definitely qualify as work. Crashing on my couch, I flip through a gossip magazine but realize this is most likely a sin, too. I vaguely recall a pronouncement against slander. The gas fireplace flickers orange over the fake

61

gray-black stones. The fireplace would have been inconceivable before today, but the rain has finally stopped, and the day has turned precipitously cold. Fall has officially fallen. The sky outside is still gray, but a cool, misty gray now. Everything looks gray in fact, like the sky sucked out all the color. Gray glossy grass, gray sodden sidewalk, silver-gray underbellies of the leaves flittering like fish scales.

The gossip mag (more a picture book than a magazine really) is finished in two minutes, and I thump my fuzzy-socked feet against the coffee table. I am officially bored, a dangerous state of affairs for an ADHDer who needs her dopamine fix. I could call Mike, but he might not want to pause from stitching up a gunshot wound to chat with me. Then it occurs to me: I could call the Nigerian girl again. The family's name was on the school website, but their machine has been "full and cannot accept new messages at this time" all week. I unfold the creased paper where the number is scribbled, make the call, and am shocked when someone picks up the phone.

"Hello?"

Even the hello has a Southern accent. "Um, hi. I was looking to speak with Sarima?"

"Can I ask who's calling?"

"Well, yes, but she doesn't know me. I'm a doctor from Buffalo. Dr. Zoe Goldman. And—"

"Oh, all right. I'll get her."

I hear a name being called. Arthur wanders by and tries to make off with the paper with her picture, and I shove him.

"Hello?" Now it's a Nigerian hello.

"Yes, hi, this is Zoe Goldman." I realize at once this will be an impossible situation to explain, especially with a language barrier, so I improvise. "I'm calling from a health agency. We just need to verify that you are in fact Sarima Balewa."

"Yes. That is me."

"And you are matriculating as a foreign exchange student in Oak Hills High School?"

"Yes, I am."

"And your vaccinations are current?" I throw this one in to sound official.

"Absolutely," she answers.

I pause then, out of things to say. "That's fine then. Thank you for your time." I hang up with a sigh. So I have proved the obvious. Sarima Balewa is in fact Sarima Balewa and not Jane. I put the paper down and lay back on the couch. My stomach growls, but it'll have to wait until sundown. Maybe it's the gray day, the fuzzy socks, or the empty stomach, but all at once I feel drugged. Pulling my blanket (Mom's old lilac blanket that she knitted herself, pre-dementia) over me, I fall into a deep slumber.

When the phone wakes me up, three hours have slipped by. My right leg has gone numb from a dog lying on top of it, and I'm starved.

"Hello?" I sit straight up, and Arthur woofs awake.

"Hi, is this Dr. Goldman?" says a woman's voice.

"Yes?"

"Yes, it's eleven north. We're having a bit of an issue here."

"Okay?" My voice is still husky with sleep.

"Our patient in 1128 is threatening to leave AMA."

"What's the patient's name?"

"Tiffany. Tiffany Munroe."

Tiffany Munroe leaving AMA. Why is this night different from any other night? "Okay, here's the thing. I'm actually not on call. Maybe the service didn't get the message, but I switched with Dr. Chang."

Papers rustle over the phone. "No, we definitely have you down."

"Yes, I can see how that might be, but it's actually a holiday. A very important Jewish holiday, and I'm not on." I'm trying to keep my voice even. "Jason is on call. Dr. Jason Chang." With fucking whom I switched one month ago, of fucking which I reminded him yesterday.

"I don't know anything about that," the nurse says, annoyed. "And your name is down here as the on-call doc. So, unless you'd rather I call Dr. Berringer—"

"No, no, that won't be necessary," I grumble. Probation Girl surely does not need that. I flick off the charming fireplace and the room blacks out like a light switch was turned off. "I'm on my way."

"Thank you very much," the nurse says with a tone that sounds more like "Fuck you very much." I slip on my new brown (seal brown, per the box) boots, and Arthur gives me a mournful "say it ain't so" look. Time to go to the hospital, to work.

I'm trying hard not to sin, but it isn't easy.

Room 1128 is empty, of course.

The bed has been stripped, leaving a stained, blue-striped mattress. The bathroom is empty, too, a mint-green toothpaste line running down the middle of the sink. Ms. Tiffany Munroe has left the building.

I march over to the nurses' counter ready to blaspheme like a drunken sailor, Yom Kippur or not, when the nurse preempts me. "I'm sorry," she says, sounding in fact sorry. "I tried to call you. Like five minutes after we spoke, Tiffany vanished."

I pull out my phone, which was conveniently on vibrate, and notice a voice mail from the hospital. "Oh," I answer, deflated. It's hard to be mad at someone who's actually contrite. And it *is* Yom Kippur, after all. "That's fine." From the chart rack, Jane Doe catches my eye. "How's Jane doing, by the way?"

The nurse squints her eyes. "The catatonic?"

"Yes."

"Nothing's up with her as far as I know. Stable."

"Oh well. While I'm here, might as well go and check."

As I walk in, her shadow looms on the wall, a camel with two humps. A soft light buzzes over her head, giving her a pale cast. Jane is the nighttime version of herself. Staring, grimacing, doing the bunny-nose thing. No change whatsoever, despite our sizable bump in the Ativan yesterday. The vision is beyond depressing. I turn around to leave and nearly slam into Dr. Berringer in the doorway.

"Hey, you," he says, like we happen to be running into each other at a shop. "What are you doing here?" He's wearing old corduroys and a pilled tan sweater. Like me, he's in "hang-out clothes." He usually wears khakis with a blazer on rounds.

"They called me for Tiffany. She left AMA. But I figured I'd check on Jane while I'm here," I say.

He nods, turning to her. "No change, huh?"

"No, unfortunately not." There is a pause. The bed moans, the IV bag whirs, her stockings fill with air and deflate again. All the sounds in the room are inanimate.

"Tough case. I was talking about her with a colleague."

"Yeah?"

"She said the next step may be ECT."

I pause. Electroconvulsive therapy. The big guns, or more like the assault weapons. His colleague is right, though. It's the last-resort treatment in the literature review on catatonia.

"But we have some time before we get that drastic," he says. "Got some more meds we can try."

"I hope so." We stand another moment. "Well, I was just leaving, actually," I say.

"Yeah, me too. Just checking up on things on the floor." We walk into the hallway together, our feet clacking two different rhythms against the tile. I don't know whether to be impressed or alarmed at his obvious workaholic tendencies. Maybe this is how he got to be "wunderkind from the Big Easy."

"Wait, isn't it your holiday or something? New Year's?" he asks.

"Yom Kippur. But they couldn't reach Jason, so I came in."

"Ah, that's too bad. I wish they had called me. Did you park far away?"

"Not too far." Though this is a lie. The resident lot is a good ten-minute walk, through not the nicest neighborhood. A neighborhood where people shoot one another.

"Let me walk you," he says.

"No, that's all right."

"No arguing. It's a Southern gentlemanly thing. I insist."

"Well." I laugh. "I suppose I can't argue against the Southern gentlemanly thing." We head into the elevator. But instead of pushing the down button, he pushes the twelve. The top floor.

"I want to show you something first, if you don't mind," he says as the elevator lumbers up.

"Sure," I answer, though I'm feeling a bit light-headed and really just want to go home and get something to eat. But I'll admit that I'm intrigued. The elevator dings open, and I follow him out. The twelfth floor, oddly, does not have the same mud-brown color scheme as the rest of the hospital. The carpet is a light pink, with tuna-colored Formica furniture, a basic block coffee table, and pink plastic chairs with scratched-up seats. A pale-pink curtain covers the large window.

"It's like a ghost town up here," I say, looking around. Dark, no patient lights, no beeping noises, no nurses calling from overhead. A forgotten, orphan floor.

"Yeah, it's been empty for over a year. They're still deciding whether or not to move dialysis up here." He gazes around, too. "You want a drink?"

67

"A drink?"

"Sure," he says, heading to the corner where a Pepsi machine buzzes softly, casting a gray-white glow on the wall. "Pick your poison. It's on me. The least I can do for them calling you on your holiday.

"All right." I tap on the Diet Pepsi window. He stares at the machine, fingering his chin in a semi-comic gesture of deep thought. "Going to have to go with the root beer." He clinks in the quarters, and the machine spits out our drinks. I spy a bag of Fritos calling out to me and push that button, too. It's as good a break-the-fast as any. He sits down in one of the plastic chairs.

"Have a seat." He points to the other one and unscrews his bottle with a loud hiss. Then he leans back, his long legs crossed in front of him. We sit a moment, drinking our drinks. The chips are heavenly. Though after a while, I wonder what the hell he wanted to show me in this musty, old abandoned floor.

"Okay, you ready for the big reveal?" he asks as if in response to my unspoken question.

I raise one eyebrow doubtfully, and he takes this for a yes and walks over to the window.

"You sure you're ready now?" he asks, and before I can answer, he rips open the curtain with a soft metal scrape. A thousand hazy city lights spring up in the window, miles of buildings and streets laid out before us.

"Wow." I walk over to the window and stand beside him.

"Amazing, huh?" he says with pride at his discovery. The glass is cool under my fingertips. The inchoate sob of an ambulance sounds out from a distance. A lone traffic light switches from red to green with no cars nearby to follow its command. After a while, I make my way back to my chair, and Dr. Berringer joins me. We sip at our soft drinks, staring out at the night. Our penthouse view from a run-down hospital suite.

"You're probably wondering why I'm not at home," he says.

The workaholic question. The unhappy couple question. "I assume you have your reasons," I say.

He sniffs out a laugh. "That's one way to put it." He scratches his knee, at the thinning dark-brown (seal-brown, if I had to say) corduroy. "You know," he says, but then he pauses and doesn't say any more.

So I don't say any more. And we sit drinking, watching the night glow and flicker, the moon a hazy pearl in the sky. And I think that this might just be a good new year after all.

Chapter Eight

I'm still an hour early for rounds when I get the idea. Dr. Koneru, the hospital pathologist, might know what to make of the scar. We bonded over cafeteria food once, when she asked me about Asperger's syndrome. I was only a first-year and shared the thimbleful I knew, then found out later she was asking about her son.

I make my way down the dank, fluorescent-lit hallway to her office in the basement and knock on the open door. She glances up from a microscope. "Why, hello there." Her face softens with a smile, and she brushes back her hennaed hair. "What brings you to this neck of the woods?" But she says "voods." She pronounces all her w's that way.

"Sort of an odd question," I say.

"Okay. What is it?"

I pull out the picture I printed. "This scar is on the left ankle of our patient Jane Doe. She's catatonic."

She takes the picture and brings it up to her face. Then

she pulls a magnifying glass out of her top drawer and gives it a better look.

"What do you think?" I ask.

"Well, it's not a cigarette burn," she says.

"Ha," I crow. "I didn't think so."

She turns it side to side. "It is funny."

"Like a circle or something, right?"

"Keloid on the rim. African American?"

"Yes."

Dr. Koneru stows the magnifying glass back in her tidy drawer and lays the picture next to the microscope. "It is hard to tell, Zoe. I think it is most likely a burn, possibly with some metal. But the keloid throws this all into question. It could just as easily be a deep cut with irregular healing."

I pause. "You think someone cut her?"

"It could even be a shaving cut, Zoe."

"Oh, yeah, that's true."

She shifts the power on her microscope. "Sorry I couldn't be more helpful."

"That's okay. Thanks for trying anyway."

She glances down at the picture one more time and shakes her head. "Just not sure. Can I keep it?"

"Sure. No problem. I can make more copies."

She goes back to her microscope, and I'm contemplating grabbing a coffee in the lobby when I see a text from Jason.

rounding early today, remember?

Oh shit, no, I did not remember. So I don't have a half hour to kill; I'm a half hour late. I take an interminable ride up the elevator after a three-year-old has a jolly old time pushing random buttons and then scramble into the nurses' station.

"P is for punctuality, Probation Girl," Jason scolds.

"And F is for fuck off."

He laughs. "We already rounded. Did you see Jane yet?"

"Yeah, this morning. No change. Why?"

He doesn't look up from his note. "She woke up."

"She—" I don't finish the sentence, tearing off to her room as fast as my legs can take me. Dr. Berringer is leaning over her with Detective Adams by his side. As I stumble in, Jane looks up at me, nervous, unsure. "Hello there," I say.

A hesitant half smile turns on her lips.

"Did she say her name?" I ask, crowding next to the bed.

"She's not quite there yet, Zoe," Dr. Berringer says, his tone betraying some annoyance at my grand late entrance.

"How long until she talks, do you think?" asks the detective, facing Dr. Berringer.

"It's variable. Sometimes right away, sometimes a few weeks."

The detective taps on his reporter's notebook, which has two words in black, sloppy writing: *Jane awake*.

I lift up Jane's arm, maybe because I'm just used to doing this, and she looks up at me and yanks it back. Her eyes are brown as raisins, fixed on me.

"She's probably scared," I say. Jane looks down at the rumpled blue blanket on her lap.

"Probably," the detective answers. "Any idea what finally woke her up?"

"Ativan, probably," Dr. Berringer answers. "Though it

could just as well be that it was spontaneously resolving anyway."

The detective watches her another second, then stashes his notebook in his pocket. "Thanks for calling me. Let me know if something changes."

"Will do," Dr. Berringer answers.

"Hey, before you go," I ask. "Did you find out any more on the scar?"

"No, I didn't. I asked our social worker who deals with the abused kids, and he wasn't sure. He said it's probably a cigarette—"

"Yeah, but here's the thing. I asked our pathologist, Dr. Koneru? And she didn't think it was consistent with that. Too perfectly round."

"It is weird," Dr. Berringer agrees. "But still the most likely explanation."

The detective shrugs. "Hopefully, pretty soon, you can ask the source herself."

Jane stares at us, not offering an answer. The detective gives my shoulder a quick pat on his way out. "Bye, guys."

After he leaves, Dr. Berringer turns to me. "Okay, Zoe. What's the next step here?" he asks, like he's testing me, not just asking.

"First, I'd see if she'll take anything by mouth, and if so, D/C the feeds."

"Okay."

"Keep up the Ativan, but lower the dose." I'm wondering if it's the correct dosing that finally woke her up.

He grabs his beat-up doctor bag. "That all sounds good."

He looks down at her then with a broad smile. "Good stuff. Keep an eye on her today. Oh, and Zoe?"

"Uh-huh?"

"Do me a favor. Try to get here on time." He says this with a smile, however, pummeling my arm in a mock punch that does actually hurt, before striding out of the room.

I stand there, staring at Jane, the beeps in the room echoing around me. Jane peers at the Halloween figurine with curiosity, and I reach up and hand it to her. She turns it over in her palms, touching all the angles like a blind person.

"It's yours," I say. "Do you like it?"

She gives the merest hint of a nod and swallows. Then out of nowhere, her eyes flood with tears, tracking down her face. And I sit beside her while she cries.

Chapter Nine

I take a swig of coffee and almost spit it out. "Blech. Is there chocolate in here?"

"Yeah," Mike says, sipping his own mug and absentmindedly petting the dog. "It's all that was left. It was that or decaf, and I figured..."

"True. Death by hanging would be preferable to decaf."

He looks up from his tablet. "Well, I hadn't considered the manner of death."

Racing around the kitchen, I rip off a banana for lunch. I would throw together a sandwich but I have to leave in five minutes, and I haven't been hungry for lunch lately anyway. Sam warned me to watch out for a decrease in appetite when he upped the Adderall dose at my prompting (begging, more like) last week. I'm pretending it's not that. "You late today?" I ask.

"Yeah. Noon. Gotta get my hair cut anyway."

I examine him. "You are looking a little shaggy."

"Thanks for the endorsement, hon."

I throw back another god-awful sip of coffee and do my checklist. Purse, check. Satchel, check. Phone…

"Shit. Where's my fucking phone?"

He doesn't look up this time. "No idea."

I march around the kitchen, tearing through magazine piles, sweeping countertops. Arthur watches me with curiosity. Mike seems annoyingly uninterested in the whereabouts of my phone. Though I do ask him this same question about ten times a day. "I'm going to be late, late, late!"

"Hmmm." Mike taps on his phone screen, then I hear my own phone going off.

Somewhere upstairs. I climb up there, and it goes silent. "Call it again?" It starts up ringing, and I play a game of Hot and Cold until I find it in the laundry room. The thing ends up in the damnedest places. I jog back downstairs. "Did I tell you Jane woke up?"

"Yes, you did." He grabs some just-popped-up toast.

"Okay." I look around one last time. "Am I forgetting anything? My phone…"

"In your hand."

"Right."

"Zoe." He scrapes butter on his toast. "I don't want to intrude, but—"

"Yes, I've taken my meds."

"No," he says, chewing. "You mentioned the dose change, and…"

"And?"

He dips his knife in the butter again. "You just seem a little up is all."

I give him a look.

"Or something."

I give him another look.

"Or nothing. Forget it. Arthur, did you hear anything? Some idiot making noise? No? Me neither."

As I grab my car keys, I catch a glimpse of Arthur panting up at him, and I could swear the dog is smiling.

My heart thumps out of my chest. I take two deep breaths and wait for it to stop, which it does. Palpitations—something else Sam warned me about.

Jane looks at me with curiosity. Maybe she can tell something is wrong. Hard to know, because she still isn't talking. My heart thuds again, then stops. I stand up and give Jane a bright smile. "I guess we'll see you later then, with the team." I'm walking out the door when I hear a soft voice.

"Where am I?"

I spin back around and look at her. She stares at me blankly, and for a moment I think I might be hearing things, when she repeats it. "Where am I?"

"Um." I'm floored. It's like a beloved doll suddenly opens her mouth and starts talking to you. "You're in the hospital."

She nods and looks around. "Why?"

"You were…" I pause, thinking of the right way to put this. "You were sick, honey. You were sick."

She nods again, like she's in slow motion.

I take a seat next to her. "What's your name?"

She purses her lips and takes a long time to answer. "I don't know."

"Do you know how you got here?"

She ponders this deeply again and finally comes up with "No."

A cart of food trays rumbles by out in the hall, silverware clinking. "The police brought you in. Do you remember that at all?"

Jane looks confused. "The police?"

"Yeah. They found you wandering around on the streets."

"The streets?" she repeats. "Where?"

"Buffalo. We're in Buffalo."

She shakes her head like she's shaking off sleep.

"Where did you think we were?"

"I don't know. New York City maybe."

"New York City?" I ask. "Is that where you're from?"

She doesn't answer but sits up and surveys the room. "How long have I been here?"

I retrace the time. "Three weeks now? Almost a month."

"A month?" She looks gobsmacked.

"Yeah." I put her chart on the foot of her bed. "What's the last thing you do remember?"

"The last thing I remember..." She pauses again, for an uncomfortably long time. "A limousine."

That's the last thing I expected her to say. "Where was it going?"

"I don't know." She picks at some tape on her arm from a blood draw.

"Were you in it?"

"No, I was watching it," she says.

"Watching it?"

"Trying to chase after it."

I pause. "Why were you chasing after it?"

"I don't know."

"Who was in it then?"

"I don't know." Jane scratches her elbow. "You know what?"

I ready my pen. "What?"

"I'm hungry."

"Hungry?" I laugh. "Hungry is a good thing! We can fix that."

She gives me a hesitant smile, which grows into a full-fledged smile. It's the first time I've ever seen her smile, and it's a gorgeous sight.

"Nancy is your nurse. I'll talk to her about grabbing you some food. Then I'll come back later with the team. You remember the tall guy? I mean, taller than me. And the one with the bow ties?"

Her expression turns nervous. "No."

"Never mind. I'll do proper introductions when we round this afternoon." I turn back when I get to the door. "By the way, you have a scar...on your ankle?"

She reaches down automatically to the left side.

"Do you have any idea how you got it?"

Jane touches the scar but doesn't look at it. I wait a long while for her answer.

"I don't know." She screws her face up in thought, then finally she says, "I'm hungry."

"Hungry, right. We'll take care of that in a jiffy." I scoot into the hallway and get right on the phone to Detective Adams. "Guess who's talking, talking, talking?"

"One second." The detective yells something muffled away from the phone. "I'm guessing it's Jane." The detective's voice sounds far away among the buzz of activity in the background.

"Yes indeed. You win a prize."

"Must be my lucky day." His voice gets louder as the phone shifts toward his mouth. "Do we have a name yet?"

"Not yet, unfortunately," I answer. "She doesn't know anything really. She doesn't even know how she got here. The last thing she remembers is chasing a limousine."

"Chasing a limousine?"

"That's what she said."

"Hmm. That's odd."

"Oh, and she thought she was in New York City."

The phone moves onto his shoulder again. "Okay, I'll get out there soon." Someone calls out his name. "Listen, Zoe, I have to get going. Thanks for keeping me in the loop."

"Sure, no problem."

There's a pause on his end. "Here's the thing. I know you care about this girl. We all do, really. But I'm working on a lot of cases right now..." He trails off.

"Okay?"

"Yeah, so feel free to call me with any big changes or updates. Like today, for instance. But"—he pauses—"you don't need to call me every day or text me reminders or anything."

I feel my face flush. I guess I did text him last week, three or four times. Or six times maybe. I lost count. It was after my Adderall bump.

"I promise," he says, "we're on it. And I'll call you if we find anything."

"Oh, sure. Sorry about that." *In other words: Don't call me, I'll call you.*

"I mean, you don't want me to try to be a doctor, right?" He laughs, to lighten the mood.

I force out a laugh, too.

"I'll call you soon. Okay?"

We hang up, and on the way back to the nurses' station, I corner Nancy to arrange for an extra lunch, then swing into the nurses' station. "Guess who's talking, talking, talking?" I ask the room, though only Jason is there. He looks up from his computer. "Did you hear me? Talking!" I reach over for a high five, and he offers only a fist bump in return. "Come on, where's the excitement?"

Jason turns back to his e-mail. "You're kind of amped up these days."

"Not really," I answer, trying not to sound defensive. But I have to admit that this seems to be the general consensus. So far, Mike has told me I'm a "little up," Eddie told me I seemed "zippy," and Scotty—less diplomatically—told me to "calm the fuck down." The slap of Dr. Berringer's walk announces him in the doorway, and Jason signs out of his e-mail.

"You guys all set?" His eyes are bloodshot, and his hair is mussed up. "Jason, who's up?"

"A new one. Ms. Clark," Jason answers as we start walking down the hallway to see the patients.

"All right. What's the quick and dirty on this one?"

"Sixteen-year-old female with new onset of probable psychosis."

"Because?" Dr. Berringer's voice is scratchy.

"Because she thinks her cat is talking to her."

He pauses. "Did you say 'her cat'?"

"Her cat," Jason confirms.

"Okay, I thought I'd heard them all. What's the cat saying exactly?"

"The cat is giving her secret messages that people want to harm her."

"By actually talking?"

Jason pauses. "To be honest, I'm not sure if the words are in English or if she's going by the meow."

"It's a feline conversation one way or the other," I break in.

They both stare at me. I find myself less patient on my new dose of Adderall.

"Yes. That's correct, Zoe," Jason says, in not the warmest tone.

Dr. Berringer knocks on the door, and we walk in to find an aide helping with a sponge bath behind a curtain. "Be ready in a second," the aide yells out.

Dr. Berringer squeezes his forehead. "We'll come back," Dr. Berringer calls to her, and we exit into the hallway. Rounding is full of such missed opportunities to see patients: They're in OT, EEG, CT—usually some sort of acronym. "All right. So we'll have to meet the cat whisperer later. Who else is up, Jason?"

A little voice inside me is dying to scream out "*Me, me.*

Call on me! I've got a new patient with anorexia!" with my arm leaping off my body like I'm back in second grade and the chair is a prison. The increase in Adderall is clearly having a paradoxical effect.

Jason swipes his gelled-up bangs, which are on the orange side today and in need of a highlighting appointment. "My next one is Brandon Gellman."

"Oh, we saw him on Friday, right? Cutter?"

"Burner," Jason says. A sixteen-year-old who burns himself with cigarettes to stamp out the less pleasant feelings swirling around in his head.

"Oh, yeah, that's right. We'll circle around to him at the end. How's Jane?" He turns to me. "Rumor has it she's talking."

"Who told you?" I ask, annoyed that someone just made off with all my thunder.

"Nancy." He looks at me funny. "Said she was asking for food. Do we know who she is yet?"

"No. Not yet. Hopefully soon. Soon, soon, soon." My foot taps out a song on the tile.

"Patience, fair Zoe," he says, his voice tired. He scans his patient list and then folds up the paper into a square with trembling hands. "You know what, guys? I'm sorry. I am just feeling like crap." He does look a pale shade of green, his forehead glazed with sweat. "My wife has the flu. I'm probably coming down with it." He puts the paper in his long lab coat pocket. "I'll get one of my partners to cover for this afternoon, if you don't mind."

"Oh no, of course, that's fine," I say. Jason and I nod reassuringly. And if we did mind, we most certainly wouldn't say. Dr. Berringer gives us a shaky smile and walks off, leaving us standing there with a cartful of charts in the middle of the hall and no one to run rounds. Our fearless leader, vanished.

"Well, ain't that just the shit?" Jason asks.

"Odd, isn't it."

"What?"

"The shit. I mean, what kind of expression is that?"

He raises one eyebrow. "Zoe, you know what?"

"What?"

"Sometimes you're really annoying."

There's no mistaking Chloe Brown's diagnosis. She wears it like a badge, a purple heart in her own private war. Painfully symmetrical collarbones, dull teeth, and sores lining her fingers from purging stomach acid.

"So, has anyone explained the rules to you?" I ask.

"Yup," she says with a loud sigh. "Been there, done that, know the drill." The war has left her ravaged but not defeated.

"So you know then," I continue, "you gain points based on participating in group and gaining weight."

"As I said, not my first time at the rodeo." She tucks a Kool-Aid-red strand of hair behind her ear with chipped black fingernails.

"Okay," I answer, ignoring her hostile vibe. I lay my pen

down on the table with a soft, slapping sound. "It might sound trite, Chloe, but we're really here to help you. That's all any of us are trying to do."

She remains slumped in her bed, staring at the whiteboard decorated with perky red marker: "Today is...Monday! Your nurse's name is...Nancy! Lunch is...mac and cheese!" I've had their mac and cheese; it's nothing to exclaim about.

I lean back in the chair, telling her with my posture that I'm open to sharing, then wait a long moment before gathering up my pen and chart. The intake has been carried out. There's not much more to discuss right now. Or at least Chloe doesn't think so. "You've had your weigh-in. Group therapy at eleven. I guess I'll see you tomorrow."

She doesn't answer.

"If you need anything in the meantime, just call me. Dr. Goldman."

"Who's the attending?" she asks.

"Dr. Berringer."

She rolls her eyes. "The great Dr. Berringer." Her red bangs hang in spikes over her eyebrows.

"You know him?"

"Yeah, you could say that. I had him last time I was here."

I nod, giving her time to elaborate, but nothing is forthcoming. "Did you have a problem with him?"

She smirks. "Yeah, I have a problem with him. He's an asshole."

Her response surprises me. Most of the patients love Dr. Berringer. The parents, especially the mothers, won't stop raving about him. "Okay," I answer, evenly. "Would you like to tell me more about that?"

"Yes, I'd love to tell you more about that, Dr. Goldman!" She claps her hands together. "He's the most egocentric individual I've ever met!"

"Because?" I ask.

"I don't know." She shrugs. "I guess you'd have to ask him. An overindulgent mother, I'm thinking. That would be the Freudian explanation anyway."

"Right." Sometimes you need to quit when you're ahead, and she is the last patient of the day. "Maybe we can talk more about that tomorrow."

"I'm counting the minutes," she says, rolling her eyes again, harder if possible. A seizure-inducing eye roll. I stand up to leave, figuring she's probably just splitting, meaning someone is either all good or all bad. Black and white, no gray zone. And this can shift. Dr. Berringer may be the devil today and her savior tomorrow.

On the elevator, a man in a turban walks on, cradling a coffee in his hands. A priest steps in on the next floor, nodding at the man in the turban and then me.

"How's the weather up there?" he asks with a broad smile. I smile in response to this question I've heard a million times. It's hard to get mad at a priest. In the lobby, health-care folks in scrubs and white coats mix it up with the civilians: patients and visitors. They all line up for the coffee shop, jonesing for their fix. People are scattered about the room in various states of disarray. A balding man in a suit, pacing with a bouquet under his arm. A very pregnant woman in sweats, staring at the vending machine. A redhead, stiff in his wheel-chair, drooling and grimacing while his mother stands next to him eating pizza. A resident talking on his phone, his scrub hat lopsided. Automatic doors slide open to a fading blue sky, and I feel a twinge of sadness at these folks in the lobby who have to stay in the hospital.

But it's time for me to go home.

Someone is sitting in my usual eggplant-colored settee by the fireplace at the Coffee Spot (annoying, but it's not like I had a sign on it), so I've settled into a bone-colored sofa chair by the window, the faux leather flaking off its arms. The night grows darker outside, a soft rain dotting the sidewalks.

Acing the Psychiatry RITE sits on one side of the table, and a thick journal article, "Catatonia: A Case Series and Liter-ature Review," is on the other. Both untouched. Eddie walks by, straightening up the table to my left. The chair knocks against the table legs. With a sigh, I open up the RITE book, flattening out the page.

> *Your patient has been diagnosed with bipolar disorder. After trials of several other medications, you decide on topiramate. What potential side effects should you counsel your patient about?*
> *a) tremor*
> *b) weight gain*

c) *hirsutism*
d) *suicidality*
e) *nephrolithiasis*

I circle *b*, because every psychiatric drug seems to cause weight gain, then immediately check out the answer below. E. Kidney stones, damn it. *Topamax is known to frequently cause significant weight loss.* Of course it is. Probation is starting to look like a life sentence. I take another sip of decaf espresso (an oxymoron, I know, but my heart has been trying to escape from my chest all day), readying myself for the next question, when Scotty wanders over.

"How's life?" He sits beside me in the French-blue chair, crossing his long legs at the ankles. The music changes to Vivaldi's *Four Seasons*, of course.

"Life is life," I answer. "How about you?"

"Similar," he says, downing the last of his coffee. "I was going to visit Mom's gravesite on Sunday if you wanted to come."

"Oh." I play with the pages of the book. "I don't think I can because—"

"Quick, think of an excuse," he says. Snarkily, I might add.

"What's your problem?"

"I don't know." He leans back again. "Sometimes it's like you care more about Jane fucking Doe than you do about Mom."

"It's not like there's a contest."

"You know what I mean."

I take a deep breath. "Obviously we just have different ways of dealing with Mom's death."

"Obviously so." He checks his watch. "The Charles Schwab thing came up empty by the way."

"What Charles Schwab thing?"

"For the bonds. I told you I was going to talk with that woman from Charles Schwab. She said they can't go back that far, but she has some nice ETFs to sell me if I'm interested."

I cackle. "I bet."

We sit another minute, not talking, and I notice my foot tapping to the music. Scotty yawns, then catches the eye of a skinny blond girl a couple of tables ahead of us. He glances at the floor a second, and when he looks back up at her, she's still watching him.

"Aren't you still seeing what's-her-name?" I ask, because I actually don't remember her name.

"I don't think so," he answers, which isn't an answer as far as I'm concerned, then strides over to meet the newest what's-her-name. Brushing his hand through his already messy hair, he bestows his trademark eyebrow raise upon her, then says something. Who knows what? No doubt a well-worn pickup line that only he can carry off, and she laughs with her friends, throwing her head back with strands of golden hair shining under the lights. Target acquired. My brother and his way with the fairer sex, one of life's great mysteries.

I turn the page, but the next question is over three paragraphs, which seems like an inordinate amount of reading right now (again, cue ADHD and utter Adderall failure), when luckily an e-mail pings onto my phone to save the day. Probably another coupon from Banana Republic, but I check anyway. It's a chain e-mail from a medical resident who barely qualifies as an acquaintance. Delete. I abhor chain mails, a gratuitous source of angst. The next question is also way beyond the pale of what I'm willing to read, so I sail on to question number five.

Anorexia is often associated with
a) depression
b) OCD
c) anxiety
d) borderline personality disorder
e) all of the above.

I picture Chloe rolling her eyes with disdain over "the great Dr. Berringer," which probably has a lot to do with answer *d*.

As I sit there, the rain hitting the window in silken taps, a sudden, overwhelming exhaustion overtakes me. It brings me back to my high school years, when we were still experimenting with stimulants, trying to get the right dose and the right combination to corral my thoughts into line. There is the surge of dopamine release.

But then there is the crash. I had forgotten about it.

Chapter Ten

I hardly recognize Jane out of bed.

She is leaning over the art table, her elbow against the scratched rubber siding, with her head on her arm like she's about to go to sleep. But she is wide awake, in deep concentration as her left hand draws out a picture. I pull in closer to see.

"That's great," I say.

She does not answer right away. "Thanks," she manages quietly.

"She's very talented," the art therapist agrees, smiling. Donna is a large woman (or zaftig, as my mother would have more gently put it) in a willowy, wine-red outfit. She always favors shapeless outfits in earth tones, like she found out her color was "autumn" at a makeup counter once and she's sticking to it. "I taught gifted and talented kids in the Williamsville school system for twenty years," she says. "And I'm always amazed that our kids here are heads and tails above all of them." She washes off some paintbrushes, a muddy purple color flowing into the sink. "I guess with burdens come talents."

The pictures are good, actually, much better than my stick-figure composition would be, my artistic achievement having plateaued around second grade. "What was the assignment today?"

"Self-portraits. It helps to see how they visualize themselves," she explains. "Tells me about their hopes and fears. That sort of thing."

The life sort of thing. I inch back over to Jane and flip through her drawings from the last week. There is one with numbers and letters. Symmetrical and straight, no bubble letters like another tween might have drawn. Plain numbers and letters interspersed with symbols of the sun. Perfect circles with spokes radiating off in glistening yellow.

"What do these mean?" I ask her.

Jane shrugs and keeps drawing.

"I told them to just draw what they wanted yesterday. This is what she came up with."

Numbers and letters and suns. Part of the recovery process? "I like them."

Jane pauses. "Thanks."

I glance at my watch, slim and silver with a pearl face. My mom's old watch. "See you later, okay? We'll be rounding this afternoon."

Her pastel crayon sticks to the paper. "Okay."

Walking out of the art room, I ready myself to see Chloe next, taking a deep breath. Every day, I walk into Chloe's room with my head up and walk out with my head down, feeling like a human punching bag. I drop the bulky chart on her table and pull up a chair. "I see you've lost a bit of weight."

Chloe has lost a pound, a major achievement in the Eating Disorders Unit, where every ounce is monitored. "Yup. Reportedly that's the big news today."

I readjust my chair with a squeak. "Any idea how that could have happened?"

She appears to think about this. "Evaporation?"

It takes all my training not to laugh.

"Or maybe not," she continues. "I'm a bit hazy on the water cycle these days."

I nod. "I was thinking more along the lines of hiding food."

"Now," she chides me, "you know that's against the rules."

"I do know that. But that doesn't mean you're not doing it." She doesn't answer my accusation. "In any case, you know the rules. You won't get any privileges for losing weight, unfortunately."

She blows her bangs out of her eyes, and they plop back down. "No privileges. Woe is me." The tendons in her wrist stick out like taut rubber bands, her pulse throbbing under her skin.

It strikes me then that I need to change my tactic here. She doesn't see me as an ally, just another pain-in-the-ass adult in her life telling her to do what she fears and abhors most: to eat. Tomorrow, I won't talk about food at all. Maybe that will buy me an inch with Chloe Brown. She is looking out the window now, a soft rain slicking the street below.

We both turn to the doorway as Dr. Berringer walks in with a perfunctory knock. He looks spick-and-span today, refreshed and fully pressed. Like he got over his flu.

Chloe refuses to meet his gaze.

"Hello, Chloe," he says. She still doesn't respond. "How are you doing?"

After a tense minute, she shrugs, not looking at him. Her face is hot red. "I'm back. So obviously it wasn't the ideal outcome."

He sits down in the chair next to me, his knee brushing against mine. His hair is damp and smells of shampoo. "It's going to take time, Chloe. But we'll get there. You were getting better, and we can get there again."

She turns her whole body away from us toward the window.

"Chloe?"

"Yeah, yeah, yeah. I've got to eat. It's not healthy. I'm not actually fat. I have a body dysmorphic disorder. Blah-blah-blahsy-blah-blah." She is talking right to the wall.

"I know you're angry," he says. "But I'm not sure why."

"Then you're not a very good psychiatrist." There are tears in her voice.

He starts to say something, then stops with a frown. He gives me a helpless shrug and motions toward the door.

"See you later, Chloe," I call out to her.

She doesn't answer. "We'll give her some time and come back," he says, once we're in the hallway. "How's Jane doing today?"

"Good, she—"

A middle-aged woman in a purple suit with a flouncy, cream-colored top interrupts us. "Hi there. Are you going to see Jane Doe?"

"Yes," Dr. Berringer says.

"I'm Tina Jessep," she says, pulling her ID tag off her chest. "The discharge planner. Just wondering what your thoughts were on her."

We both stare at her. "For discharge?" Dr. Berringer asks, making no attempt to hide his disbelief.

She nods with a tight smile. "Well, it's been nearly a month. She's not catatonic anymore. She's not suicidal."

"That's true. But I wouldn't expect her to be suicidal. She wasn't depressed."

"Okay, but my point is, there's nothing acute going on here. Nothing she necessarily needs to be hospitalized for."

"Yeah, but it would be nice if she knew her name, don't you think?" he asks. Tina doesn't answer the rhetorical question. "Seriously, this is egregious. She doesn't even know who she is. Where exactly are you going to send her?"

Tina tugs on one of her flounces. "I guess that's my job to figure out. The hospital is just looking for a more appropriate placement at this point."

"A cheaper placement, you mean."

"Listen," Tina entreats. "Don't shoot the messenger. We're all part of the same team here. We all want her to get better, but we also want to get her out of the hospital as soon as it's safe for her." This sounds suspiciously like a talking point.

"I just don't think she's ready," he says. "She just started speaking, for God's sake."

She nods. "I understand. I do. Keep me posted with how things are going. On my end, I'll be looking for a good place for her."

"Where might that be?" I ask.

She turns to me, like she just noticed the six-footer to her side. "I'm not sure yet. Probably Gateway or Father Baker. A home for children with emotional disturbances. Maybe foster care if we have any further progress."

We both pause to process this, and she gives us another fake smile and walks off as we get ready to see our patient. The girl who may or may not be leaving soon, whether we know her name or not.

"Where the hell would they send her?" Detective Adams asks.

Static sounds over the car phone. Mike is navigating our route via Google Maps when the detective calls for the latest update. "Gateway," I say. "Or Father Baker. They're calling her emotionally disturbed."

"Oh, please," the detective groans. "That's not going to be a good fit. Some of those kids are..." He pauses. "How do I put this delicately? Really fucked up."

I wonder what the indelicate way of putting that would have been.

"To the left," Mike calls out. "Left!"

"I was going left," I argue, swerving as Mike hangs on to his seat belt for dear life.

"It's not subjective, Zoe. You're either going left or you're going right, and you were going right."

"You guys okay over there?" the detective asks over the speaker.

"Yeah, she's just trying to kill me," Mike says.

I jab his ribs.

"Tell her that's illegal," the detective says. "People go to jail for that."

"Yeah, yeah, I got it." I pull into the driveway. "We're fine. Just checking up on some things."

"Okay, I'll let you go," the detective says. "But do me a favor, Zoe. Talk to the girl. Find out who the hell she is, would you? Before they send her somewhere she'll get eaten alive."

"I'll do my best," I promise. I don't mention that I've inveigled Mike into my dilettante investigation plans, starting with the limousine companies. As I hang up, Mike unbuckles his seat belt, and we make our way into Party Hearty Limousines. The building is cold and smells of cigars.

"Can I help you?" The man has a thick black mustache with matching curly chest hair and a thick gold chain. He could be an extra in a seventies movie.

"Yes, my name's Zoe Goldman, and this is my friend Mike."

"Hey, I'm a Mike, too!"

My Mike gives him a no-nonsense handshake.

"So what can I do you for?"

"We're looking for a missing girl," I say. We go with a less confusing story than the catatonic-Jane-Doe one, which didn't work the last two times. I'm hoping for the charm thing on the third. "I was just wondering if you've seen her before." I flash him her solemn, unsmiling picture.

He takes a long look but shakes his head. "Don't think so. Nothing that jumps out at me anyway. Did she go missing around here?"

"Maybe. She was last seen in a limousine in Buffalo. In September. September fifteenth to be exact." Actually, by her account, she was chasing the limo, but I don't get into all that.

He holds up the picture. "She looks young."

My Mike leans against the wall, playing with his phone. He's keeping me company but letting it be known this is entirely my folly.

"Here, come on in back. We'll look at the books," Mike II says. We wander back to a room that smells even more strongly of cigars. A space heater rumbles at our feet. Mike II flips through a thick, well-worn book to the correct page. "It was a Sunday, so that's usually pretty slow." He lays a fat finger on two names. "Connors was a bachelorette party. Threw up in the limo but tipped well," he says, almost to himself. "And Newberger was a fiftieth birthday party. Jewish people, you know. They were very nice."

My Mike coughs through a smile.

"How about the day before?" I ask. "Just in case."

"Yeah, sure." He trails his finger over a date. "So that's a Saturday night, and we had every limo booked." He lists off the names and an anecdote for each. His memory is shockingly good. "We didn't have any black folks that night." He pauses. "Not that we don't accept black people. We do business with anyone of course—black, white, purple…" He grins. "As long as their money's green."

"Right," I say with nothing more to add to this soliloquy. "Well, thanks anyway."

"Sorry," Mike II says. "Wish I could help you."

"That's okay, you've helped a lot."

More than the last place, where the direct quote was: *Listen honey. I don't know what you think this is. But we do weddings, proms, and bachelor parties. We don't go carting around twelve-year-olds.* Mike looked like he was about to throttle the guy.

I push the door against the wind as we leave, sniffing my sweater for any lingering cigar smell.

"Are we done yet?" Mike says. "It's past dinnertime."

I examine the list on my phone. "Three more."

He groans.

"You won't starve."

"But I'm hungry," he says, in a perfect toddler whine.

"Come on. They're trying to discharge the poor girl. This may be our last chance to figure out who she is."

Chapter Eleven

The next morning on the way into work, I check my e-mail at a red light. I know it's illegal and dangerous, but right now I can't handle sitting through twelve seconds of unaccounted-for time. Plus the limousine companies promised to write if anything came up on Jane. Unfortunately, the e-mail box remains barren. A horn beeps and I lurch ahead, when the phone surprises me by ringing in my hand.

No caller ID, but it could be one of the limo places. "Hello?"

"Bonjour."

My heart flutters. I'm not sure whether it's from the Adderall increase or hearing Jean Luc's voice again for the first time in over a year.

"Bonjour," I answer back as casually as possible.

"How are you doing?"

"Good, good."

"How is Mike?"

He always asks this. Perhaps out of politeness, but also verifying that I am now safely ensconced in another relationship, just in case I was getting any ideas. "Great. And Melanie?" I ask, though I don't actually care.

"Great." So now we've established that everyone is either good or great. "Did you get the save-the-date?" he asks.

"Oh, yeah, I did. It looks terrific. Really."

"So are you coming?" The hope in his tone is almost pitiful, like a kid asking his workaholic dad to come to his baseball game just this once.

I pause too long. "Probably."

"Probably?" he laughs. It's probably not the answer he expected.

"I mean, I want to, of course. It just depends on flights and vacation and all that, so..."

"So probably."

"Right." I get to a red light, and my phone pings with an e-mail. I fight the urge to check it while I'm still talking to him.

"Okay. Well, I should let you go then," he says.

"Yeah. I'm driving anyway, so I shouldn't really talk. I'll call you. Later. Okay?"

"Yes, this is good. Say hello to Mike for me."

"Sure thing." I hang up, thinking, "Asshole." Yeah, I get it. You're with Melanie, and I'm with Mike. And guess who won in that little exchange? That's right: I did! And no, I'm not going to your fucking wedding! Someone honks at me and I realize the light's been green for a little while now as the driver leans out the window. "Get off the fucking phone!"

101

I simultaneously flash him a bright smile and give him the finger. Showing uncharacteristic patience, I wait until the next red light to check the new e-mail. It's a message from the Black and Missing website.

Hi, Dr. Goldman. This girl looks a lot like my friend Destiny. She went missing two years ago. They think her sister's boyfriend killed her, but no one's ever found her. I'm not sure, but it could be her. Didn't have a scar I know of, but she could have gotten one. Don't know how she would have ended up in Buffalo. - Jasmine.

She left her number so I give her a call. The phone rings five times, and then a message comes on. "I ain't here. You know what to do." Short but sweet. I leave a cringingly awkward white-girl message and hang up. For a second, I'm tempted to text Detective Adams the information, but then I remember our conversation, in which he informed me I didn't have to text him every five minutes with an update. Then again, he did ask me, personally, to find out who Jane was. I debate, but the better part of valor wins out, and I hide my phone in my purse for safe-keeping for the rest of the ride to the hospital.

Because it occurs to me that I haven't exactly told him I put her information on the Internet.

Brandon has a hundred burn marks up and down his arms. I don't mean about a hundred; I mean a hundred. He counted them.

"I promised myself I'd stop at a hundred," he says. He gives the floor a dejected look. "But I don't think I can."

"What's he been on?" Dr. Berringer asks.

"Luvox, Lexapro, Effexor," Jason lists, leafing through the chart.

"Any antipsychotics?"

"I don't want an antipsychotic," the patient interrupts.

Dr. Berringer puts an "attaboy" hand on his shoulder. "But you don't want to keep hurting yourself, do you?"

Brandon shakes his head, his eyes brimming with tears.

"Let us help you, okay?" Dr. Berringer asks.

Brandon rubs his eyes hard with the heels of his hands. His eyes are red and puffy when he looks up at us again. "If it were all over, then I wouldn't have to worry about this any-more."

It, being his life.

"True," Dr. Berringer says, surprising me with the answer. "You wouldn't have to worry about a lot of things: the sun on your face, scoring a goal in soccer, getting popcorn at a movie, hanging out with your friends." He pauses for effect. "There are good things you would miss, too."

"I don't have any friends."

His words hurtle me back to eighth grade, lying in my bed with my mom stroking my hair, my desk piled up with unfinished homework. *I don't have any friends,* I am sobbing. She doesn't argue with me, knowing it will only provoke my full ire. I am a rage of hormones and dopamine deficiencies, forever the tallest kid in my grade, thorny and miserable and ready to strike at one false look. *You'll have friends*, she says. *Someday, Zoe, people will see how beautiful you are.*

Before I know it, we're halfway down the hall. "So what are you going to watch for in this patient, Zoe?"

I missed all the back and forth, but it appears Brandon grumblingly accepted the idea of an antipsychotic, and we are moving on to the next patient. I bite my lip. "I'm sorry, what antipsychotic did we end up using?"

"Seroquel," Dr. Berringer answers with forced calm.

"And you're asking for common side effects?" I ask.

"That I am."

Every thought in my head evaporates while Dr. Berringer examines a scuff on his tan bucks and Jason draws blue doodles on his patient list. So the Adderall boost has given me palpitations, loss of appetite, and pressured speech, but no boost in my brain speed. "Weight gain," I say.

"Okay," Dr. Berringer says with encouragement that verges on pathetic.

"You have to watch for suicidal ideation in young adults and teenagers."

"Uh-huh. Anything else?"

"Tardive dyskinesia. Rare, but it can happen."

He nods. "Excellent. Can you think of anything else, Jason?"

Jason looks up from his doodles. "Nope, that's all I got."

"Me neither. Okay, Zoe, you're off the hook." He grabs

my shoulders, leaning in so close that I can see gray flecks in his irises. "Pay attention next time!" he jokes, giving me that white-bright Chiclet smile, then lets me go. Jason is doodling again. "Let's go see Jane?" Dr. Berringer asks.

And we're off. On our way down the hall, I wonder at his admonition. *Pay attention!* Seems an odd thing to say, even in jest, to someone who just admitted to struggling with ADHD. But then again, he's my attending, not my doctor. Jane's room is empty, and Nancy informs us she's in speech therapy. Time for a group journey to the speech room.

"I just have to grab something." Dr. Berringer goes off toward the nurses' office, and Jason and I lean against the wall, waiting.

"He's in a good mood, huh?" I ask.

"Mr. Happy," Jason remarks, playing with his gelled-up bangs. "Especially with you."

"What's that supposed to mean?"

He yawns. "It means you two should get a room somewhere."

I roll my eyes. "I'm not even honoring that with a reply."

"That was a reply," he says, then we both shut up as Dr. Berringer comes back our way.

"It sounds like we need to back down on the Adderall."

I plow through some sand. I've been telling him my symptoms. My cocaine-like pressured speech, five-pound weight loss, palpitations. "Yeah, I guess you're right."

He leans back in his chair, fingering his glossy, thin, but fully grown-in goatee. "How do you feel about that?"

His question makes me think of a cranky elderly woman I saw last year. *What's all this crap about how I feel? I feel with my hands. And that's the last thing I'm going to say about it.*

"Fine, I guess. It didn't help much anyway. Just made me keyed up."

"How about other stuff? How are you doing with your mom?"

"Okay, I guess. Scotty wanted me to go with him to visit the gravesite the other day."

"And?"

I scratch the back of my neck. "I couldn't do it. I don't know."

Sam looks at me but doesn't speak.

"I guess I just don't want to see her there."

He nods. "You know, I do think that starting to accept it, on whatever level you can, may be helpful for you. Running away from it won't help."

"I know." Scotty, for whatever reason, is handling it better than I am. My immature kid brother is outshining his accomplished, luminary, Yale-graduate big sister. Who's on probation. "I told you about his thing with those stupid bonds, right?"

Sam nods.

"It's weird. He's never been like that before. If anything, the opposite. He never gave a shit about money."

He leans back in his office chair. "Maybe he finally feels the pressure of working while he's going to college."

"Maybe."

"Or it could be his way of coping. Trying to find meaning out of something which essentially makes no sense."

I stifle a yawn. "I guess."

He looks down at his yellow legal pad. Sometimes I wonder if Sam and I should really be going out for tea instead of having a psychiatric relationship. But then again, maybe that's just how it always goes after a couple of years—the bloom fades.

"Have you been running yet?"

"Well…" I hesitate, guiltily picturing my new running shoes, swathed in tissue paper and stuck in their box.

"Get running, Zoe. It'll help."

The ship-wheel clock ticks out the remaining minutes until "It's time," and I walk outside to a bright fall afternoon. Finally the rain is giving us a reprieve. I had to leave work early today for the appointment, but Dr. Berringer didn't mind. It turns out he had to leave early for some appointment, too. The coppery leaves of an oak tree sway above me as I step into my car. Staring at my phone, I consider leaving another message for Jasmine, but since I've already left three jacked-up messages throughout the day, I should probably hold off. The poor girl's going to think I'm a stalker.

I'm pulling on my seat belt when a black Jeep swerves into the parking lot, missing my side-view mirror by a few inches. I'm half a second from pulling down my window to berate the guy, when I realize that there is someone I know who drives a Jeep just like that and duck down just in time to catch his unmistakable form in my rearview mirror.

Emerging from his Jeep, with a brown leather jacket and sunglasses on, is none other than Dr. Tad Berringer.

Chapter Twelve

I'm finishing my coffee, about to run out the door, when she calls.

"Hi, it's Jasmine."

Dropping my satchel, I put my coffee down. "Jasmine, yes."

"From the missing people website? I was calling about Destiny." The voice sounds young.

"Yes, hi, this is Zoe. Zoe Goldman. Dr. Goldman," I add, for no obvious reason.

There is a pause. "And how do you know this girl?" Jasmine asks.

Like a Jewish-sounding white doctor knowing her friend Destiny seems a bit implausible. "Here's the thing. I didn't want to get into the whole thing on the website to protect her confidentiality and all."

"Okay."

"But she's actually my patient. I'm her doctor. She came

109

to the hospital because the police found her and she wouldn't speak."

There is another pause as she processes this. "Okay," she repeats. Her voice is full of doubt, like I might just be some crazy person trying to insinuate herself on a missing persons case. The amateur-sleuth type. And my coked-up, Adderall-enthused messages from yesterday probably didn't help matters.

"Um, she is talking now, actually. But she still doesn't know her name. She doesn't know who she is at all."

"That's weird."

"Weird yes, but not unheard of. Likely she's been through some kind of shock or trauma maybe."

"And so you think she got amnesia?"

"Sort of."

She pauses. "Sounds like some kind of soap opera."

I laugh. "It does, doesn't it?"

My laugh wakes up Arthur, who launches on a mad dash around the family room, knocking over last night's wineglass in the process. "Shit."

"What?"

"Nothing. It's my dog, I mean." I grab a paper towel. At least it was white wine. Arthur spilled an entire bottle of red last month, and the place looked like a crime scene.

"Well," she says. It sounds like she's deciding whether to trust me or not. "She does look like Destiny. And she would be the right age and everything."

"Yes." I'm dabbing the carpet with a paper towel, which Arthur keeps trying to grab like I'm playing a game of keep-away, unaware he's at the top of my shit list.

"Who knows?" she goes on. "Maybe she did go through some kind of trauma with him."

"Who?" I ask.

"Her sister's boyfriend. Maybe he holed up in Buffalo. Not that far from Philly."

"No, I guess not."

There is another pause on the phone, where I guess she makes the decision to trust me. "How you want to handle this?" she asks.

I think a minute. "Could I have her call you?" Maybe just hearing her friend's voice could jog her memory.

"What, from the hospital?"

"Yeah."

She pauses. "I guess I could do that. I don't see a problem with that."

"How old are you anyway?" I ask. "You seem pretty mature for your voice."

She laughs. "Fifteen. We was twelve when she went missing. Well, I was thirteen, 'cause I got held back."

The math fits, age-wise. We set up a time for the phone call, and I take a last gulp of now-chilly coffee and grab my keys. I was running a little late before, but now I'm undeniably so.

Another golden moment for Probation Girl.

Jane was in physical therapy today so our threesome took a group trek to the PT room, only to find out she was having therapy outside today. We exit the lobby to a cool but sunny autumn day. Cars roll by in front of us like a parade, discharging wincing, bent-over passengers for the ER or picking up smiling but still slow-moving patients from their wheelchairs to go home at last.

Jane is farther up ahead in a wheelchair (unneeded, but I'm assuming hospital regulations prevailed) with Jeremy, the physical therapist. We walk over, past the gaggle of smokers— all wearing scrubs, incidentally—with Dominic among them. He may or may not be flirting with one of the female nurses. He glances up when we pass, and we pretend not to see each other. I notice Jason not noticing him, too. Finally we reach Jane, the sweet sound of her laughter ringing out. It's a sound I've never heard from her before. Jeremy is popping wheelies with her wheelchair on a sunny patch of grass.

"Hello there," Dr. Berringer says.

Jane beams up at us.

"We thought we'd play hooky and have a session outside today," Jeremy says. He is handsome in the typical physical-therapist mold. Brush cut, square jaw, perfectly proportioned muscles in his golf shirt with the hospital logo on the chest. "And I think we've just about graduated PT. She can walk up and down thirty feet. Actually, she beat me in the last five races."

Jane looks down at the grass, smiling.

"I think OT is still doing some work on writing, getting those hands back into fighting shape." He grabs her hand and wiggles it teasingly, and she grins again. (I'm sensing a crush on said physical therapist.)

"That sounds positive," Dr. Berringer says.

A gust of wind rushes by, and the smokers huddle, while Jane pulls her blanket over her lap.

"Getting cold?" Jeremy asks.

"A little," Jane admits. "But I don't mind. Let's stay out here just a little longer?"

"Why not?" He stretches his back, his chest straining the buttons of the polo. "It's good to get some sun."

The wind picks up again, whispering through the papery, dried-out, pink petals of the hydrangea bush in the planter. The base is littered with cigarette butts. A long, black car pulls up, nearly as long as a limousine, and idles in the driveway. A girl and her mother get out and glance around nervously before heading in, with no obvious physical ailment. I wonder if this girl will be my next patient. The sun glints off the license plate, and a little girl in the back window waves slowly at us, a somber look on her face. The car pulls away, and Jane looks up at us.

Her eyebrows are furrowed, and her face is different somehow, like she just awoke from a long slumber.

"My name isn't Jane," she says. "It's Candy."

"So Jane has a name?" Mike takes a swig from his dark Dos Equis.

"Jane has a name," I say, delving into the chip dish again. "Jane is Candy."

"Don't eat them all," Mike says, whacking my hand.

"We can get more," I argue.

"Fine, eat them all. Eat all of the chips. But don't eat your hand."

My appetite has rebounded nicely with my Adderall back down. "So what do you think? Her name is Candy. The last thing she remembers is chasing a limousine."

"Hmm." He dips a chip in guacamole. "A really bad prom experience?"

"Ha, ha, ha."

He shrugs. "I've had my share. But I've got my pride, you know. I never actually chased after the limo."

"No last name still. But I did hear from Jasmine." I take a long drink of margarita.

"Jasmine?"

"The girl from the Black and Missing website."

"Oh yeah. What did she have to say?"

"She thought she could have been a girl named Destiny. Her friend who went missing, from Philadelphia."

Mike takes another chip. "Doesn't sound like a fit."

"No, probably not. We'll see."

A round of laughter floats over from the bar as we keep plowing through the chips. Mike taps his nearly empty beer bottle on the table. "So, about next year."

"Not to change the subject or anything," I say.

"Of course not." He spins the bottle. "Any thoughts?"

"Thoughts? Lots of thoughts. Just no concrete decisions."

"Uh-huh." A man with a sizzling platter swoops by us and on to a different table. "The thing is, they're talking about jobs now. So I really do need to figure this out. Jeff told me he could pretty much guarantee me a job at the County."

"That's good."

"But some of that depends on your decision, you know? I could just as easily go with that urgent-care center in North Carolina, where Mom is."

I nod. "I just don't know. Fellowship-wise. Definitely not child psych. That I know. And I was thinking maybe addiction, but Jason told me the burnout rate is through the roof. And geriatrics is just too depressing." I slurp my margarita. "I don't know."

"You could do a year of practice and figure it out?"

Mike, the ever-practical. "Yeah. The fellowship thing may be a moot point anyway. My loans aren't going anywhere, so maybe it's time to just face the music."

He scrapes the bottom of the basket for some chips. "One more year of loans won't kill you. And I could help out," he adds in a quiet voice, "if need be."

Mike, the ever-kind. "That's sweet of you, but..." I let the sentence trail off, and we sit in silence for a moment. A basketball game plays on the TV overhead. "You know, even if we do end up in different places," I say, "it doesn't mean we have to break up or anything. If you go to North Carolina and I'm here, let's say... we can still be together." I steal the last chip. "They have these things called planes nowadays."

He toys with the beer bottle again. "Yeah, I guess."

But he doesn't sound so sure. And I must admit that it didn't work so well with Jean Luc. "We'll see. I just feel like the answer will hit me someday. Hopefully, someday soon."

"Hopefully." His tone is vaguely annoyed as he stares into his beer. "But you know, Zoe, sometimes doing nothing ends up being the same thing as doing something."

I don't answer.

"Here we go!" A cheerful waitress in a billowy Mexican shirt comes to our table, her arms raised high with our own sizzling platters. The smell makes my mouth water.

"Thank you, Lord," I say.

"That's right, come to Papa," Mike says as the fajita plate descends to him. Digging into our food, with the mariachi music blasting through the speakers, I feel like I've been given a momentary reprieve.

Chapter Thirteen

By Monday, it is clear the name Candy doesn't bring us any closer to an answer.

Half of the puzzle is solved, but we still don't know where she's from or her last name. Detective Adams does a fresh round of neighborhood canvassing and hangs up new missing-child posters with a smiling "Candy" instead of the stone-faced Jane Doe. Nothing comes of it. Meanwhile, Discharge Planning is still breathing down our collective necks. "We may not know who she is or where she belongs," Tina Jessep said to me yesterday in a rather icy tone, "but she doesn't belong in the hospital."

Today I catch up with Candy (I keep wanting to call her Jane) in group "share" therapy. Jason and I are sitting at the back of the room, watching our respective patients.

"Miss Judy" leads off the discussion. She has an unfortunate habit of ending all of her sentences with "uh-huh? uh-huh?" so that it's brutally annoying to listen to her for more than five consecutive minutes. This has also earned her the patient-wide nickname of "Miss Uh-huh."

"So today," she starts, flipping back long, dyed-black hair that reaches to the back of her thighs (how she doesn't get a basilar dissection every time she sits down, I'm not sure), "I'd like to focus on positives. Uh-huh? Uh-huh?"

No one answers. Chloe is chewing her fingernails. Brandon is tracing over the scars on one arm. Candy watches intently, like there might be a quiz.

"We always focus on what's going wrong—the negatives, uh-huh? So today I want to focus on the positives, uh-huh? The things we can think about to get us over the bad times, the humps in our lives. Uh-huh? Uh-huh?" She waits about ten seconds, but no one offers any response. Chloe chooses another nail to decimate.

"Because if there's one thing we know, uh-huh, it's that there's going to be tough times, whether we like it or not—tough times that we have to get through. Uh-huh? Uh-huh?"

I don't know how they get through twice-weekly share therapy with this woman. I would turn homicidal in a jiffy.

"Chloe?" Miss Judy asks.

Chloe looks around the room, like there might be someone else named Chloe who could save her from answering the question. Sadly, there isn't. "Yes?"

"I'd like you to tell me something positive you can focus on."

"Positive?"

"Uh-huh. Positive. Like, maybe, a favorite perfume?"

"Perfumes give me migraines."

"Or a favorite color then?"

"A favorite color. Let's see." She pauses, pretending to think deeply. "Black. Black is my favorite color."

"See now, that's a nice color, uh-huh? Uh-huh? Black?"

"Yes, I like black," Chloe continues, "because it symbolizes death, depression, depravity, negativity. Basically everything I feel most days."

Miss Judy looks at Chloe and debates whether she is being played and decides probably so. She turns to her next victim. "What about you, Candy?"

"Yes?" she answers without delay. Her speech has improved vastly this week since she figured out her name.

"Do you have a favorite color?"

"Yes, I do. Purple," she announces.

I sit up straight in my chair. So she knows her favorite color but not her name?

"Uh-huh. Purple. What do you like about purple?" she asks, pleased to have someone finally responding to her.

"I don't know," she says, shrugging. "I just do."

"Now see, purple is good. That's a terrific start here. Uh-huh, uh-huh? Any other positives in your life?"

Candy leans back in her chair and thinks. "I like pizza. And leopard skin. One of the aides on the floor bought me a purple leopard-skin purse from the gift shop. I love it."

"Good, good. Uh-huh. Now this is what I'm talking about. Positives, everybody, positives."

It's odd, hearing her go on about how much she loves her new purple leopard-skin purse, like Little Orphan Annie is singing "Tomorrow" to a roomful of Eeyores.

"It's good to start with little things. Your favorite colors, foods. Then, you'll find, the good things start to take over. Take root in your garden. Remember we said last week how your brain is like a big garden? Well, it's time to weed out the bad thoughts and let the good things grow. Uh-huh?"

Candy is nodding right along while the other patients stare at Miss Judy in disbelief. *Let the good things grow?*

It's just about time to round, and Jason and I manage to escape as Miss Judy attempts to pry some answers out of Brandon. I'm starting to wonder if the dreaded discharge planner is right. Maybe Candy doesn't belong here, dealing with the likes of Miss Judy.

Dr. Berringer is waiting in the room, flipping through charts. "I have a bitch of a headache," he says, grabbing another chart. His eyes are glassy, and he's wearing the same clothes today as he was yesterday, a wrinkled blue checkered shirt with the second button undone. Must have put in a tough night, though I was on call last night and caught all my winks—didn't even get a Tylenol order. He turns to Jason. "How's Brandon the Burner doing? Can we discharge him yet?"

"I'm not sure about that. He was cutting himself with a sharpened toothbrush yesterday," Jason says.

"Well, maybe we should just—" A text interrupts him, and Dr. Berringer whips out his phone, his face turning into a scowl. He shoves it back in his pocket. "Sorry, what were you saying about Brandon?" The phone buzzes again, and he grabs it. "Sorry," he says, standing up and marching out into the hall to call someone. When he leaves, a strong smell hangs in his wake. A bitter scent that it takes me a second to recognize. But I've smelled it many a time on many a patient before. On young men with ripped shirts and bruised knuckles in the ER on any given Saturday night. On the impeccably dressed lawyer in my Thursday-afternoon clinic who assures me she never goes over two bottles of wine at dinner.

I'm about to ask Jason if he smelled it, too, when Dr. Berringer returns. "Okay, let's hear about Brandon."

Jason goes on about Brandon's self-mutilation while Dr. Berringer listens but doesn't, his jaw clenching and unclenching, and I'm left half wondering if I imagined it, the scent still hanging in the air.

"Hello," Mike calls out. "Honey, I'm home."

I laugh at the corny line, turning a page in my RITE review book. "How was work?"

He leans down to pet Arthur, who is doing his happy "Mike's home" dance. "Not too bad. One MVA, four headaches, and about a hundred sinus infections."

"That time of year."

He drops his coat on the kitchen chair and starts rifling through the refrigerator. I catch his silhouette in scrubs in the gray light. "We have any food?"

"There's some leftover Chinese in there."

"Ah, yes." He takes out some lo mein and dumps it on a plate to microwave it. "So what's new with you?"

"Not much."

"Have you solved the curious case of Candy yet?"

"Nope. But hopefully we'll talk with Jasmine tomorrow."

After a bit, the microwave chimes and he grabs his plate. "You didn't talk to her yet?"

"No. I still have to explain it to Candy." I take a sip of my wine. "Tomorrow."

We sit for a bit as Mike digs into his lo mein and Arthur watches him with a mournful "feed me" expression.

"So I have a question for you."

"Hmph?" he asks, still chewing.

"What would you do if you thought your attending had a drinking problem?"

He takes a gulp from a bottle of water. "Is this a theoretical question? Or do you think your attending has a drinking problem?"

"The latter."

"Hmm." Another gulp and the bottle is empty. "Honestly, I probably wouldn't do anything."

"Really?"

"Well." He looks around a second. "You have any wine left?" I point to the island, and he pours himself a glass and sits back down. "How sure are you about this?"

"I don't know." I refortify my glass as well. "I don't have any definite evidence. But he looked like crap today, like he could have been hungover. And I could swear he smelled of alcohol."

"Uh-huh." He doesn't sound impressed.

"Plus, he's seeing my psychiatrist."

Mike gives me an odd look. "How do you know that?"

"I saw him come in the other day when I was leaving."

"Huh. That's weird." He pushes his plate to the side. Arthur takes a lightning-quick chomp and races off to another room, leaving Mike staring at an empty plate. "I wasn't actually done with that."

"He means well. Have some more wine." I pour the last drops from the bottle into his glass. "So you wouldn't say anything? About the drinking?"

"I don't know," Mike says. "Do you think it's affecting his judgment?"

"Maybe. Maybe not. Candy is getting better, so maybe he's on the right track there."

"Yeah."

"And he is smart as hell. That's pretty much common knowledge." Arthur wanders by, a piece of lo mein stuck to his nose. "You think I should call the Chair and get her opinion?" I tap my glass. "I'm not excessively fond of her, though…"

He yawns. "I wouldn't."

"No?"

"No, you're on probation."

"So?"

"So this could seriously bite you in the ass."

I yawn, too. It's contagious. "I suppose."

He twirls his wine in a spiral. "Trust me. You don't want to do anything stupid here. You could get in some real trouble."

Mike's right. It's an apt description of my modus operandi

throughout life. It could be my gravestone inscription: "Zoe Goldman. Did stupid things. Got in real trouble."

"Yeah, but what about if I—"

"Zoe?" He throws the rest of his wine back, then faces me, his eyebrows scrunching together in a way I've always found rather cute.

"Yes?"

He moves closer to me on the couch, warmth radiating off his body. As he leans in to kiss my neck, his breath smells of sweet white wine. "I have a question for you."

His stubble tickles my face. A trace of cedar cologne that I bought him. "What?"

"Do you want to talk about your attending?" His hand, resting on my thigh, starts crawling up by inches. "Or do you want to do something else?"

Chapter Fourteen

She's all set for Monday," the discharge planner tells me, then starts booking down the hall.

"Wait, wait." I run after her and she stops, bracing herself. "Monday?" I ask.

"Yes. Monday."

"But can't you just give us a little more time? She remembered her name. She's remembering more every day. I think if I can just work with her a little more—"

Ms. Jessep shakes her head, resigned. "We just don't have any more time. Administration cleared it. I've covered all the bases. She's excelling at art therapy and group therapy, graduated from PT and OT. The only issue that's been holding things up is placement."

"Well, her identity, too," I add. "That might have been holding things up a bit."

"Yes, that's true," she answers, unsure if I'm being sarcastic or not, which I am.

"Where is she going, might I ask?"

"A foster family. The Watsons. They're nice people."

So they're not sending her to a pack of maniacs. That's a relief. "And will she be going to school?"

"Dr. Goldman," she sighs, "I know you want the best for Candy. We all do. We're not throwing her to the sharks. She'll get therapy. She'll have siblings. A new school. Much better than we can offer her growing up on the psych floor of Children's Hospital, don't you think?"

I think back to her therapy with Miss Uh-huh and grudgingly agree.

"It's not until Monday," she adds. "You'll have a chance to say your good-byes." Ms. Jessep gives me a brisk farewell nod and escapes down the hall. I don't chase her this time.

When I go to see Candy, she's rummaging through her purse, like each new item in there is a treasure. She sniffs the wand of the lip gloss, then fits it back in. She snaps the silver makeup mirror open and shut.

I remember doing this myself as a child. Sitting up high on my mom's scratchy fabric stool, rifling through the makeup drawer, which seemed so chock-full of marvels and intrigue. Sky-blue eye shadow. Coral-red lipsticks. Fluffy makeup brushes with flakes clumped on the ends.

"Hi," Candy says, seeing me come in.

"Nice purse," I say.

"Thanks." She taps her fingers on it. "The discharge lady came to see me."

I nod. "Did she talk to you about going to another place on Monday?"

"Yeah. The Watsons, she said."

I nod again, giving her time to talk, but she just stares at her purse. "How do you feel about that?" I prompt her.

"Okay, I guess." She doesn't offer any further opinion.

"Better than getting hospital food every day, right?"

She laughs, to humor me I think. "The pizza isn't bad. I forgot how much I liked pizza."

I pause. "So you remember liking pizza?"

"Yeah, I do remember some things. It's weird. I don't remember being at the police station, or my parents, or any of the big things. But I remember eating pizza one night in front of the TV."

"What were you watching?" I ask, hoping to stimulate more memories.

"I don't know," she says. "It's like I remember and I don't remember. You know? Like I'm watching a movie of me eating pizza, laughing, but that's all. I don't even know for sure that it's real." She frowns.

"And the limo? Did you remember any more about that?"

"The detective guy asked me the same thing. But I don't remember. I just remember seeing a limo pull away. Trying to chase after it. That's the last thing I remember before waking up here." She chews on her lower lip. "The discharge lady told me more will come back to me over time."

"She did, did she?" Just then my phone rings, and the number on the top of the phone is Jasmine's. We had arranged for her to call this afternoon. I turn the ringer off. "Candy?"

"Uh-huh."

"If there was someone who thought she knew you from before you came to the hospital, would you want to talk to her?"

"Like a friend or something?"

"Yes. I'm not sure, but it could be someone who could help you remember where you came from, your family and all that."

"I guess that would be okay," she says. "How do you know her?"

This is a tricky one. I sit down next to her and decide to chance it. If she doesn't know Jasmine, that's that. But if she does, it might keep her from being released before she's ready. "I put your information on a website for missing kids."

She stares at me in silence for a moment, until I think she might be angry, but then her face breaks into a soft smile. "You did that for me?" she asks, in a whisper.

A pulse of joy surges through me, and I pull out my phone. "Shall I?"

She nods, and we wait only two rings before Jasmine answers.

"Okay," I say. "It's Zoe Goldman. I've got my patient here. I'm putting her on speaker."

"Hello?" Jasmine's voice is fuzzy over the speaker.

"Hi," Candy answers back, unsure.

"You don't have FaceTime, do you?" I ask.

"No, not on this phone," Jasmine apologizes.

"That's okay," Candy says, leaning in to the phone.

"It's Jasmine," the girl says, her voice excited. "Is this Destiny?"

"Um." Candy looks at me. "I don't know. I'm sorry. I don't remember a Jasmine."

The phone is silent for a moment. "We went to School 78 together. We had Mr. Benton, who was a total asshole. Oh, sorry for cussing."

"That's okay," I break in.

"I...I don't remember," Candy stutters.

"You remember the song we loved in chorus? 'I Will Always Love You'? The Whitney Houston song?"

"Oh, I know that song!" Candy says. She starts singing the chorus, her voice cracking and a bit off tune. She stops then, frowning. "But I don't remember singing it with you."

"No." Jasmine's voice is deflated. "I'd remember Destiny's singing anywhere. She sounded just like Whitney Houston."

"I really don't think my name is Destiny," Candy says, sounding disappointed as well.

The call ends with well-wishing on both sides, and my own sneaking suspicion that my meddling may be making things worse, not better.

Later that day, we are finishing off charts in the nurses' station, waiting to round.

"He looks fine today, doesn't he?" I ask.

Jason keeps writing in his chart. "And who are we talking about?"

"Dr. Berringer."

"Yes, Zoe. He looks fine," he says, in a weary voice. "I'd do him myself if I didn't have a boyfriend." He pauses. "A pseudo-boyfriend," he corrects himself.

"No, I mean..." I tap my pen on my chart but don't say anything more. Maybe I smelled alcohol on him, maybe I didn't. Maybe he was hungover, maybe he wasn't. I certainly don't want to tell Jason the town crier about my suspicions or it would be all over Children's within the half hour.

"Actually," Jason says, "that French-blue shirt is rather becoming on him, I'll admit."

"Wow." I stack up my charts. "That was gay."

"More gay than saying I have a boyfriend?"

"A pseudo-boyfriend."

"We all set?" he asks, the French-blue-shirted Dr. Berringer himself poking his head into the room. We set off to see Candy, who is sitting on her perfectly made bed, reading *The Catcher in the Rye*. On the table beside her is a blue folder with silver cursive writing that says "Foster Care and You: Everything You Ever Needed to Know!"

"You about ready to leave us?" Dr. Berringer asks.

"I think so," Candy says, putting the book in her lap.

"It sounds like a nice foster family," Dr. Berringer assures her.

"Oh, I'm sure it is."

He lifts up her latest drawing on the bed stand. It's a bright red maple leaf. The actual leaf she used as a model wafts down to the floor, spotted with mold.

"Nice picture," he comments.

"Thanks," she says. "I figure since it's fall and everything..."

"Right." He crosses his arms. "We're gonna miss you, girl. But you've outgrown us."

She smiles her megawatt Candy smile. "I'm going to miss you guys, too."

We pause, all staring at each other, then she turns back to her book and is engrossed again in seconds. So much for good-bye.

"Taper her off the Ativan," Dr. Berringer says to me as we're leaving the room.

"Completely? In one weekend?"

"We don't really have a choice. She can't exactly be on it out there." He hands me the chart. "It's sink or swim, Zoe. You'll learn that about child psych. Sometimes you have to make tough decisions."

I start writing the order. Sink or swim. I just hope she doesn't drown.

⟵

We have an hour before we're officially done at five p.m., and leaving early is just tempting an ER call, so I head to the library. My RITE book is patiently waiting for me to read it, but I hop on a computer first. Having assured myself that there is nothing new in Facebook, Instagram, or my Twitter feed, I have no choice but to open the RITE book.

A 60-year-old-male comes in with his wife, who complains he has been "making up things" and "walking around like he's on a boat." He states he has met you be-fore, though this is a new patient visit. He smells strongly of alcohol . . .

Smells strongly of alcohol. An image of Dr. Berringer crosses my mind from yesterday, his shirt wrinkled, his eyes glazed. On a whim (and perhaps to avoid answering the question), I decide to do a quick Google search on the good doctor. I glance around the room to see if anyone is watching, but there's only one medical student in the room with me. She doles some red Tic Tacs out onto her hand and turns to her computer again.

After crossing out one from Alaska and another from Massachusetts, I zero in on the right child psychiatrist. Healthgrades gives him four and a half out of five thumbs up for patient ratings—not too shabby. He went to a decent medical school and residency in New Orleans. The website, meanwhile, assaults me with ads for ADHD medications, smartly assuming a person searching for pediatric psychiatrists might be concerned about this, though it feels Big Brothery and more than a little close to home. Then the site asks, "Do you want to check out Dr. Berringer's background?" I hit yes. Why not?

Pending lawsuits? No.
Criminal investigations? No.
Medical license waived? No.
Sanctions? YES.

Yes? That is unexpected. I read on.

This may indicate that the physician has been cited for alcohol or drug abuse violations and is currently successfully engaged in a voluntary treatment program. Full inquiries can be made via the Department of Health at the following number.

Just then I hear Jason's voice. "Wassup girlie girl?" He grabs the computer next to me and straightens his chair.

I close out of the website in an instant.

"What, are you looking at porn or something?" he asks.

The medical student, who has been making impossibly loud sucking noises with her Tic Tacs, glances over at us then back at her screen.

"No," I say with annoyance.

"What? I look at porn all the time. But not in the hospital library. That's just gross."

"I was *not* looking at porn."

"Oh yeah?" He opens up his e-mail. "Then why were you all *Oh my God, let me X out of this site as fast as I can?*" He mimics my panicked face, whipping around the mouse.

"None of your business," I mutter, pulling up my e-mail.

"Oh," he says, like he just figured it out. He smooths his thin lavender tie, his bow tie replaced today. "It was Jean Luc."

"Wrong."

"Mike?"

I don't say anything, figuring it's a lie of omission.

Sandra Block

"Fine. Be like that. Next time, I'm not telling you any-thing about Dominic."

"Dominic's an asshole."

"Nonetheless."

I close out of my e-mail and stand up. "See you later."

"Later," he answers, leaning in to the computer to look at something.

I grab my bag. It's 4:45 p.m., but I'll risk the wrath of the ER consult by leaving early. Heading out, I walk past the lobby, past velvety rust-and-gold mums, to my car. My mind keeps traveling back to the Healthgrades website on Dr. Ber-ringer. Sanctions? Yes.

So my nose was right. He *was* hungover, with the telltale scent of last night's bender. Maybe this is what Dr. Berringer meant then, with his hand over his heart, telling me that's how the light gets in.

Chapter Fifteen

Bright and early Monday morning, Candy is sitting in her street clothes, a plastic bag full of her belongings perched at the foot of her bed. I can't put my finger on it, but something is different about her. Maybe because she is no longer a patient but a person now. Her own person, ready to start a new life and literally discover herself.

And it's our best bet at this point, since Black and Missing was a dead end and none of the limousine companies had gotten back to me with further information. "You ready to go, Candy?" I ask, realizing that I will miss her.

Her eyes are like daggers. "Who the fuck is Candy?"

My breath catches, and I stare at her. "Excuse me?"

"Who the fuck is Candy? I ain't no fucking Candy."

"You're...not...Candy," I repeat, feeling distinctly like I've entered the Twilight Zone, like I'm the one who's been catatonic for the past month.

"Candy," she huffs. "Sounds like some stripper's name. My name is Daneesha."

"Daneesha," I repeat stupidly, wondering if this is some kind of sick joke. But Candy doesn't joke like that. Sweetness and sunshine, our Candy. No sick jokes and definitely no f-bombs.

She pivots her legs so they are hanging off the side of the bed and looks around the room like it's the first time she's been here. "And who the fuck are you?"

"I'm...Dr. Goldman."

"Dr. Goldman?" she asks. "What I need a doctor for?"

I shove my hands in my lab coat pockets. "Do you know why you're here?"

"I don't even know where the hell I am," she says, standing up to look out the window for a clue. "Running away from some white dudes is the last thing I remember, and now I'm in some hospital. That's all I know."

Running away from some white dudes. Detective Adams might be interested in that.

"Do you remember a limousine perchance?"

"A limousine?" She looks at me like I've grown a third head. "I ain't playin' with y'all. White guys, running after me. Now I'm here, and I want out."

"Can you tell me more about those white guys?"

"Yeah, right, lady. How about you tell me something?"

"Okay."

"When am I leaving?"

I take a step away from her. "Soon, very soon," I say, which was true five minutes ago. "I just have to talk to the right people, and we'll get that going."

"Yeah, you do that. You talk to whoever y'all need to talk

to, and you get that going. I can't be waiting around here all day."

"Just one second," I say with my pointer finger in the air, then tear out of there like the room is on fire. Down at the nurses' station, Dr. Berringer is standing with coffee in hand, chatting with one of the LPNs.

"Oh, yeah, he took a *punishing* hit," Dr. Berringer says, his voice animated.

"Marion ain't doing all he should, though," the man answers back, his face serious with the discussion of insider football.

"He's still a rookie, really," Dr. Berringer says. "You guys look good. I'll root for them, but my heart still bleeds for the Saints. You know what I'm saying?"

"Oh yeah. They got a good team, too. Nothing to sneer at."

I clear my throat.

"Why hello, Zoe!" he says with a big smile, dapper in his khaki sports coat, his eyes fresh and sparkling blue. Looks like he's staying on that wagon. "And how are you today?"

"Um, there's a problem with Candy."

"What is it?" He takes a long swallow of coffee. "Some screwup with the foster home?"

"No." I circle my finger around the white plastic button on my lab coat. "I think you better just come see her. It's hard to explain."

"Okay." He tilts his head in good-bye to the LPN, and we march down the hall to see Candy, or maybe Daneesha.

Dr. Berringer swings through the door first. "What's up there, Candy?"

She takes one look at him and leaps off the bed. "My name is Daneesha!"

"Okay, Daneesha," says Dr. Berringer, who I note with some satisfaction has lost his composure and is staring at her with the same expression I must have had a minute ago. "Let's just calm down there, my girl."

"I ain't your girl!" she screams. "You get away from me!"

Dr. Berringer steps in closer, which is a mistake, as she lunges at him, scratching one side of his face, then landing a fist on the other side of his head with an ugly *thump*. He puts up his arms to ward off more blows. "Hey, could someone get security in here?"

"You get away from me, motherfucker!" She is half snarling, half screeching, her arms windmilling out punches. "Don't you fucking touch me!" A nurse rushes into the room and then out, and we hear security called overhead. Time crawls, and I move in toward Daneesha to try to reason with her, which is also a mistake and results in a well-landed punch in my left eye. Sparks shoot through my vision as footsteps pound outside of the door and the security guards rush in. It takes two burly guards to keep this twelve-to-fourteen-year-old down.

"Get off me! Get off me! Jesus, help me!" She is squirming out of their grasp, her legs kicking out at whatever she can connect with. By now, a group of nurses has circled around the door to see what the commotion is all about. Not that commotion is all that uncommon in the psych ward, but so far it's been notably absent in Candy's room.

"Nancy!" Dr. Berringer calls out into the hallway. "We

need five milligrams Ativan, ten milligrams Haldol in here, stat."

"Coming right up," she says, scurrying through her co-workers.

We move away from Daneesha's squirming, screaming mass, which the security guards have managed to pin to the floor. "She's a live one," one of the guards puffs out, leaning a muscled arm on her shoulder.

"I see what you mean about a problem with Candy," Dr. Berringer remarks, his face bloody with three parallel scratch marks, like a still from a horror movie. His cheekbone is swelling on the other side already. He laughs a little, and I start laughing with him.

"Are you okay?" he asks me, reaching up to touch my eye, and my hand goes up at the same time, brushing his knuckles. The skin around my eye tingles, and I can see in the room mirror that it's pink and swelling already.

"It's fine," I say.

He nods, admiring my face. "Gonna be a shiner for sure."

Nancy hurries back, ripping an alcohol pack open, and finds a bare spot on Candy's (Daneesha's?) shoulder. She taps the bubbles out of the syringe and shoves it in.

"Bitch!" the girl is screaming out now as the nurse stands up from a squat. "Fucking whore of a bitch!" One of the security guards shifts to get a better hold. "You all fuckers! You all fucking motherfuckers!" she yells out in a hoarse voice, the last words slurring as the drugs finally hit. After a couple of halfhearted kicks, she stops. Her eyes roll up, and she relaxes. The security guards lighten their grip but don't let her go. Her breathing steadies.

"Phew," one security guard says to the other, sweat running down his temples. They stay on the floor for a minute. "What should we do?" the guard asks Dr. Berringer. "You want to put Sleeping Beauty back in her bed?"

"Yes, let's do that." He turns to me. "Can you put an order in for four-point restraints?"

I start writing it. "I guess she's not going anywhere today?"

"I'd venture to say." He dabs his scratch with a tissue from her nightstand.

Sink or swim. It looks like Candy drowned and left us with Daneesha.

"So she has an alter?" asks Sam, who despite his best intentions, perhaps, is interested. He leans forward on his glass desktop, his brown eyes lit up.

"So it appears."

"That's something," he says, nodding. "I didn't see that coming."

"You and me both." I laugh. "She was like ten minutes from leaving the hospital!"

He pauses. "You know, maybe that's why it happened."

"What do you mean?"

"It makes sense, actually. If there was a trauma which was the cause of her catatonia, maybe she wasn't really ready to leave the safety of the hospital. Candy didn't know how to tell you, so Daneesha stepped in."

Wind bangs against the window. The sky is white gray with clouds in charcoal swirls this late afternoon. I left work early because Sam had to change the appointment. Dr. Berringer didn't object, and I didn't bother to mention my psychiatrist's name.

"Interesting theory," I say.

"Yes, theory is all it is, really. Most people agree that a dissociative disorder is caused by emotional trauma. But we can't seem to agree on much more."

"And it's a bitch and a half to treat," I add.

He shrugs. "Multiple personalities are tough. But maybe with some cognitive behavioral therapy—"

I cackle at this one. "CBT?" I point to my eye. "Does this look like it's going to respond to CBT?"

He gives a half smile. The wind shakes the pane. A swath of pink-orange leaves flutter down from a sugar maple.

"So how's the concentration? Stable?"

"Yeah, I guess. It's not great, but it's probably as good as it'll ever be."

He twirls his fake Montblanc. "And how's everything else going? Things with Scotty?"

"Fine. As long as we don't discuss Mom or Treasury bonds." I hold back a yawn.

"Any more from Jean Luc?"

"Well, he called me. Wanted to let me know all about his wedding."

"And how did that make you feel?"

I think for a moment. "Surprisingly shitty."

He lets a smile escape. "That's an honest answer."

"Yes, well. Brutal honesty has always been my strong suit." I pick at the rake in the sand. "Doesn't always work so well in psychiatry."

"Or life, even," he adds.

Which is true, though I could do without the editorial.

"What the hell?" Mike says as I walk into his apartment, which is soothingly warm and smells of garlic.

"Long day," I say, dropping my satchel.

He walks over to take a closer look at my eye. "What happened?"

"Daneesha hit me."

"Okay." Mike throws some ice in a bag and hands it to me. "And who might Daneesha be?" A touch football schedule flaps up under a Sabres hockey magnet as the freezer door closes.

"You remember Candy?" I sit at the kitchen table, maneuvering the ice cubes on my face.

"Yes, I remember Candy."

"Candy has an alter."

"A what?"

"An alter," I repeat. "It hurts more with the ice."

He answers this with an eyebrow raise and drops a handful of pasta into boiling water. "You were saying something about an alter."

"Yes, she's dissociating." I take the ice bag off to let my skin regain some feeling.

"Which in English means...?"

"Split personality, in the old parlance. And the other girl is named Daneesha."

He stares at me. "So tell me if I got this right. Candy turned into Daneesha, and Daneesha hit you?"

"Yes, that is correct."

He adds some more garlic to the tomato sauce. Mike makes sauce instead of using the canned stuff. He actually wrinkled his nose when I picked up a jar at the grocery store. "And why, may I ask, did she hit you?"

I shrug. "It was my fault, really. I did get in her space. And the girl doesn't even know who she is."

"Huh." The sauce starts sizzling, and he turns down the heat. "Is this common, then?"

"Which—disassociation or being hit by your patient?"

"Um, either one, I guess."

I ponder this. "No, neither are common. But they both happen."

He takes a taste off the spoon and adds another shake of salt. "You know what's really surprising?"

"What?" I ask, grabbing a paper towel for the dripping ice bag.

"You said she's twelve or so?"

"Yeah, thirteen maybe."

"So you must have, like, fifty pounds on her. I figured you would have kicked her ass."

"Very funny." I laugh, which hurts my cheek, reminding

me to put the ice back on. "Is the food almost ready? I'm starving."

He hands me a loaf of Italian. "Cut up some bread, Rocky. It'll be ready soon."

"You know," I say, slicing in, "after a hard day of work, I expect dinner to be on the table when I get home."

"Shut up," he says with affection, "or I'll punch you in the other eye." Leaning in, he kisses me, his five o'clock shadow scraping against my cheek. I put down the bread and kiss him back as the water bubbles beside us. And pretty soon, I've forgotten all about my eye.

Chapter Sixteen

Chloe looks up from her *Catcher in the Rye* (which Candy devoured in one day), the paperback cover shining in the sun. She gained two pounds, which means book privileges at last.

"What happened to you guys?" she asks drolly. "Out fighting crime again?"

"Something like that," Dr. Berringer says, smoothing his Band-Aid. I am quite sick of being asked about my shiner. "And how are you today?"

"Same as yesterday, and the day before. Actually, I could just put a hologram in here, and you could ask me the same questions and I could give you the same answers, and then I could be off doing something valuable with my time."

That *would* be clever, I think. I could have a hologram, too, so it could go to the hospital every morning while I sleep in.

"And what valuable thing would that be?" he asks.

She shrugs. "Don't know. Anything is better than rotting here."

"You know the way to get out, Chloe."

"Hey, didn't you hear the big news? I gained two pounds! Woo-hoo! Party time!"

"I did hear that. That's good. That's what we want."

"A fat patient," she says morosely.

"A healthy patient," he corrects.

She glances back down at her book, surely connecting far more with Holden Caulfield than the likes of us. I can't say I blame her.

"Keep it up, Chloe," Dr. Berringer says.

She gives him a rock-on horn hand gesture, not looking up from her book.

"Okay." He turns to me. "Let's go see Daneesha. Or Candy. The suspense is killing me." We get to her room, and by her slouched posture I can tell it's Daneesha. Detective Adams is standing next to her, grinning. Dr. Berringer must have called him.

"She's a live wire, isn't she?" he asks.

"Whatever," she says. "Just tell me what I need to do to get the hell out of here." She has calmed down, though, probably from the Haldol and Ativan cocktail still on board from last night.

When Daneesha turns away, the detective motions to my eye with a questioning look. I mime a punch, pointing to her, and he stifles a smile. "I've been asking her about her story." His notebook reads, in black scrawl, "running away from white dudes."

"And I been telling him, *I don't know*," she answers with frustration. "If I knew, don't you think I'd tell you already so I could get out of this shit-bag of a place?"

"Hey," he scolds.

She rolls her eyes. "Please, that is the nicest way I could say it." But I notice she doesn't drop any f-bombs around the detective. "Like I told him. Running away from white dudes trying to rape me and shit. Then I sort of remember some nice lady in the police station, and that's it. And I wake up in some ratty-ass clothes with y'all calling me Candy, shoving me out the door to some foster home, which I'm not even hearing about, and that's it. Present day. I think we all caught up now."

She is definitely more vocal than Candy. And, I have to admit, more entertaining.

"How old are you anyway, Daneesha?" I ask.

"Come on. Tell me you people don't have all that in your big doctor charts."

I shrug.

"How old you think I am?"

"Fourteen?" I guess.

"Close. Thirteen. Everybody thinks I'm older, though. Heaven said I was sixteen by the time I was two."

"Who's Heaven?" the detective breaks in.

"My momma."

"Heaven?" Detective Adams asks, writing.

"As in, her name is Heaven, or she's *in* heaven?" I ask.

"As in, her name is Heaven. I ain't being all metaphorical and shit."

"And where is Heaven from?" the detective asks, pen in hand.

"Who the hell knows?" she answers with disdain. "I ain't seen my momma in years."

"Okay," he says. "Well, where were you living?"

"I don't know." She sits up in the bed, getting agitated again. Her wrists are lined with red marks from fighting the restraints all night. They're finally off now, but she's been warned they could go back on at any time. "When we gonna talk about me getting out of this place?"

The detective pulls up a metal chair with a squeak and sits down so he's at her level. "Think about it, Daneesha. Where are you going to go?"

She snorts. "I can take care of myself."

He shakes his head, kindly. "I think that's how you ended up in here."

"Then I'll go find my momma, or my momma's people."

"Who you haven't seen in years."

"Whatever," she says, but some of her fire has faded.

Dr. Berringer steps closer to the bed. "We're all trying to get you out of here as soon as humanly possible."

She looks at him like she just noticed him in the room. "Who you supposed to be? Doctor somebody or another?"

"Dr. Berringer."

"I know you from somewhere?" she asks.

"I was in here yesterday."

"What happened to your face?" Then she looks at me. "You two get in a fight or something?"

"You don't remember?" he asks.

148

She throws him a sidelong glance. "Would I be asking you if I remembered?"

"Never mind. It's a long story." He turns to me. "How did it go overnight?"

"Okay. She got two more Ativan and five more Haldol." Daneesha watches us warily.

"Can we talk more about those white guys, Daneesha?" the detective says. "I'd really like to find them."

"And I'd really like to stay away from them."

He smiles. "I can understand that, but we also don't want them to hurt anyone else. And it might help us find your home."

"I don't need no help finding my home," she shoots back. "I got a home. I just ain't discussing it with y'all right now."

"Well, Daneesha," the detective says, "the quicker you feel like discussing it, the quicker you can get out of here."

She huffs and crosses her arms, looking like a thirteen-year-old for the first time since I've seen her. She refuses to answer any more questions, so we all leave the room, Detective Adams heading back to his office.

As soon as we get to the nurses' station, Dr. Berringer says, "So what should we do with her?"

"Maybe...cognitive behavioral therapy?"

He gives me the same look I gave Sam at the suggestion, then reaches into his pocket and tosses a blue gumball into his mouth. (A gumball? Who carries around gumballs?) "Multiple personalities," he says with a grin. "Read up on it."

149

Three hours later, Candy is back.

I can tell as soon as I walk in the room. Daneesha is all movement, sitting up, tapping her foot, pacing, and looking out the window for any activity. Candy is content to sit in bed, hands folded. She gives me her bright, wide smile.

"Candy?" I ask with some hesitation.

She lets out a sweet laugh. "Yes. Who'd you think it was, silly?"

"Uh, I'm not sure." We stare at each other. "Do you by chance know a girl named Daneesha?"

She purses her lips a second, thinking. "I don't think so."

"How about Heaven?"

"Oh sure, I believe in heaven," Candy answers.

"No, no. I mean, do you know anyone named Heaven?"

Her face flashes a hint of recognition, but then it's gone. "No. That's a weird name, though." She starts tidying up her nightstand. Daneesha left it a mess. "Why do you ask?"

I sit down next to her. "I don't know. We thought it might help figure out your identity."

"Oh yeah, like my last name and where I'm from and stuff? I don't know. I'm sorry I can't be more help with that."

It strikes me then, for the first time perhaps, that Candy doesn't much care who she is or where she's from. Or if she cares, she is certainly laissez-faire about the whole matter. La belle indifference.

"So what happened to the Watsons? My foster family. Did that fall through or something?"

"Yes, it sort of did."

She shrugs, then smiles brightly again. "Oh well, that's okay. I'm sure we'll find someone else soon. And the hospital's not so bad," she says, channeling Little Orphan Annie again. The contrast with Daneesha couldn't be more stark. "Hey, what happened to your eye?"

You hit me. "Long story," I say, stealing Dr. Berringer's line.

Candy nods, content with my nonanswer. My cell phone rings. Detective Adams's name pops up on the screen. I mouth "one minute" and leave the room. "Hello, Detective."

"How's Daneesha doing?"

"Candy. She's back to Candy."

"Oh, crap."

"What do you mean, oh, crap? Candy's perfectly nice," I say, feeling defensive for the less flamboyant personality. "She doesn't hit me, for instance."

He laughs. "It's not that I don't like her. She's just kind of"—he pauses—"useless. That's all. I felt like we were getting somewhere with Daneesha."

"Don't worry," I say. "If I know anything about multiple personalities, Daneesha will be back."

Chapter Seventeen

I was right. The next few days are a Candy-Daneesha parade. Today, Daneesha is up.

"I seriously don't know what you're talking about," she says, staring at me like I've gone crazy. Cognitive behavioral therapy is going about as well as I thought it would.

"Split personality," I explain. "That's one name for it. The other one is dissociative identity disorder."

She scratches her leg, now covered with a sheen of light brown hair, a fact she has complained about already. ("My legs are looking nasty, girl. You got to get me a razor or something. I promise I'm not gonna go all suicidal or shit.") Candy has yet to notice.

"So let me get this right. You trying to tell me I have more than one personality. Sometimes I act all crazy and shit, like someone else. Not Daneesha."

"Sort of," I say.

"Some bitch named Candy," she adds.

"Again, kind of," I say, not entirely comfortable with her characterization of the situation.

"You know what I think?"

"What?" I scoot my chair in closer for our breakthrough moment.

"I think all you people crazy. And I mean *crazy* crazy. Out-your-dang-skulls crazy."

"I can see how you might think that Daneesha, but—"

"But what? I ain't no split personality. I'm telling you some fat white guys chased me. Probably fell and smacked my head is all. So I don't remember everything, but that doesn't mean I'm crazy," she says, her voice rising. "Why ain't you found those white dudes yet?"

"Detective Adams is on it. I promise."

She scoffs. "He ain't on it very hard, is he? You know, if I was some *white* girl with a name like Candy, and some brothers were trying to rape her, them niggers be in the chair already, and that's the truth."

"I don't disagree with you."

"Maybe, you find those assholes, and I start remembering some shit better. You ever think about that?"

I pause a minute. "Did Detective Adams ever ask you your last name?"

"Jones. My last name Jones. Don't you people have all this in your charts and shit? Y'all don't seem to know very much about your patients," she grumbles.

To say the least.

"Whatever. Y'all can keep asking me these stupid questions. Just be sure you get me the hell outta here and quick."

"We're trying."

"Girl, you got to step that shit up. Foster me up if you need to. I ain't planning on spending my entire young life in this place, you know."

I allow a smile. "We want to get you out of here, Daneesha. But we want to get you back with your family, too, with Heaven."

"Good luck with that one," she snorts. "Heaven in jail or dead by now, no doubt." She stands up to check out the window, then, finding herself barefoot, sits right back on the bed. She swats the bottoms of her feet with disgust. "Where the hell my socks at?" Candy hates socks, would rather walk around without, though she's been warned against it.

"Um, in your drawer maybe?"

"Man, that floor is nasty." She yanks the drawer open and finds the socks neatly balled up. Candy is forever tidying up clothes that Daneesha leaves lying around. Daneesha throws on her socks, then springs up to look out the window again, at the cars zooming around the parking lot. The sky is a dazzling blue after weeks of gray rain. The trees are nearly ready for winter, half their leaves shed, with muted yellows, reds, and browns left over. God's fireworks show is wrapping up.

Daneesha turns away from the window and looks at me, like she just noticed something. "You sure are tall. You play basketball or something?"

"Nope. Common misperception. Volleyball neither."

"An unathletic tall chick," she muses.

"Sort of. I like running." (Or used to anyway, before I got lazy and spent every last minute studying for my RITE.) "You remember any more about the guys that chased you?" I ask, changing the subject.

"Not really. White guys, kinda old. Like forty. They all dressed up in ties and shirts, like they just came from work or something. Fat motherfuckers, too. Couldn't catch me 'cause they too fat." She laughs. This is the first time I've heard Daneesha laugh. It's different from Candy's musical laugh. There's an edge to it, raucous, not cautious like Candy's.

"Hey, one other thing," I say. "You know that scar you have?"

She reaches right down to her left ankle, though I didn't say where it was.

"Yeah, what about it?"

"I just wondered how you got it."

She looks puzzled a second. "I don't know. Probably cut it on something."

"Was it a cigarette?" I ask.

She throws me a look. "No, it ain't no cigarette. I ain't fucking crazy like that Brandon dude."

I spend the rest of the visit unskillfully avoiding the topic of her discharge date, and once out of the room, I call Detective Adams.

"Did she tell you her last name?" I ask him.

"Why, is Daneesha back?"

"Yeah, how'd you know?"

"Because Candy is clueless. And no, she didn't tell me her last name. Are you going to grace me with that information?"

"Jones."

He groans. "Perfect. I guess it would be asking too much to have a name that isn't shared by a million other people."

"Who knows if it's even true, but it's something, huh?"

"Yeah," he sighs. "It's something. I'll run it through, let you know if I come up with anything."

I decide to check Facebook before I venture in to see my newest patient: Donny Thomas. He's a seventeen-year-old psychopath who tortured his neighbor's dog. I'm kind of putting it off. There's nothing blazingly exciting on Facebook. My third cousin once removed (I think) just had a baby and got about a million likes. Which is reasonable, honestly. I mean nine months and then all that labor. Right at that moment, a very bad idea pops into my head.

I could post her picture on Facebook.

The idea flashes all sorts of alarm bells I've been taught to watch out for as an ADHD veteran. "BEWARE! NOT A GOOD PLAN! COULD SPELL TROUBLE!"

So, of course, I take three seconds to consider it, ignore my wailing superego, and create a Facebook post. I upload her picture with the title *Who Is This Girl?* Then I fill in the profile with "Missing Teenager. May go by Daneesha or Candy Jones." I take a deep breath and then, before I can think about it anymore, post it, sharing it with all the waiting Facebook public out there.

Pushing open the door, I lay eyes on my newest patient. He is standing with his shirt off, sporting an impressive six-pack. He could double as a male model if he weren't a psychopath, though I suppose the two aren't necessarily mutually exclusive.

"Donny Thomas," he says, shaking my hand. I immediately think of Donny Osmond, the polar opposite of a psychopath.

"Do you mind putting your shirt back on?" I ask.

"Why? Am I making you uncomfortable?"

I don't bother to answer, keeping my face impassive. Donny shrugs, flexing muscles I can't even remember from Anatomy, and puts his white undershirt back on slowly, like a backward striptease.

"Okay, I wanted to ask you a few questions, if I could," I say, sitting down.

"I'm all yours." His smile is slippery.

"Right. Can you explain to me why you killed the dog?"

He rolls his eyes. "I already made this very clear in my statement to the police."

"Yes, but I want to hear it from you."

He sits down on the edge of the bed, and I move the chair back, leaving a few crucial feet between us. I'm not forgetting what happened with my last psychopath, and I've already been hit in the face once this week.

"The dog," he says.

"Yes."

"I was putting the thing out of its misery. The neighbors just didn't understand."

"What didn't they understand?"

He stretches his arms up with a yawn. "I told the officer already. The dog was sick."

"Sick? How do you know it was sick?"

He smiles again. "I know a lot of things. I've got a hundred fifty-five IQ."

"Hmm." I'm probably going to hear about his MENSA membership next. "But you still haven't told me how you knew the dog was sick."

Donny leans back, flexing then retracting his biceps and gazing at them with pure absorption. "You know what? I'm done with this discussion."

"I'm just trying to understand how—"

"Done. With. This. Discussion."

I nod and walk out of the room backward so I can keep an eye on him, plotting how I can pawn this one off on Jason. In the hall, I open Facebook again and wait forever for the page to update. There's one comment already, and I click on it to see.

"You have seriously fucking lost it." From Scotty.

Arthur opens one eye, then closes it again with a nosey sigh, assured that I am just getting in the bathtub and not doing anything that involves food. After a long week, I am more than ready for my bath. Which took some preparation, mind you. I had to choose exactly the right bath oil (English lavender), the right candle (China Rain), and the right glass of white wine (Russian River Chardonnay). Actually, the wine didn't matter; any 14-percent alcohol would have worked. I am submerged at last, the hot water swirling around my body like a balm, when the text quacks. I peer over at the ledge where my phone is propped.

whatcha doin? It's Mike.

in a bath

oh good, let's face-time

hahaha

you coming over later?

on call, so wasn't going to. Call u later, I write.

sounds good

xo

xo, he answers back.

I lay back farther in the tub. The candle flickers as the wick sizzles in the pool of wax. I stick my feet out at the top of the tub (the previous tenant must have been rather short), when my phone quacks again. I look over at the ledge.

some issues up here. Can u come in? It's Dr. Berringer.

I groan. Loudly. Arthur pops up his head, confirms there is still no food in the offing, and lays it back down. Sure, I answer with a sigh. Taking a bath was just tempting the on-call gods anyway. Of course Probation Girl can come in.

any problem?

will discuss when u get here

ok. B there in about 10

I text Mike to let him know I got called in already and throw on a pair of scrubs. Ten minutes later, I am walking what feels like a hundred miles from the residents' parking lot. The air is foggy and cool with a milky-white sky that makes the night look eerily like day.

r u still here?

12 floor, he answers.

Right, the twelfth floor, where there are no patients. This must be quite an emergency. I am growling to myself all the way up the stairs, then I shove the squeaky door open to the dim, ghostly, empty room. The curtains are open already this time to the grayed-out night, soft, fuzzy lights splayed out below.

"Hi." He is sprawled out in the little chair. This time, there is no question as to whether he smells of alcohol. He is drunk. Drunk as a skunk. "Thanks for coming," he says with just a hint of slur to his words, his New Orleans accent stronger than usual. The scratches on his face are just visible. "I couldn't think of who else to call."

"It's not about a patient?"

"No, I'm sorry. It's not."

I take the chair beside him. "So what's up?" I say, making no effort at any counseling niceties.

"My wife is leaving me," he answers with similar bluntness.

"Oh." I peel off my leather coat because, despite being a ghost town up here, it's still hot as hell. "Do you…um… want to talk about it?"

He turns to me and laughs. "Do I want to talk about it? I don't know. Considering I dragged you out here on a perfectly nice Friday night, I guess I probably do." But he doesn't say anything for a moment. He just stares down at the rose-pink Formica tabletop. "She wants a divorce," he says finally. "And to be honest, I don't blame her."

"You want something from the bar?" I ask, standing up and heading toward the vending machine. "My treat this time."

He twists his body toward me. "Okay, I guess I'll have my usual." I come back with a root beer for him (though I'm sure he'd rather skip the root) and a Diet Pepsi for me. Too late for caffeine, but then I'm going to need it to drive home anyway. He takes a big sip and sighs again.

"Was this a surprise?" I ask.

He pauses. "Not really. It shouldn't have been a surprise in any case. She's put up with my shit for too long now." He takes another sip.

"Any particular issue going on?"

He stares ahead. "Issues, plural. She misses New Orleans. She doesn't like Buffalo. I don't make as much money as her daddy used to." He pauses, then recaps his drink and places it on the table. "Of course, it doesn't help that I'm a drunk."

I twirl my bottle in my hands. "Yeah. I've noticed. It seems like that might be a problem."

He takes another swig with a laugh. "Good observation, Dr. Goldman." He exhales then. "Leaving Tulane, though. That was the last straw."

I nod, staring out the window. A siren bleats in the distance.

"I had it under pretty good control until this damn thing with my wife. She's been spying on me. Thinks I'm having a goddamn affair."

I nod again. In my limited experience, this usually means you *are* having an affair.

"I'm not," he says, "since you asked."

"Hmm," I answer.

"Anyway, she packed up all her stuff. So the place is empty. It's as depressing as hell at my house right now." He takes a drink. "So that was a surprise. Saying you want a divorce is one thing. Moving out the next day is another."

"Dr. Berringer," I say.

"Tad. Oh God. Please call me Tad. Dr. Berringer sounds like my father."

"Was your father a doctor?"

"Yeah. Retired now. He was a radiologist. A *real* doctor." He puts air quotes around "real." I'm guessing he has some issues with his father, and I wouldn't even need to be a psychiatrist to suss that one out.

"Okay, Tad," I say, though the name feels funny to say. "Maybe you just need to give her some space for now. And let her come back when she's ready."

"Yeah, maybe. But I don't think so." He twists the cap on and lobs the empty bottle toward the garbage. It misses entirely, though he doesn't seem to notice. "I don't think she's ever coming back."

We sit in glum silence for a while, and then he gets a text. The phone is sitting on the table between us, so we both see it.

O-club tomorrow?

He rolls his eyes. "That's my sponsor, Oscar. Our stupid name for AA."

"The O-club?"

"Yeah. There's an Omar and an Ozzie we hang out with there. So we took to calling it the O-club."

"So you messed it up with a T."

"Huh?"

"T for Tad."

"Oh yeah, guess I did."

We fall into silence again, staring outside, when he stands up, stretching. "Zoe, I've kept you long enough. I've gotta get back home." He fishes in his pocket for keys. "I'll walk you to the lot."

"You know what, I'll drive you."

"Oh, please, Zoe. I've been far worse."

"That may be true, but I'm still driving. We can take my car."

"You don't even know where I live."

"My Google Maps is very smart."

He finds his keys finally, debates, then drops them back in his pocket. "You're one tough broad, ain't you?"

"Yup, that's me."

He follows me to the elevators, and I pick up his mis-thrown bottle and toss our drinks in the trash, which smells sour, like the bag hasn't been changed in months. How we get to my car, I'm not exactly sure. He leans heavily on me, probably more heavily than he needs to, and we lumber slowly over the gravel road to the residents' lot. It's an awkward slough, some odd approximation of a three-legged race at the fair, his thigh rocking against me. His sweater is scratchy and smells like sweat and gin with notes of root beer—not a bad smell, actually. I type his address in my GPS, and we're on our way. Within minutes, he is dead asleep beside me, his head lolling back and forth like a rag doll. With no small effort, I am finally able to wake him up when we get to his house.

"You ready?" I ask.

He falls back asleep on my shoulder, which gives me the answer.

"Come on," I say, giving him a shove. I get out of the car and open his door. "Tad," I whisper, as loud as I can whisper. "Come on."

"Okay," he mumbles. "I'm fine, I'm fine, I'm fine."

"Then get out of the car."

It takes him a few tries, but he lumbers out of my little car like he's overplaying a drunk in a movie. We do our three-legged shuffle up to his doorstep, and he manages to fit his key in the slot after a couple flubs. The door opens to a dank, cold house. I have to agree with him: It's depressing as hell. "Haven't you turned on your heat?" I ask him.

"I keep meaning to," he answers, gazing around his house. His face looks on the verge of despair. I don't know if I can handle him crying.

"Where's your bedroom?"

"Upstairs," he says and lopes off that way, banging his knee on a coffee table. We climb up the stairs, him leaning on the rail and me supporting his other arm. His room is neat but bare, like someone just moved out and took all the pretty things away. Staggering over to the bed, he sits down, putting his head in his hands. "I really fucked up this time, didn't I?"

"It's not so bad," I lie.

He shakes his head and looks up at me, his eyes shiny with tears. "Did I ever tell you about that Leonard Cohen song?"

"Yes, you did."

Unexpectedly, he grabs my hand. His hand is warm, despite the cold drive home and the cold house. I swallow, my heart rate elevating. He pulls me closer to him, and I stand there awkwardly with his shoulder digging into my ribs. Heat radiates off his scratchy sweater. I sit on the bed and pat his shoulder. "Zoe?"

"Yes?"

He grabs my shoulder and pulls me in closer. The smell of root beer, gin, and wool. "Don't ever let me fall in love with you, okay?" His whisper is hot on my neck. His words are mumbled, barely intelligible. I could have misheard them. "Promise me that, okay? Because I am some bad, bad news."

"Okay," I answer, gently pulling away from him before I do something stupid like lie down beside him.

When the phone rings, the clock says 10:00 a.m. My mouth is dry as cotton.

"Hello?" I croak out.

"Sounds like someone had a bad night," Mike says.

"Yeah, sort of."

"I figured. So I let you sleep. Whereas I, on the other hand, have already put in two hours at the gym."

"Oh, okay, Mr. Show-off," I say, sitting up stiffly.

"That's *Dr.* Show-off to you."

"Ha." I shove on my slippers and make my way to the kitchen. "You working today?"

"No, I'm off. You want to do something?"

I set up my coffee, a one-cup jobber that Scotty gave me for my birthday. I love the thing, though he told me it would probably put him out of business. "Sure. I'm on call, though, so we can't go far."

"We could drive up to Letchworth," he offers. "Prime time for leaf peeping."

"No, too far. And don't ever say that again."

"Don't ever say what again?"

"Leaf peeping."

"What?" he objects. "That's what they call it."

"A movie maybe?" The coffee hisses to a close, and I pour in my fixings. As I take my first sip, my brain comes to life.

"I already checked. Nothing good up. Just a couple of action movies."

"What kind of action movies?" I ask.

"The kind with elderly heroes in bad toupees."

"Oh, no. You're right. No interest." I take another lovely sip. A huge linden tree glows yellow outside the window, the leaves flickering in the sun. "How about a walk?"

There is a pause while he thinks about this. "Sure, we could do that. Where do you want to go?"

"Surprise me," I say, "within a ten-mile radius."

"Okay. It's a deal," he says. "Pick you up in ten minutes?"

"Ten minutes? I haven't even finished my coffee. I still have to put my face on." We both know this is a joke. I barely remember to use ChapStick. Once I wore foundation to cover my freckles for a medical school dance with Jean Luc. He told me I looked "beige."

"Pick me up in an hour." I hang up the phone in a good mood, 8.7 at least, ready to spend a gorgeous fall day with Mike. But the guilty thought still surfaces, that I didn't tell him the truth about last night, about Dr. Berringer.

And I'm not exactly sure why.

Chapter Eighteen

Any idea how her picture ended up on Facebook?" the detective's voice booms into my Bluetooth.

"Whose picture?" I turn left at a light that was almost still yellow, and someone honks at me.

He guffaws. "Whose picture? Zoe, a word of advice: Don't take up a life of crime. You're a terrible liar."

"Yeah, um..."

"I assume you're pleading the fifth?" he asks.

"Can I do that?"

A laugh comes over the speaker. "Don't you watch any cop shows?"

I take a sip of coffee, which I swallow wrong and cough all over my just-dry-cleaned sweater. "Fuck." I'm going to need some of Scotty's magical Treasury bonds to deal with my mounting dry-cleaning bills.

"Don't swear in the phone, please."

"Sorry."

"Well," he says, "as much as I hate to admit it, your little stunt might have provided our first lead."

"My *alleged* stunt."

"Yes, your alleged stunt. A woman recognized the picture."

"Oh yeah?"

"But she's says the name isn't Daneesha or Candy. It's Monica. Monica Green."

"Monica Green," I repeat, pondering this. She doesn't look like a Monica Green.

"She's a girl from North Carolina, missing about a month now. Her uncle picked her up from school one day, and she was never heard from again."

"No one looked for her for a month?"

"No, they looked for her, just in North Carolina. The Amber Alert was a no-go, and then all the leads went cold. But it just so happens her cousin is friends with someone who's friends with someone, et cetera, however the hell these things work, and saw the post."

"Aren't you on Facebook?"

"No, I'm not on Facebook," he says, offended. "My wife's on that thing all the damn time. It's the last thing I need."

"How did you hear about it then? I didn't see any comments on it."

"On the post you didn't write?" he asks. "She thought it might have been a hoax, and she saw the post was from Buffalo, so she called us. She's sure that's her."

I pull off the exit to the hospital. "How could it get missed all this time, though? Don't you guys share missing person photos across states?"

169

"Of course." Boisterous laughter rises up in the background. "It got missed somehow, Zoe. I don't know. It might not even be the same girl. But it's worth a look."

"What does her mom say?"

"The mother's deceased."

I stop at a red light. "Was her name Heaven by chance?"

"No. I checked that out already. Her name was Vonya. She died of breast cancer. The girl's being raised by her aunt."

"Huh."

"The aunt's a solid citizen, but I can't say the same for her abusive asshole of a husband."

"And the aunt thinks it's her niece?"

He clears his throat. "She's not sure honestly, because it's a crappy picture. Said she's ten pounds thinner and pale as a ghost, but says it could be her."

"Wow." The light turns green. We may have finally solved the puzzle of Jane.

"The aunt's flying in soon to confirm. We're still firming up the date. So I guess we'll see."

"Why don't you just Skype?"

"I suggested that. She said if it's her girl, she wants to be able to hold her."

The nurse supervisor, a sixtysomething-year-old with a light-brown beehive hairdo, pokes her head in the charting room. "Did any of you guys write a Demerol order yesterday?"

"I was shooting up yesterday," Jason says, "but not with Demerol."

"You're awful, you know that?" she titters, heading back to her desk. "I'll have to ask Dr. Berringer. It's recorded as taken from the Pyxis, but I don't have any orders for it."

"Nancy, did you waste any Demerol?" she calls down the hall.

"No," Nancy calls back.

Dr. Berringer on Demerol? He's been hungover before, but not strung out. No pinpoint pupils or mini-nods. No scratching at his skin as the day wears on. I vote yes for Jim Beam but no for the opiates. If anyone wants my opinion. As if to answer for himself, Dr. Berringer appears in the doorway, wearing his famous French-blue shirt. Dr. Berringer confirms that he, too, did not order any Demerol.

"Hmm," the nurse says. "I also have insulin taken out without an order. Did any of you guys order that?"

"No insulin, no Demerol," he answers. "Call the pharmacy. Maybe there's a problem with the machine." He grabs a couple of charts. "Let's go," he says, up and happy, with no sign of the downtrodden man from Friday night. I notice he doesn't say a word about it either. But then again, what's he supposed to say? "How's Chloe doing?"

"Not great. Lost a pound and some privileges. Extra-hostile today," I answer.

"Sounds fun. And Candy? Or should I say Daneesha?"

"It was Daneesha this morning. Daneesha Jones."

He stops walking. "You got a last name?"

"Oh yeah, I forgot to tell you. It was before the weekend."

He nods, scratching at his head.

"But that might not even be her real last name. The detective's got a lead. He thinks she might be a missing girl from North Carolina. Monica Green."

"Monica Green?" he repeats with some confusion. "Well, whatever, let's go see her." When we walk in, she's sitting in a chair with her socks off, flipping through *Gulliver's Travels*. It's got to be Candy.

"You like it?" I ask.

"It's kind of boring, actually," she says with a nervous laugh.

Daneesha's response when the acne-ridden, mousy volunteer handed her the book from the bare offerings on the roller shelf: *What's this shit?*

"I didn't like it much either," I say with a vague memory of a giant peeing on a fire and my frustrated English teacher telling me that's perhaps the least relevant thing in the whole book. I was skilled at frustrating English teachers.

"By the way," Candy starts, her voice soft. "I don't mean to pry. But do you know when the foster home thing might happen again?"

So now both of them are badgering me about getting out. "We're trying our best, Candy. It's great of you to be so patient."

She nods and blushes, pleased with the compliment. "Okay. Just wondering is all." We don't get much further. She doesn't remember her last name being Jones, still doesn't know a Daneesha, has no recollection of an aunt (though is excited to meet her!), and as for fat white guys chasing her, no clue. I have to agree with the detective that, if this case gets solved, it's going to be by Daneesha.

I leaf through the artwork on her desk. The newest picture is rows of purple decorated with repeating letters, numbers, and suns, much like the one Jane Doe did for her first art project. The paper is warped, still drying. "What was the assignment for this one?"

"A quilt," she says.

I nod. It does look like a quilt. Donny Not-Osmond likely drew rows of disemboweled puppies. Farther down in the art pile is a work in multicolored, zigzagged, polka-dotted bubble letters that reads "FUCK THIS SHIT." Wonder who wrote that one?

"We'll see you later, okay?" Dr. Berringer says.

"Yeah, that sounds good." She offers a shy smile. "Your eye looks better, by the way."

"Thanks." I reach up automatically to touch it, the tenderness almost gone. We get back to the nurses' station, to a pumpkin bowl full of hard candies and a loop of alternating smiley ghosts and grinning pumpkins spanning the counter. Last year, they decided the mummies and spiders were "mentally inappropriate" for a psychiatric floor (yes, a committee took the time to determine this), so this year, it looks like all the decorations are on Prozac. Not to mention that it's over two weeks past Halloween now, and no one's bothered to take them down yet.

"Should we be doing more?" I ask.

"What do you mean?" Dr. Berringer asks.

"It doesn't seem like we're getting anywhere with CBT.

173

She just keeps streaming Candy and Daneesha. It's pretty unstable."

"Or we could be heading for a breakthrough," he says.

"Maybe," I answer, doubtfully.

"What do you think, Jason?" he asks.

Jason shrugs. "I don't know. We could try something."

"Okay," he says, weighing our opinions. We residents appreciate this. Unlike most of the attendings, Dr. Berringer at least pretends to listen to your suggestions, even if he doesn't usually follow them. "And what would you suggest?"

Jason purses his lips. "Increase the Ativan?"

"How about adding an antipsychotic?" I ask. "They say if benzos aren't working, you might want to add an antipsychotic."

"Who's they?"

"The *Journal of Clinical Psychiatry.*"

He leans his elbow against the Formica countertop, drumming his fingers. "All right, here's what we're going to do. Keep working the CBT. It may not be helping much, but it can't hurt. Look for triggers. We can try some anti-anxiety techniques if we can identify a trigger."

"Okay."

A nurse walks by us in her scrubs, black with glow-in-the-dark skeletons. I wonder if she had to run those by the committee. ("You can wear them during the day, but at night, definitely mentally inappropriate.")

"Let's increase the Ativan to two mgs q six. An antipsychotic's not a bad idea, but let's wait. You should always make one change at a time. But if we're not seeing any movement with the benzos, we'll try it."

Chapter Nineteen

I don't know. I just feel kind of fucked up or something,"
Daneesha complains. "Like high but not high. A bad kind
of high."

"You've gotten high before?" I ask, surprised.

She smirks. "Dr. Goldman, you sure ain't from where I'm
from."

"No, I guess not." But then again, neither of us knows
where she's from.

"Maybe I should get high, then at least I could get out of
this place. That boy Donny wasn't stupid."

"What do you mean? What happened to Donny?" I didn't
get to see Donny Not-Osmond yet today. Again, sort of
putting it off after Jason said "Hell no" to the suggestion that
he take him on.

"Don't you people know nothing in here? Off to baby jail.
Good riddance is what I say. That boy gave me the heebie-

jeebies." She crosses her legs, her hospital gown billowing against her knees, and smooths a hand up and down her leg absentmindedly. She did get to shave her legs, to which she huffed "Finally." Yesterday Candy kept rubbing her legs together in wonder. "What were we talking about? Oh yeah, me feeling high."

"Maybe it has to do with what we talked about, losing yourself to another personality?"

"Nah," she says quickly. "I don't think so. I just feel dizzy or some shit. I don't know. Maybe I'm just coming down with something."

What she's coming down with is the double dosing of Candy, since Daneesha has been refusing her meds. "So what do you think about what I said?"

"About what?"

She does seem a bit hazy today. "Your aunt," I remind her.

"Oh, well." She looks down at the floor. "I guess that's cool. I don't remember no aunt, to be honest with you. But I could talk to her."

"Do you remember any family? Besides Heaven. Siblings or cousins or anything?"

"Cousins, sure, I got cousins. No brothers or sisters, though." She is rubbing her forehead, when something seems to occur to her. "Hey, if this lady my auntie, she get to take me outta here?"

"Well, yes," I say. "That's how it would work."

She smiles then, a Candy-bright smile. "All right then, bring her on. Let's meet this auntie of mine already."

"What happened to Donny Not-Osmond?" I ask Jason.

"Got caught smoking weed in the bathroom," he says.

"Oh. Why am I always the last to know these things?"

Dr. Berringer is in the nurses' station with Jason, working on charts. Neither of them answers me, and the sound of pages flipping and pens scratching on paper fills the room.

"You see Candy yet?" Dr. Berringer asks.

"Yeah, I just did. She was Daneesha, though."

He frowns. "Obviously the benzos aren't having enough effect." He runs his hands through his hair, which looks freshly shorn.

"We could try the antipsychotic," I suggest.

He stares ahead, biting his bottom lip. "All right. Let's give her some Risperdal."

"All right," I say with some gusto. Finally. "Maybe we should decrease the Ativan, though. Daneesha's feeling it pretty good."

"One thing at a time, remember?" He gets up from his chair. "I'm going to grab some coffee. You want anything?"

"No, I'm good," I say, and he leaves, the cologne scent trailing him, mixed with the unmistakable scent emanating off his skin. Though he didn't look at all hungover today. Either I'm imagining things now or we have a case in point of a functioning alcoholic. Once Dr. Berringer's down the hall, I clear my throat. "Do you think maybe he smelled a little like—"

Jason answers with a vaudevillian mime of tipping back a bottle.

I glance around the nurses' station. "You think anyone else knows?" I whisper.

He stares at me. "You're kidding, right? Zoe, the man smells like a brewery. It's like the worst-kept secret ever."

My jaw is quite open.

"You *didn't* know?" he asks, astonished.

"Well, he did sort of confess it to me," I say, without going into more detail about that night, which Dr. Berringer still hasn't discussed with me. "And I saw he had sanctions against him on Healthgrades."

"You were Googling him?" He laughs.

My face turns red. "It was research."

"Yeah, well. He's on his own probation. I heard he's got to see a psychiatrist. All sorts of shit."

And now I know why he's seeing my psychiatrist.

"And he's getting a divorce," Jason adds.

"He told you?"

"Oh, honey, he tells me everything. That man totally overshares."

I feel an undeniable prick of jealousy, thinking back to that night. His scratchy sweater, his whisper in my ear. *Zoe, don't ever let me fall in love with you, okay?*

My phone quacks out, and I look at my text.

Melanie driving me crazy! Never get married :)

"Who's that?" Jason asks.

"No one," I grumble. I don't feel like chatting about Jean Luc right now. My oh-so-sensitive ex plying me for sympathy on his wedding.

I answer with a smiley face, then stare at the text another moment, waiting for a reply. I don't know why. I can't help it. I'm like a rat that keeps pushing that lever for my reward pellet. And Jean Luc was my reward pellet. I think of his perfect body in my bed while I watched him breathing, not quite believing he was there with me. I have never dated anyone who looked like him before and never will again. And vice versa. He doesn't have to share his bed with an Amazon-tall woman, her nose dotted with ridiculous freckles, boring brown hair covering the pillow, her feet nearly touching the edge. He has the perfect match in his perfect Melanie, with her perfectly sized everything and golden-blond hair that mirrors his.

I shove the phone in my pocket.

"Now I don't want you to get your hopes up too much. In case it isn't her." We are waiting for Detective Adams, who just called that they are on their way up.

Candy is beaming. Her hopes are surging. "What if I don't recognize her? You think I'll recognize her?"

"I don't know," I say, honestly. "Maybe seeing her will spark a memory for you."

"Maybe," she answers, too hopeful again. She rubs her hands together. "It's cold in here, isn't it?"

"Yeah, it's supposed to snow today."

"Amy took me outside for lunch yesterday. It was chilly, but great to be out."

"That's nice," I answer. But that wasn't yesterday. Daneesha was here for lunch yesterday. Candy has accepted the idea that she loses time sometimes, and that some other girl could be there when she doesn't remember. But she doesn't fully embrace it. She can't identify triggers that provoke the switch, and we certainly haven't been able to control it. Anyway, all of this is better than Daneesha, who threatens to stop talking any time I bring up "that Candy shit."

"How are you feeling with the new meds? Any side effects?"

She shrugs and sits up in bed with her arms around her knees, grabbing her toes. Candy is ultraflexible, rubbery. She could have been a gymnast. She's got the Olympic smile down at least. "A little tired maybe. Not too bad, if it'll help me get my memory back."

We started the Risperdal. Daneesha is having headaches, and Candy barely notices. A knock rings out on the door. "Hello, hello," Detective Adams calls out.

"Hi," Candy answers as he walks in. She likes Detective Adams. Even Daneesha likes Detective Adams. He's like a big Papa Bear; it's hard not to like him.

"I want to introduce you to someone." He motions to the woman next to him. She is fiftysomething, overweight, but not obese. She wears a cream-colored turtleneck, a cranberry cardigan with matching polyester pants, and a string of gold beads. The clothes look well worn but chosen with care. Like she might have dressed up for the occasion. "This is Mrs. Green."

Candy grants the woman her brightest smile but obviously doesn't recognize her. And by Mrs. Green's bewildered expression, it's clear she doesn't recognize Candy either. "I'm sorry," the woman whispers.

Detective Adams reads the situation, and his face falls. "This isn't her?"

"No, it isn't," she says, trying to hide her disappointment for Candy's sake.

"I don't recognize anyone really," Candy says apologetically. "Not even myself really, so I wasn't sure."

"Well, honey," Mrs. Green says, her voice a million years old, "I'm sure. And unfortunately, you aren't my niece."

Candy scratches at her knee. "You seem very nice anyway."

"You do, too, darling," the woman responds with a warm smile.

They stare at each other for an uncomfortable, unscripted moment. Detective Adams and I glance at each other, and he raises his eyebrows in resignation. So she isn't Destiny, and she isn't Monica. And I've broken two hearts, a friend's and an aunt's. Three, if you count Candy.

I consider it a small grace, at least, that Daneesha wasn't here.

⌒

"Zoe!" Dr. Berringer calls out, catching up with me on my way out of the hospital. I wait for him in the doorway of the lobby. The cold air shoots by me as people come in and out. Dr. Berringer turns the corroding brass knob on his bag. "You heading home?"

"I was. Why, are there any issues?" I glance back up toward the escalators, hoping to hell not.

"No, no. I was just going to walk you out if you were going that way."

"Sure." I button up my jacket. The sky is a dimming blue. The wind kicks up leaves at our feet. We pass a row of flowering crab trees, wine-red berries glistening in the sun.

"Zoe," he says, breaking into the silence, "I never really got to apologize to you."

I pull up my bag, which is slipping off my shoulder. "That's okay."

"No." He stares down at the pavement. "It's not. It's not okay. I should never have called you that night. I should never have let you see me that way, or gotten you involved at all." It sounds like he's been scolding himself with this speech lately.

"Maybe not. But you needed help. And I'm happy that I could help you at all. If I did. Help you, that is, in any way." Verbal diarrhea, my specialty.

"You did," he assures me. "You definitely did. The problem is, I should never have asked you to do it."

The whine of a leaf blower rings out in one of the yards behind the parking lot. "How are you doing with it all, anyway?" I ask.

He sighs. "As good as can be expected, I guess. My wife isn't being very helpful with the divorce, but I guess that would be too much to hope for. Helpful divorce—kind of an oxymoron, huh?"

"Yeah." We walk in silence a bit.

"How'd the aunt thing go?" he asks.

"From North Carolina?"

"Right."

"Dead end. It wasn't her."

"Didn't think so."

"Me neither," I admit.

We keep walking toward my car, which I can just see peeking out in the corner, the sun shining it candy-apple red. A red Mini Cooper. Completely unsuitable for Buffalo and my height, but my mom bought it when she was dipping into dementia, and I'll drive the thing until it's ready for the junk-yard.

"And the drinking?" I ask, not sure if I should.

His cheeks, ruddy from the cold, turn ruddier. "Working on that one, too." He kicks a crumpled-up Coke can out of his path, and it clanks off to the side. "This divorce thing has me thrown, though."

We get to my car. "It'll get better," I offer lamely.

He smiles. "One day at a time, right?" He stares at me, putting his hand on my shoulder, as the wind swoops my hair into my face. He tucks a piece behind my ear, almost unconsciously, then drops his hand back down. "Zoe, you know, I just wish…"

I wait for him to finish, but he doesn't.

"It doesn't matter. Just, I'm sorry," he says. "For everything."

As he walks away, I feel my breath going fast, like I've been jogging.

Chapter Twenty

Daneesha paces back and forth in the room. The Risperdal doesn't seem to be agreeing with her.

"I am done with this," she spits out. "Done with speech therapy. Done with art therapy. Done with 'sharing' therapy"—she uses air quotes for this one—"with Ms. fucking Uh-huh. Share my problems? I don't have any fucking problems! Only problem I have is being here locked up in this place because no one believes me that some white dudes were trying to rape me!"

"That's not why you're here," I say, in a calming voice.

"No?" she yells back. "I don't know about that. Because no one can tell me why I'm here, and no one can tell me when I'm leaving."

"We'll let you go as soon as we have a place to send you."

"What happened to my auntie? When she gonna get here?"

"Um, that didn't work out in the end." It's easier than explaining that she didn't recognize Candy.

"Okay then. How about something else? I thought the discharge planning lady was all up in that shit."

"I wish I had a better answer for you, Daneesha. We're working on it."

She sits down on the bed finally, putting her head in her hands. "And I feel like crap," she says. "Some kind of flu. Got the runs. Got one fucking monster of a headache." She shoves her legs under her blankets. "Ain't y'all supposed to be doctors or something?"

I reach over and grab her vitals sheet. Her blood pressure is 128/88, her temperature 37.8 C. A touch high for both, but not excessively for an agitated, pacing young girl. Maybe she is coming down with something, though. "We'll keep an eye on it, Daneesha."

"Yeah, you do that," she grumbles.

I stand up to leave and glance down at her table, adorned with her newest self-portrait.

"Someone of y'all made me a picture, too," she says, seeing me evaluate it. "Looks like me, if I was skinny." She laughs halfheartedly.

Which is strange, because she *is* skinny. But I guess Daneesha doesn't see herself that way.

"Before I go," I say, "you mentioned white guys trying to rape you?"

"Yeah, what of it? I been saying that since I got here, and none of y'all seem to care."

"Were they in a limo? Those men?"

She cradles her head in her hands. "No offense, Dr. Goldman. But you're driving me nuts with that fucking limo."

⌐

"Guess who we found?" Detective Adams asks.

"No idea." I shift the phone onto my shoulder, grabbing Chloe's chart.

"The real Monica Green. In North Carolina."

"Alive, I'm hoping?"

"Alive and kicking, yes, thankfully. So the aunt has forgiven me."

"Well, that's good for you at least."

"So I take it there's nothing new on Candy or Daneesha?"

"Nope. We're adding more meds to see if it will help. So far, not really. Just sedating Candy a little and pissing off Daneesha."

Yelling and laughter ring out in the background.

"Sounds like a party over there."

"It is, actually. My fiftieth."

"Hey, congrats." A party horn blares out.

He sighs. "Five more years until retirement."

"I've got a good forty left if it makes you feel any better."

"It doesn't," he answers with a laugh. "I'll let you know if we find anything out." We're hanging up as Jason comes in. He plops down in the chair and leans back, the front legs lifting with a creak.

"God, I can't wait until this pediatric rotation is over. I can go back to dealing with depressed adults. Depressed kids are just too depressing."

"I know. I'm not loving the under-eighteen set myself."

"I got this poor kid today," he says, "in foster care because his parents were abusing him. Now it turns out the foster dad was abusing him, too. The kid tried to commit suicide. Ten years old."

"Hideous. Some people should not be allowed to have children." I shake my head.

At that moment, Dr. Berringer walks in the room, surveying his residents. "It looks like somebody's funeral in here."

"Oh, we're all depressed for various reasons," Jason says.

"No time for that," Dr. Berringer calls out. "Buck up that serotonin, we've got a job to do." He leans against the file cabinet and wipes a stripe of dust off the top with his index finger, spreading who knows what kind of bacteria. "Let's start with Candy. How's the Risperdal working?"

"Not too well," I say, opening her chart. The heater bangs in the stuffy room. "This morning Daneesha was pretty agitated. Complaining of a headache, diarrhea."

He taps his finger against his lips, and I notice he's still wearing his ring. "Let's bump up the Risperdal. No improvement tomorrow and we'll add some Effexor."

"Okay. What about the headache and flu stuff?" I ask.

"Watch it. We can always call an ID consult. Meanwhile, let's run a CBC and a CMP."

"Got it."

"Okay, Jason, who you got?" he says, turning toward him.

Jason gathers up his papers. "Ten-year-old Caucasian boy with a suicidal attempt," he starts.

Dr. Berringer leans back against the wall, crossing his arms. "God help us."

I am suddenly reminded again of the man who stood watching Jane with the saddest expression, his hand on Jane's head. It feels like a hundred years ago.

At 2:37 a.m., the phone rings, and I jump up in bed. "What? What? What?" I yell out, only half awake. Arthur growls in response. I look around the room and see nothing familiar, until I remember I'm not in my room.

Mike has my phone, squinting at the light on the screen. "It's the hospital. Eleventh floor."

"Fuck," I grumble, taking the phone as he turns right back over to sleep. "If I don't get back, take Arthur for a walk?"

"Yeah, yeah, yeah," he mumbles.

"The leash is on the washer," I whisper. But he's already in dreamland, so I throw on some scrubs, pull my hair back in a ponytail, and head out.

When I walk onto the psych unit, La-Toya (one of my favorite night nurses) meets me. "I'm sorry," she says, in her squeaky, Minnie Mouse voice. "I wouldn't normally call you just for a fever, but Jane's really acting loopy." The nurses all still call her Jane. Otherwise it's too confusing to figure out which patient is asking for what.

"That's okay," I say, scrolling through her med sheet and then heading down to see her. It's Candy, and she looks awful.

"Hello," she mumbles, in an effort to be polite. Her smile is weak.

"Heard you're not feeling so well, huh?"

"Yeah," she admits. "Not great." She shivers and pulls her sheet taut over her.

I flip through the vitals on her clipboard. "Looks like you're running a little fever."

She nods and hugs the sheet tighter.

"Sore throat? Stuffy nose? Vomiting?"

She shakes her head to all of these. "I have had some… diarrhea," she says, embarrassed.

"Is that right?" Probably the flu that Daneesha was starting to feel.

"And I had the weirdest dream," she says.

"Oh yeah? What was it?"

She rubs her forehead. "Men were chasing me down the street."

"Yeah?"

"White guys, in suits," she continues.

A chill runs through me. I wait, but she doesn't say any more.

"That's all I remember. Probably just a nightmare, huh?"

"Maybe." I put her clipboard back on the bed. "But Daneesha was talking about the same thing before."

"Really?" She opens her eyes wider and sits up a bit. Candy is always interested in Daneesha, even if she doesn't fully believe in her. Like asking after a good friend. She rubs her forehead again.

"Headache?"

"A little." Her eyes start closing. Grabbing her chart off the table, I see the self-portraits again. Candy added some artistic flair to hers, light reflecting off her irises. Daneesha's picture looks like a child's version of Candy's, broader face, same color eyes. But looking at it closer, I notice there are other differences, too. Daneesha's chin is pointier, with a notch in it. A cleft maybe? And on the left cheek, a dot. It could be a smudge, but could it also be...a birthmark?

"Candy, do you have a cousin maybe, or a sister?" I realize that I asked Daneesha that question before, but never thought to ask Candy.

She looks straight at me, and it's as if a veil falls away from her eyes. Candy bolts upright in her bed, clutching at the guardrails. Her bony hands are trembling.

"Janita!" she screams out, high-pitched, shrill. So loud it hurts my ears. "The limousine took her!" she screams out.

"Where? Where did they take her?"

"Janita!" she wails out again, and nurses start running toward the room. She is hyperventilating now, her chest rising and falling. "They've got Janita!"

Chapter Twenty-One

"S he's got a sister?" Detective Adams asks.

We had to sedate her overnight. By the time he gets there this morning, she's sound asleep, our angelic Candy again.

"Look at this," I say, handing him the two pictures. We sit around her bed, talking quietly while she sleeps. "I always assumed they looked so different because Daneesha was the worse artist. But then I noticed something else." I point out the cleft and the birthmark, though he's not as convinced as I am. "And when I asked if she had a sister, she went ballistic."

"Wait." He puts the pictures down. "She didn't offer the sister spontaneously? So it may not even be accurate."

"Maybe not. But I didn't give her a name. And I didn't coach her to go off the rails like that."

He nods with a sigh, flipping to a page in his notebook. "And you said Candy was talking about the white guys, too."

"Yeah. She said they were in suits and everything."

"Huh." He picks up the pictures again and pulls them away for a far-sighted look, then puts them back on the table with a shrug. "We'll see what we can do. I'll put out an APB on Janita Jones. Maybe we'll get something. Maybe the father took them and then decided against it and dumped them somewhere."

"Maybe he's a limousine driver," I suggest.

"This case is so screwed up, who in holy hell knows at this point. But I'll send some people out to lean on the limo companies."

Dr. Berringer jogs in then and looks down at Candy asleep in the bed. "What happened?" he asks.

"Oh." I stand up from the chair. "Candy got pretty agitated last night. We had to sedate her."

He looks startled. "On whose order?"

"Mine." I sound defensive. "I tried to call you, but nobody could reach you. And she was getting violent toward herself." I swallow. "It's only ten of Valium, a one-time order."

"It's okay. You did the right thing." He lifts his hands up, immediately conciliatory, and walks over to the foot of the bed. "I'm sorry about last night," he adds, not looking at me. "I was exhausted. I ended up crashing hard, and my phone was on vibrate."

Translation: He was drunk as hell. "Do we know what got her so upset?"

I explain what happened with the pictures and how it turns out she has a sister.

"A sister?" he asks, his voice stricken.

"We don't know for sure. But it sounds like she might. Janita."

Dr. Berringer puts a hand out to lean against the desk. "A sister," he repeats. "This is just horrible. Now we've got a missing girl *and* a sister?"

Detective Adams turns to him, nodding. "I'll admit I was thinking the same thing." He frowns. "But on the other hand, if it's true, it gives us more to work with. This could be just the break we needed in this case."

"I was thinking—could we add a reward?" I ask. It hit me last night: Why was there no reward?

He slaps his notebook shut. "I can try, but I'll tell you, there's barely money on the books to pay for coffee at the station right now. Usually the family does that."

"Obviously that's not going to happen." I grab the arm of his blazer. "Come on. It's a young girl's life at stake here."

"They might have some stashed away at the FBI branch," he grumbles. "I'll try, Zoe. It's the best I can promise you."

Chloe hasn't eaten in three days. I've been so focused on Candy and Daneesha that I barely registered this. She told the nurse she's on a hunger strike, though I'm not sure what she's protesting. Herself maybe.

"If you lose any more weight, you're not going home. You understand that, right?" I ask as patiently as possible.

Chloe shrugs, her collarbones jutting out with the motion. "My insurance only pays for three months. I'll get out of here one way or another."

"Maybe not," I point out. "You don't eat, and it's a transfer to the medical floor for a feeding tube. Brand-new insurance mandate, Chloe. No maximum on that one."

She blinks her eyes and pulls her blanket up. I can tell this got her thinking.

"I don't understand. You were doing great. You were participating in group, gaining some weight... What happened?"

She stares out the window, brooding. "'Great' is a relative term."

I flip through the notes over her last week. Slow weight gains on her log. Less "hostile" in share therapy. *First family visit*. "Was it the family visit?"

"No."

"Sometimes that can bring up difficult emotions, set people back a bit."

"It's not that," she mumbles.

"Okay. Maybe something you heard from a friend?"

"No."

I close the chart. It feels like we're playing Twenty Questions. "Anything you can think of?"

She chews on her lip. "Yes," she answers, to my surprise. She does not meet my eyes.

"Do you want to tell me about it?"

Her breath quickens, her cheeks turning a blotchy red, and she bites her lip harder. The teeth gouge into her bottom lip. A tear falls onto her nose. "No one will believe me."

I lean in another inch and put my hand on her shoulder, her birdlike, bony shoulder. She doesn't flinch. "I'll believe you."

"They didn't believe me last time."

"It'll be different this time, I promise. But you have to tell me. I can't help you if you don't tell me."

She moves in her bed, and the gown twists, revealing four bruises on her arm. Four circle, blue-gray bruises in a row. A handprint?

"Is someone hurting you?" I ask, trying to hide the shock in my voice. I lightly touch the bruise, and she jerks her arm under the covers.

"No," she barks out. "I've got a million bruises. The nurse did that to me the other day getting my blood." She sticks her other arm out of the sheets to prove this, and indeed there are bruises and pinpricks all over.

"Okay, but what did you want to tell me?" I ask.

She pauses. "Nothing. Forget it."

The psych ward is up in arms. More Demerol has gone missing. Police are wandering around interviewing people.

"Drama, drama, drama!" Jason says to me as he walks into the nurses' station, squeezing his hands together in mock excitement. Or real excitement, hard to tell.

Dr. Berringer walks in next, past the buzzing cluster of nurses. "What's going on?"

"Demerol. Someone's stealing from the Pyxis," Jason says.

"Wow." He glances around the room. "There really is a war on drugs."

"Yeah, they're talking about urine-toxing everybody," I say.

"I'll pee in a cup anytime," Jason says, grabbing for a chart. "This boy's clean as a whistle."

I pause. "Is a whistle clean really? I've always wondered about that phrase. You know, with all the saliva."

"How's your kiddo doing?" Dr. Berringer asks Jason, ignoring my linguistic musings. He sits down and leans back in the chair with his long legs crossed. His tan buck shoes are rimmed with brown scuffs from the light snow lining the streets this morning. An early-season snow already melting outside into irregular patches.

"Stable," Jason answers. "Off one-on-one. I think the Prozac's finally kicking in."

"Good, good. And Zoe, what's your status?"

I give him the update on Chloe and my suspicions about abuse of some sort.

"Very common in these cases, unfortunately. You think it's someone in her family?"

"It seems coincidental. She just saw them, and then she suddenly changes."

"Yeah."

"She's not very open to discussing it right now."

"Too bad," he says, grimacing. "She may need a medical transfer if she's still not eating tomorrow. Get one of the GI nurses to come in and show her the feeding tube. That might change her mind at least."

I nod, impressed. "That's a good trick."

He gives me a wry smile. "Been in this business a little while now. Got a few up my sleeve."

Just then, a portly policeman walks inside the room. "Excuse me. I don't mean to interrupt."

"Yes." Dr. Berringer stands up.

"I was just hoping you guys could take a look at this guy, see if he looks familiar at all." He hands us paper copies of a black-and-white image taken by one of the floor cameras. It's a priest, on the heavy side, with a close-shaved white beard. The image is fuzzy and shaded.

"I think so," Dr. Berringer says. "Maybe. I might have seen him a couple of times on the floor."

"Great." The policeman pulls out a pad. "Can you describe him?"

"I guess." He taps his fingers in concentration. "I didn't pay that close attention to him, though. Figured he was just a priest. I don't even think we said hello."

"I understand, but anything you remember could be helpful."

Dr. Berringer nods. "Okay. Let's see, he was kind of...overweight," he says, not wanting to insult the overweight cop.

"Okay." The policeman writes this down. "Anything else?"

He looks over the picture again. "I remember the gray beard, too." He shrugs. "He looked like a priest. Honestly, that's all I really remember."

"Thanks," he says, handing Dr. Berringer a business card. "How about either of you guys? Recognize him?"

"No," I say. Jason shakes his head. I don't recall seeing any priests on the floor either.

"Okay, thanks." He turns back to Dr. Berringer. "You think of anything else, just let us know."

"Sure, of course." He sits back down. "Do they think he's stealing Demerol?"

"Well," the policeman says, scratching a bushy eyebrow. His eyebrows are so thick they look like two centipedes stuck on his face. "I don't want to get into it too much, but one of the cameras caught him near the medication dispenser. So he's a primary suspect right now."

"A priest?" Dr. Berringer laughs.

"Well, that's the thing. We checked with Human Resources, and he's not listed in the clergy personnel. So they think he might be impersonating a priest."

"A drug-dealing priest," I say. "Clever."

The cop gives me a look like he doesn't think it's so clever. "Thanks again." He shakes Dr. Berringer's hand and walks back out into the hall. I stuff the priest's picture into my satchel.

"Okay, back to the grind," Dr. Berringer says. "How is Candy and the mysterious sister?"

"She is still Candy," I answer. "Coming around a bit now."

"Has Daneesha been back yet?"

"Not yet."

"You know," he says, stretching his long arms above him in a yawn. His sky-blue boxers peek out in the process. "I've

199

been thinking about this one. We really don't know if she even has a sister."

"True," I admit.

"And either way, I think we're finally making some progress."

"How so?"

"No Daneesha. And maybe Candy's confusion means she's getting closer to her true self."

"Maybe," I say, doubtfully.

"So I say we keep the Risperdal on and start some Effexor. See if we can get to a breakthrough."

I scratch my head. "She did seem pretty drowsy, though."

"Her defenses are down," he answers. "Seventy-five BID. If she's too tired, we can back off."

My text quacks, and I grab my phone.

$500 reward. It's from the detective.

"Five-hundred-dollar reward for Candy," I announce.

"Huh," Dr. Berringer says. "Seems kind of low to me."

"Yeah, me too," I admit. I guess beggars can't be choosers. Thanks, I text back.

Jason starts cleaning his teeth with a toothpick. "Would have been five K if she were a white girl."

I hold up a music box that just about fits in my palm. "What about this one?" I ask, opening it. The box lets out a few twangy beats, then stops, the dancer bent over like she's got lordosis. I remember buying this at the mall in fifth grade for Mother's Day.

"Put it in the maybe pile," Scotty says. Everything so far has gone in the maybe pile.

"I don't know. I might keep it."

He shrugs. "You could get it fixed."

We're in his stuffy walk-in closet, sorting out Mom's belongings. Most of the big stuff we already divvied up when we moved her into the nursing home. Scotty took the dresser, and I got her cherry rolltop writing desk. All that remains are five extra-large boxes. A life stuffed into five boxes. He lifts up a ratty, red blanket from the nursing home.

"Toss," we say at the same time.

"So I've been putting together a few photos for your website."

"Oh, good." He shoves a damaged boom box in the toss pile without asking. "Kristy and I looked everywhere for those fucking bonds by the way."

"Kristy?"

He rips the tape off a box. "The girl from the Coffee Spot?"

"Oh, right." Must be the girl he wooed while I was talking to him. "Sorting through Mom's stuff—sounds like a fun date."

He picks up a little nightstand clock. "Keep?"

"Sure." I sort through the maybe pile. "So Jean Luc keeps texting me about his damn wedding. That's fun."

"That guy's such a fucking douche bag." He throws knitting needles in the discard pile. They clink together and roll off. "What's up with Mike?"

"Nothing really. We're fine."

Scotty burrows arm-deep into the next box. "That 'fine' sounded hesitant."

My brother would make a good psychiatrist. "No, we are fine. It's just figuring out next year. Kind of weighing on me. On us, I guess."

"What are the options?"

"Your basic 'should we stay or should we go' scenario. If we stay, it could be trouble."

"Yeah, yeah. And if you go, it could be double." He tosses another item in the maybe pile. "You got a job lined up here?"

"I could. With the university maybe. But I don't know. I was thinking about a fellowship maybe. But then again, maybe I should go private and start paying off loans. I don't know."

"Sounds like a lot of maybes."

I finger the little heart pillow that Mom made at the nursing home. Purple with crooked black stitching that says "I love you." Definitely a keep. "And Mike's basically got an offer here already and a couple of leads down in North Carolina. So that's the debate."

"Hmm." Scotty folds over a recalcitrant box flap. "You're smart. I'm sure you'll figure it out." He cleverly doesn't offer his own suggestion.

I brush off a dusty Venetian-glass paperweight, deep blue with gold spirals reaching into the center, flanked by koi fish and orange flowers in dizzy rows. Like a kaleidoscope or a happy LSD trip. Mom and Dad brought it back from a trip to Italy. We stayed home with a babysitter, an elderly woman with only half a pinkie, which fascinated me beyond all reason. "You mind if I take this?"

"All yours."

I move on to the next box and start ripping tape. "Scotty, did you ever think maybe she was mistaken about those bonds?"

Scotty throws out an old pack of playing cards. My mom was a poker superstar, oddly enough, until she forgot how to play. "Yeah." He rolls up the sleeves on his T-shirt. "I've pretty much come to that conclusion."

"Toss?" I hold up a couple of old cookbooks.

He takes one to examine it and hands it back. "Yeah, I guess so."

"Oh, by the way," I say, hurling some pantyhose onto the pile, "I might need to make use of your world-renowned computer prowess again."

He rolls his eyes. "For Jane Doe? Or Candy or whatever her name is?"

"How'd you guess?"

He shakes his head, combing through the next box with me. "I already tried the facial recognition stuff."

"Yeah." I grab some frayed pink ribbons and throw them out. "But I had another thought. If I send you the photo of her scar, could you do a search on it?"

"What kind of search?"

"I don't know. Just on the Internet? It's a really weird scar.

Maybe if we could figure out what caused it, it would help us figure out who she is."

"That's a reach," he says, his voice echoing in the box. He tosses out an old skein of almond-colored yarn.

"It is. But would you do it?"

Chapter Twenty-Two

When I walk into Candy's room the next morning, my heart falls. She isn't any better. She's worse. She's catatonic.

"Candy!" I call out.

No answer. Her big brown eyes stare out, dead, her dazzling smile gone. "Candy!" I jog over to the bed and take her hand, which is warm though not feverish. Squeezing it, I get no response. I run my hand across her field of vision. No blink, no response. Her vitals sheet reports nothing new. Fever is gone, though the temp is up just a little. Heart rate up, but not abnormally so. I lift her arm, expecting it to stay up in the pose, but her arm is stiff. It resists me. I try the other side, and it's the same. I run into the nurses' station, and Dr. Berringer is already there.

"Did you see Candy yet?"

"No, I just got here. What's up?"

"She's catatonic."

His face crumbles. "Really?" He starts toward her room, and I follow. Immediately, he begins the same testing, checking visual fields, the tone in her arms. "These things do recur," he says. "It's not that uncommon unfortunately."

"But she was getting better."

"I know." He sounds as disappointed as I am.

"Should we get an ID consult?"

"What for?" He glances over her vital sheet. "She's not feverish."

"No. But she was. And she's diaphoretic."

"You can see that with Effexor, though." He pinches her nail bed to check for any response. She doesn't even moan. It seems cruel, but it's part of the exam. "I spoke with a few colleagues about her again yesterday."

"Okay?"

"They couldn't think of anything else we weren't doing. Said we should be thinking ECT."

I move a lock of hair from out of Candy's eyes. "You think we're there?"

He stares at her. "I think we're almost there. We got her out of it before. Maybe hitting her with some more Ativan could do it again."

"God, I hope so." I close her chart, which is getting heavier by the day.

"How's Chloe?" he asks, washing his hands.

"Eating," I answer. "Minimally, the nurses said. To avoid an NG tube." I wait for him to move from the sink and run my hands under the faucet. "You were right. The NG demo worked."

He winks at me, ripping some paper towels off. "Always does." We head back to the nurses' station. "Got to wrap up some stuff in my office. See you in a bit."

Settling down at the table, I start plowing through Candy's chart for some clues, anything that could lead me back to catatonia. But there have been no changes. Ativan same. Effexor same. Risperdal same. Jason saunters into the room, whistling.

"What?" I grumble. "Are you seeing Dominic again?"

He stares at me. "How the hell did you know that?"

I look back through the chart. "You're whistling."

"Ooh, nonverbal clues. Look at you being all psychiatric."

"Yeah, well. I'm not in a whistling mood today unfortunately."

"Why?" He pops a cherry cough drop in his mouth. "What's wrong with you?"

"Candy. She's catatonic again."

He looks up from his chart. "That sucks." The faintest triangle of a goatee is growing in under his lip. "Any more on the sister?"

"Still missing."

"Too bad Daneesha's gone."

I grab another chart. "Why?"

"She would have known where Janita was," he says, and walks off whistling again.

I flip through Candy's latest labs. CBC doesn't show any sign of infection, so Dr. Berringer's right: An Infectious Disease consult will be pointless. Pulling out my phone, I hesitate. I know it could piss the detective off, but I do it anyway.

"Hi, Zoe," Detective Adams answers, his voice resigned to my hundred weekly calls by now. "What's up?"

"Just checking if you heard anything on the reward?"

"Not as of yet. How's Candy?"

"Not great." I pause. "In fact, she's catatonic."

"Oh no, really?"

"Yeah. And we've pretty much maxed out the meds. They're talking about doing ECT this time."

"ECT, what's that?" he asks.

"Electroshock therapy."

He lets out a long, high-pitched whistle. "No shit."

"Yeah. I'm not loving the idea, to be honest. But we're running out of options."

The pause grows over the phone. "I best leave all that up to you guys. Docs usually know what they're doing, I've found."

I chuckle. "Thanks for the vote of confidence." I tap my pen on the paper. "Maybe if we increased the reward?"

"Zoe, take care of Candy. I'll call you the minute I hear anything."

After rounds, I'm hanging out in the library, wasting time on the Internet. No hits on my Candy Facebook post, which I updated. The sun is setting out the window in creamy-pink streaks across the sky. Scrolling down to earlier Facebook posts, I see a Vine posted from Melanie (which Jean Luc has shared!). Because I am fond of torture, I open it. Six seconds of lameness, with them both laughing and Melanie feeding him sushi. Which he hates. Or claimed to hate. Her ring is blinding. I close out the Facebook app with an inward groan. What is Vine-worthy about feeding someone sushi anyway? My phone rings then, saving me from any further pangs of envy.

"Got a new one," Jason says. "Bed Five. Possible steroid psychosis."

"Cool. I'm on it."

"Oh, and guess who else is back?"

"Tiffany?"

"You got it."

"Oh, I can take her while I'm down there."

"They didn't ask for a consult yet, just wheeling her in. Giving her Narcan, I think. She looked pretty bad, actually."

"Give her a few days," I say. "Same old dance. They'll stabilize her, send her to us, and two months later she'll be back."

"Aren't you all jaded today."

"Just realistic," I mutter. Heading into the ER, I run into Damien, one of Mike's fellow residents. The shift has just changed, so the place is buzzing. I always thought Damien was trying to date me on the sly and hinted as much to Mike. "Yeah," Mike said thoughtfully, "he's kind of a snake." But they're friends.

"Hey, how's the big man?" Damien asks, referring to Mike. Damien is five feet four, so this is the joke. "Been stuck in Children's hell for a while now, so I haven't seen him lately."

"He's good."

"You guys still…?"

"Yup," I answer. "How are things going around here?" I gaze around at the usual suspects: nervous-wreck parents, athletic teenaged boys with arms twisted the wrong way, vomitting toddlers, and a crying high school girl who's about to lose her appendix.

"Same old," he says, gazing around, too. He takes a drink of coffee from a metallic travel thermos. He's just starting his day while I'm ending mine. "Just coded a twenty-five-year-old." He points to the curtain we're standing in front of. "On some kind of drugs. I've seen her a couple of times down here. Had a seizure, went into cardiac arrest. Pregnant, too. Fucking awful."

Dread fills up my chest. "She died?"

"Yeah, unfortunately. We coded her over thirty minutes. V-tach right into asystole. Shocked the hell out of her."

"Can I? What's… what's her name?"

"Oh, don't remember. Terry? Tammy?"

"Tiffany?"

"Yeah, that's right. Tiffany. Why? You've had her before?"

Trauma Team, Room One. Trauma Team, Room One beckons over the loudspeaker. "Got to go," he says, putting his thermos on the table and looping his stethoscope on. "Say hi to Mike for me." He trots off, following a troop of scrub-clad men and women chasing after a gurney.

I head over to Tiffany's bed, pushing the curtain aside to a brightly lit room, like the room forgot the person in there isn't alive anymore. The bedsheet is over her face, and I lift it up. It's Tiffany for sure, eyes closed now, patches of hair missing from her yanking it all the time, sores on her face. Like she's been dying for years and this was just the final step. Her foot sticks out of the sheet at the foot of the bed, her baby toe with a silver-moon pinkie ring, and a crack running through the crescent.

I cover her foot back up with a blanket and hear yelling followed by a flurry of nurses in Bed Five. Must be my steroid psychosis. I close Tiffany's curtain and make my way over to my next consult.

⟵

Mike is not a graceful runner. He is a football runner, a wrestler-runner, not a runner-runner. But then again, I'm not exactly a gazelle myself. And I'm the one huffing and puffing, while he could seemingly chat through a marathon.

"So they're thinking ECT?" he asks.

"Yeah," I answer, my voice ragged.

"Maybe it could help."

"Maybe," I manage again.

Mike takes mercy and doesn't ask any more questions for a bit. I called him earlier tonight, not fully in distress but close to it. After Candy, then Tiffany. I felt trapped in my living room with the fake fireplace and its well-planned precarious logs, and my cozy red couch. Like I was in a dungeon. I started pacing around, to no avail. I have hours like this, days sometimes, when my brain and my body don't align and my limbs are a restless extension of my head. This is when I used to row, back in college and medical school.

But instead I called Mike, who suggested we go for a run. So I agreed, remembering Sam's frequent admonition. I unwrapped my new, fresh-smelling running shoes from their box, tightened my laces, and met him at the park.

Sweat wicks under my shirt, and by the end of the first mile I realize I dressed too warmly. The afternoon thunderstorm emptied into an unseasonably warm night. As we keep going, I relax into the run. My footsteps pound out a rhythm, and the tight coil in my brain starts to unwind, ceasing its useless roiling and spinning. Never-ending circuits, mazes, flying thoughts. Candy staring out, dead-eyed. Tiffany's pinkie toe ring. The xiphoid pointing out of Chloe's chest. My mom's purple puffy pillow. Spiraling over and over. Snippets of songs, conversations, thoughts. Probation. Probation. Probation.

"So did you ever find out any more on Berringer? And the drinking thing?"

I shake my head. Sweat sticks to my forehead. "Just what I found out on Google. And what Jason said. He hasn't smelled like it lately, but that's not saying much." I still haven't gotten around to telling him about putting him to bed that night. And truthfully, I probably never will. "I told you about that stupid sushi video, right?" I ask, to change the conversation.

He answers me with an eye roll. "And I was just so interested."

I laugh. "Okay, okay. I get it." As I run, I'm feeling better already. Lighter.

"You hear any more about the priest?"

"The priest?"

"I thought you said a priest," he says, wiping off his forehead with his shirt and gracing me with a nice view of his abdomen.

"Oh yeah," I say, "the Demerol guy. No, no more word. I think they're crazy, though. It's gonna be a nurse or something."

We run in silence awhile, through the almond sheen of the streetlights against the pavement, the moon glowing through a seam in the clouds. A dog tears by on the lawn across the way, yipping madly.

My mind slows then, like it usually does at this point in a run. I don't notice my breathing anymore, or my burning legs. Images pop up, and I don't bother to bat them down. Candy. Daneesha. Janita. Candy's purple leopard-skin purse. Effexor. Risperdal. Catatonic. Dr. Berringer's bloodshot eyes. The night unfolding on the ghostly twelfth floor. Chloe's sunken eye sockets. Jason's budding goatee. Purple. Purple. Hospital art projects. Sisters. Art quilt. Candy's art quilt: numbers, letters, suns. Daneesha's quilt: FUCK THIS SHIT.

Numbers, letters, suns.

I stop. The soft wind whistles, swaying the pines. Numbers and letters—of course. *A limousine took her!*

"Holy shit."

Mike stops short. "What? Did you pull something?"

"Why didn't I think of it before?"

He wipes his sopping forehead with his sleeve. "Zoe, what are you talking about?"

"Numbers and letters," I tell him. "It's a license plate."

Chapter Twenty-Three

Donna is in a flowing, lemonade-pink outfit today, a break from her usual autumn palate. She riffles through the awkward, bulky files. It turns out she had one for Daneesha and a separate one for Candy. ("They just seemed so different to me.") The newest art projects hang drying on a laundry line with clothespins. It looks like a kindergarten art room with morbid themes.

Detective Adams cocks his head at the line. "Looks like a handy way to hang yourself," he says, half joking.

"The room is monitored at all times. And locked at night so that— Wait a second," she interrupts herself. "I found it." She pulls out the quilt picture with the scratchy noise of dried watercolors rubbing against each other. Candy's quilt is just as I remembered: numbers and letters and suns, all in shades of purple. There's no pattern I can discern, though.

"You think this could be a license plate?" he asks.

"It was a thought."

He takes the paper and stares at it, like he's trying to see through it. "It's not enough digits, though."

"Yeah, I noticed that, too."

"Did you guys see this one?" She pulls out a stack of blank index cards, held with a loose, red rubber band, and lays them out on the table in rows like a memory game. Numbers, letters, suns. All the same numbers and letters. A V D 1 4 7.

"If it's a New York plate," the detective says, "it's going to have three letters and four numbers, unless it's personalized."

I lean an elbow on the table, next to a faded blue paint stain. "And what's the sun supposed to mean?"

We pause, and the detective chews on his bottom lip, his eyes squinting.

"What if," Donna says, "the sun represents something, like happiness? A feeling."

"But that's so vague," I argue. "It could mean so many things."

"Or," the detective says, "it could just be the sun." He shifts the cards into a line. "Put these together and we have three letters—let's say VAD, for instance—with four numbers. Maybe there's only three numbers, not four, because she couldn't see one of the numbers in the glare of the sun." He grins. "Huh? What do you think?" He looks so self-satisfied that I fear he might don a plaid hunting cap and pull out a pipe.

"It's possible," I admit. "Can you run through the numbers and letters?"

"We can get a partial at least, try some different combinations." He shakes his head. "It's going to take time, but we'll try."

I think for a moment, playing with a corner of one of the index cards. "I might have another idea."

Candy is dazed but somewhat responsive when we come in to see her. So maybe Dr. Berringer is right. Tincture of time and she'll come around. Or maybe the Effexor is breaking through. She's still not speaking, but she's not doing her bunny-nose twitch. And she's making some eye contact and tracking.

I walk over to her with the cards in hand, the detective following me like an oversized shadow.

"Candy, I've got something for you," I say.

She looks up at me, her cheeks flushed, still sweating.

"These are some pictures you drew. We were wondering if you could help us figure them out."

She watches us intently but doesn't answer.

"We weren't sure what these meant." I show her the quilt picture first, then lay the cards on the table. "We were thinking a license plate number maybe?"

She looks down at the cards without expression.

"We were hoping it might help us find Janita," Detective Adams adds.

Her brown eyes open wider with the mention of her sister's name, but she keeps staring at the cards, so long that the room feels stifling. I steal a glance at Detective Adams, who gives me a somber half grin. *Well, we tried.*

I'm a second away from picking the cards up when she reaches out, sluggishly, like a robot. Slowly, methodically, she arranges the cards in a new row.

D V A 1 4 Sun 7.

Then she sinks her head back in her pillow, spent with the effort of engaging with us. Or maybe the effort of remembering.

The detective writes the combination in his notebook, then scoops up the cards and puts them in a baggie from his briefcase. "Evidence," he says.

"Thank you," I say to Candy.

And she doesn't answer, but her eyes meet mine. Her stare is strong, angry, like Daneesha, not Candy. Then she closes her eyes and falls back to sleep.

My grandfather clock gongs out nine chimes. Otherwise, Arthur, Mike, and I are sitting in companionable silence watching the newest PBS mystery. The true killer (I think it's the farmer's wife, but Mike is set on the soldier's estranged grandson) is about to be revealed. Right then, my phone pings with a notification. I grab the remote to pause the TV.

"Aw, come on," Mike objects, "I was finally getting into this stupid show."

"Yeah, well, remember how you kept doing that to me," I remind him, "with *Downton Abbey?*" I check my e-mail.

"*Downton Abbey*? Please. Pausing that was just a kindness."

YOU HAVE A RESPONSE ABOUT YOUR MISSING
LOVED ONE.

"Hey, it's the Black and Missing website," I say. Mike moves closer, reading over my shoulder as I zoom to the website. The response is under Candy's picture.

Zoe,

I think this is my daughter. Her name is Candice Jones.
Please call me, and we can discuss it and the reward.

"Huh," Mike says. "Odd that she was remembered after the reward was posted."

"Agreed," I say. I tap my finger on the remote, chewing on my lip.

"Just call," he says. "I'll make some more popcorn." Arthur trails off behind him. I think he actually knows the word *popcorn*. Somewhat leery, I dial the number.

"Hello?"

"Hi, this is Zoe Goldman."

"Oh, child. Thank the Lord. Thank the Lord, you called me back. I been praying on this moment since I saw the picture. Thank you, Jesus, thank you."

"Oh...great. Um, it's about Candy?" I ask, taken aback by the effusive response.

"That's right. Candy. I think that's my daughter you got posted up on that website. Candice Jones."

"Okay, and who am I speaking with?"

"Heaven," she answers. "Heaven Jones."

I sit up straighter and catch Mike's eye, pointing to the phone. "Heaven," I mouth to him. "Your name is Heaven?" I ask her.

"That's right. My momma named me that. I used to hate that name, oh my Lord, but now I like it. Now it suits me just fine."

The pendulum swings on the grandfather clock. So Heaven is real. "How did you find out about the reward?"

"My friend told me all about it, honey. She tell me somebody found Candy. Put up a reward and everything. Praise be to Jesus."

"That's right, I—"

"Is she all right? You said she in the hospital? She okay?"

I pause. "She's okay," I lie.

"Oh, thank you, Jesus. Thank you, Lord. I thought I never see my babies again. How about Janita? How she doing?"

"We don't know. We're actually trying to find Janita."

"Oh." The word is laden with unease.

"When was the last time you saw them, Candy and Janita?"

"Oh, girl. It's been more than two years now. I was drugging. Had to give up both my girls when I lost the baby. But I'm done with all that now. I've been saved."

"Okay. Good. That's good. So where are you now?"

"In Toronto," she answers. "Living in a nice house. God

blesses me every day. Now I just wanna get my girls back when they ready."

Toronto, just a short drive over the border to Buffalo. "Do you know, did Candy have a scar on her ankle? If you remember?"

There is a pause as she considers this. "You know, I wasn't the best mom. I wasn't always there when they got hurt and all that." Her voice goes low and serious. "But I don't think she had any scar on her ankle. Unless she got it in the last couple of years."

"Okay." I get up and search for something to write on, miming a pen to Mike, and he hands me one. I grab the vet receipt from when Arthur had his stomach pumped after eating a huge bag of M&M's. "Let me take down your information so I can have the detective call you back about that reward."

She gives it to me, and I pin the paper to the corkboard in the kitchen. As we hang up, I sit back on the couch with Mike. He throws Arthur a piece of popcorn.

"So you think that's her?" he asks.

"It's got to be her."

"You going to tell the detective?"

"Yeah." I scratch my chin. "How to explain it without him killing me, however, is the question." Mike chuckles and grabs the remote to unpause the television detective and let him resume with the final revelation of the killer and how he cleverly sussed him or her out (the farmer's wife or the estranged grandson). Arthur nudges my hip with a new toy, a green monster that lost its squeak. I give the thing a halfhearted throw, and Arthur comes back proudly with it in his jaws, then flops to the floor and gnaws on it with the apparent hope the squeak will be somehow resurrected.

It turns out that Mike was right after all. It was the grandson.

Chapter Twenty-Four

I'm sorry to hear about Tiffany," Sam says. "Addiction can be so hard. I've lost a few patients to it."

"Yeah," I say. "I just wish I could have done something more."

"It's certainly a hard disease."

We pause, him mindlessly tapping his fingers on his yellow pad and me watching the wind blow some leaves in a circle under a cement-gray sky. "We finally went through my mom's stuff," I say.

"That sounds like a good thing."

"It was a good thing. And we didn't mutilate each other in the process, which is also a good thing."

Sam smiles. "And how is Candy?"

"So the plot thickens." I explain the relationship with her sister and how Heaven called me.

His expression is as startled as Dr. Berringer's. "What does the detective have to say?"

"He's going to call me later this morning." I yawn. I'm not used to eight-a.m. Saturday appointments, but it's all he had available this week. We cover the basics—Adderall fine. Lexapro fine. Concentration okay, could be better. Life okay, could be better—the usual fare, until my twenty-minute follow-up has run its course.

"You know, Zoe," he says as we stand up, "since you've been so stable, I was actually going to propose going down to every other week for now."

I feel a shot of anxiety at the thought, but have to admit he's right. He's more of a security blanket right now than anything. And a few less co-pays wouldn't hurt either. Pretty soon, I'll graduate to every month, then three months, every six months. Yearly? And by that time, I'll have graduated the psychiatry program myself. One full-fledged psychiatrist to another.

I pass by a smiling turkey decoration on my way out. It will be my first Thanksgiving without my mom. Though the last Thanksgiving with Mom was pretty miserable. Scotty's date was some double-D blonde who talked like she just had a lobotomy, Mom spent the whole time in a recliner staring out the window, and my first-ever attempt at a turkey was so burned we ended up ordering pizza. Scotty's cooking this year, so that's something at least.

A handful of raindrops topple down from the sky as I head out to the parking lot.

Sam's office is behind a nondescript storefront sandwiched between a guitar shop on one side and an ever-changing shop on the other. Last year it was a consignment shop. This year it was Patty Cakes, a cupcake store that died in six months. (And come on, who's driving through a blizzard for cupcakes?) Now there's a sign for "Crazy Heart Jewelry. Coming Soon!" Worst-case scenario, Sam could prescribe something for the hearts.

On the way to the car, I soak my foot in a freezing cold puddle. I'm removing my sock with a groan when my phone rings. It's Detective Adams, which is a good sign—it means he's still speaking to me.

"Yeah, hi, Zoe. Heaven's story sticks. She showed us pictures, and it was definitely Candy. I have to assume the other girl in the photo was Janita."

"Heaven's in Buffalo?"

"No, we went to see her in Toronto this morning. She can't get through customs with a record." He rips open what sounds like a bag of chips, which seems appalling at this hour of the morning.

"She can't come to the US?"

"No. Before 9/11 maybe, but not now."

"So it's definitely the girls?"

"Yeah, the picture was from Candy's sixth birthday. You could tell it was her. And Janita looks a lot like that other picture she drew, actually." Crunching sounds in the background.

"Did she have a birthmark?"

"Yes. And a cleft chin," he adds before I can ask.

"Hmm," I say, just holding back an I-told-you-so.

"You'd make a good detective, if you ever feel like a career change. Did I mention I'll be retiring in five years? There'll be a spot opening up."

I laugh. "No thanks."

Crunching rings out again. "Did she tell you about the baby that died?"

I think back to the conversation last night. "She did mention something about that. Said she lost her baby."

"Uh-huh. Turns, out she had a two-year-old. Thought Mommy's pills were Skittles and died from an overdose. That's when Candy and Janita went into foster care."

I tap on the steering wheel. A few raindrops thud onto the windshield. "That's sad."

Lightning flashes through gray clouds ahead. "Did she tell you what the baby's name was?" he asks.

"No, she didn't. What was it?" The rain builds up, pelting the windshield now, as thunder bangs in the distance.

"Daneesha," he says.

Chapter Twenty-Five

J ason is whistling again. "What are you up to for Thanksgiving?" he asks.

"Going over to Scotty's. How about you? You going down
to see your parents?"

"Nah. Going over to Dominic's."

I sit up in my chair. "Shut the front door."

Jason raises one eyebrow. "You can say the word 'fuck,'
you know."

"Seriously, Dominic's house? As what? His good friend?"

"Boyfriend." He shrugs, a smile tugging his lips. "He came
out to his parents last week."

I turn back to my review book. "That ought to be a comfortable meal."

Dr. Berringer joins us to round then. "How about we start
with Chloe for a change?" he asks.

She sits in her bed, reading a long letter with pages of
flowery handwriting. She has gained two more pounds, which

is a leap for mankind when it comes to Chloe. Five more and she can be an outpatient. It's a one-eighty-degree turnaround from her hunger-strike stance.

"Don't even say it," she warns us. "I know what the scale says, and I don't want to dwell on it." She has on thick, black eyeliner, which means she must be feeling a millimeter better.

I mime like I'm zipping my lips and earn a black-eyelined eye roll. "I'm happy for you. Am I allowed to say that?"

She allows herself a smile. "You want to know my secret?"

"Sure," I answer.

Dr. Berringer busies himself with her chart, giving us space, and Jason stands by him.

"I made the decision that I *had* to get out of here. Even if I didn't feel well, I had to *pretend* to feel well so I could get out of here."

"Fake it 'til you make it kind of thing?"

"Whatever you want to call it," she says.

"We don't have to label it. Just keep it up."

Another eye roll.

We spend another few minutes going over her various therapies, talking about her latest family visit, then it's off to the next patient.

"What do you think she meant by that?" I ask Dr. Berringer, once we're well down the hallway. "*Pretending* to feel well?"

He shakes his head with a cockeyed grin, his own version of an eye roll. "You know what, Zoe? I've given up trying to figure out that girl."

While this may be true, it seems an odd admission for a psychiatrist, and I'm still pondering this when we get to Jason's patient Manuel, a sixteen-year-old who moved from Puerto Rico as a freshman. Decided to kill himself when his parents read text messages from his boyfriend and discovered he was gay. Luckily, he went the pill route. One good stomach pumping and he was no worse for wear, but he earned himself a stay at the County. Jason shared his own coming-out story with him. When his mother didn't speak to him for a year. Manuel called him "simpatico." Jason fairly glowed. For the very first time, I could see why Jason went into psychiatry.

"Manuel," Jason says, "how're you doing?"

"Good."

"Did you see your parents yet?" Dr. Berringer asks.

"Yeah, they come in this morning," he says with a heavy accent.

"How'd it go?" Jason asks.

He shrugs. "Not too bad, actually. They say they not exactly happy about it, but they going to get used to it."

A semi-happy coming-out story. We spend a few more minutes with him, plan out his pending discharge, then make our way over to see Candy. She had been lethargic but responsive all weekend and through this morning, when I saw her. But when we reach her room, she is lying stiffly on the bed, moaning.

"What...how...?" I stammer. "This morning she was—"

"Not like this," Dr. Berringer answers, madly flipping through her chart. "Did someone give her sedation?"

"No. I didn't order any."

"Jason?"

"No. I didn't hear she was agitated or anything."

"Aaaagh," she moans, repetitively, her mouth cartoonishly open. Not like she's in pain, more like a motor.

"She was so much better this morning," I say.

"Aaaagh. Aaaagh. Aaaagh." It sounds like a mantra.

Dr. Berringer shines a penlight in her pupils and lifts up her head to test for meningitis. No sign of stiffness there. He crinkles his lips, like he just tasted something sour. "This is a fluid state, Zoe. Things can go up and down in an hour."

"Yeah, but…" I shake my head, at a loss for words.

"Hit her with some more Risperdal. If it doesn't work, we're trying ECT."

"You think it's time?" I ask.

The room answers with her moaning.

Chapter Twenty-Six

The little girl bounds up to me, her sparkly red-beaded corn-rows swaying around her head. A smile fills up her face, and she cradles a mound of pills in her hands, so many they are slipping through her fingers.

"No!" I call out. "Daneesha!"

But before I can stop her, she pops the whole handful in her mouth and starts chewing.

She chews forever, her dazzling smile fading, dimming. I watch her helplessly then, as her chewing slows.

"Daneesha?"

She stares at me with confusion and sadness, her head falling, her knees bending, collapsing to the floor like a dropped puppet. I run to her, try to lift her up, but she's too heavy.

"Dr. Goldman," she whispers, her lips glazed with blood.

I lean in to hear her. The bitter scent of the pills hangs around her mouth.

"Dr. Goldman?"

"What?" I am an inch from her face.

Her eyes are flickering shut, but she opens them wide for one second. "Find my sister."

Chapter Twenty-Seven

I'm halfway through some god-awful cafeteria chili when my phone rings. I don't recognize the number.

"Zoe? It's Dr. Koneru."

I take a quick swallow. "Oh, hi!"

"I'm calling about that picture you brought me. You remember, with the scar?"

"Yes, of course."

"You know, it was bothering me, this picture. I couldn't stop thinking that I'd seen it somewhere before."

"Okay?"

"So I was looking through my files, and I found one that was very similar. From a girl who died of an overdose two years ago."

"Really?"

"Yes, how can I...?" I hear her fumbling with the phone. "Can I text you the picture?"

"Sure, that'd be great."

Her voice echoes onto speaker. "Wait, I can't figure out this stupid phone. My daughter said 'It's so easy, Mom,' but it's not easy at all. I like to just push the buttons and you talk to someone. I don't need all of these apps things—"

The phone quacks in my ear. "Wait," I interrupt her. "I think it came through." I examine the picture. There's no doubt. Same circle, same scar. "Is it on the ankle?"

"Left ankle. Just like your girl."

Some nurses walk by with fried chicken, the smell wafting up from their trays. "Do you have a name on her?"

"Yes I do. Eliza Sapierski. Sixteen years old." She gives me her date of birth and medical record number. "She was Jane Doe for a long time until someone called the hospital looking for a missing girl. She was an overdose, so I don't think the police worked very hard on it."

"Who ID'd her?" I ask, shifting in my chair and somehow spilling chili on my sleeve in the process.

"It was a cousin, I think. The girl was adopted."

"Adopted?"

"Yes, that's what I have written down. It's my own file system I keep. I don't have that much information, but you can get the chart from Medical Records if you need it. I'll text you her photo at least."

I have an hour before we round, so I throw away the rest of my chili and decide to make a trip down there.

Medical Records is a stuffy little room, full of anguished doctors in cubicles laboring over piles of charts. And of course, we doctors always leave them until the last minute, when we're fifty charts late and about to lose privileges, before venturing down into this circle of hell. It could be a scene from a Bosch painting.

An officious, middle-aged woman with a diamond-shaped birthmark on her cheek grabs my slip with the patient's information. "Eliza Sapierski," she reads off, and takes a quick look at her computer screen. "We'll have to get these in Archives."

"Archives? Really? It was only two years ago."

"Archives," she repeats.

"How long will it take to get it from Archives?"

"Ten to fourteen days," she says as if she's given this answer a hundred times already today, which she probably has. I take my sheet back and slump down in one of the chairs. A GI doctor nods at me and continues his rapid-fire dictation.

I give Scotty a quick call, and he confirms he's found nothing on the scar.

"Just some scar fetish sites came up. So thanks a lot for that one."

I laugh.

"And I got ahold of some more banks, too."

"Banks?"

"Yeah, you know, for the Treasury bonds."

The GI guy fumbles through another chart, whipping through pages, dashing off signatures. "I thought you were done with all that."

"Yeah, I just gave it one more try. Called some places in Syracuse. They said they have a record of his account but can't do anything without his death certificate."

"Hmm. I have no idea where that would be."

"Yeah, me neither. I'd probably have to get another one from city hall, and that's going to be a fucking nightmare."

"And so continues the hunt for the phantom Treasury bonds."

"Yeah," he says with such utter dejection that I could hug him through the phone line.

"Well, keep up the good fight," I encourage him. As we hang up, a doctor plops an armful of charts onto the desk behind me. Grumbling, he cracks open a chart. I decide to call Detective Adams to let him know about Eliza Sapierski.

"Zoe!" he answers. "Got an update on Candy."

"Oh yeah?"

"Yeah," he says, crunching again. The man must live on potato chips. "I got in touch with the adoption agency that Candy and Janita were processed through. It's a place called New Promises, in Toronto."

"Where Heaven's from," I say.

"That's right. It appears they were sent to a foster family in Toronto and adopted soon after. But then the trail goes cold."

"Who adopted them?"

"Brown. Linda and James Brown. But the number they gave us is disconnected. So we're still looking. Isn't easy. There's fifty-seven thousand Browns in Canada."

I grab my patient list and write some notes on the back. New Promises. Linda/James Brown. "But I don't get it. They just lost track of them?"

"It appears so. The woman at the agency said it's not that

uncommon. Sometimes a family moves, and they don't really keep tabs." Someone calls out his name, and he shouts back at them. "Zoe, I have to get going."

"Wait, before you go," I say. "I found something, too." I tell him about Eliza Sapierski and the scar. "I can text the picture to you, if you want."

"Go ahead. I can have someone look into it, but honestly, Zoe, it's not a lot to go on. A similar scar. There could be a million reasons for that."

"Maybe. But it's weird, isn't it? And she's adopted, too."

"True. But it's still not much of a link." His name is called out again, this time with annoyance. "Okay, I really do have to go. Just caught a case. But I'll let you know if anything comes up."

The answer jumps out at me while I'm sitting in the library.

An 18-year-old-woman comes in with moaning and confusion. She had been depressed and was recently started on Lexapro. She was also on Elavil for migraine prevention. In the ER, her heart rate is found to be elevated at 120 beats per minute with a low-grade fever. She is diaphoretic and appears anxious and agitated.

Serotonin syndrome.

I know the answer before I even look at the choices. Not

catatonia. Serotonin syndrome. I dial Dr. Berringer's number as fast as my fingers can dial.

Hi, you've reached Dr. Berringer. I'm not here right now . . .

Grabbing my satchel, I run up to the floor, hoping to catch him before he leaves for the day. When I get there, he's on his way out, buttoning his long navy coat.

"Serotonin syndrome!" I blurt out, breathless from racing down the hall.

He loops a merlot-colored scarf around his neck. "I assume you're talking about Candy. And yes, I've considered it."

"It fits. It does. She's moaning, confused, diaphoretic. She's on an SSRI."

"All true. And a good thought in the differential." He spots his untied shoe and perches his foot on the chair to tie it, unraveling his scarf in the process.

"But?" I ask.

"But it doesn't fully make sense," he says, rewrapping his errant scarf. "We just started the SSRIs. And she was only febrile once."

"But we can't just ignore it." I take a deep breath. "We've been focusing on catatonia. But what if it's not catatonia? What if it hasn't been all along? What if it's encephalopathy?"

He stuffs his hands in his pockets. "Confused, but not catatonic?" he asks, seeming to consider it.

"Right."

"I don't know," he says, debating. "I've stopped her benzos. Her labs all look good. Nothing smells like encephalopathy to me."

"Let's repeat the EEG," I say, thinking of it just then. "If it's consistent with encephalopathy, maybe we can take off the SSRIs for a bit. Just in case it's serotonin syndrome."

He shrugs. "Fine. It can't hurt. And we'd need one before ECT anyway." He pulls his hand out of his pocket, looking at the blue-and-red watch. "Off to AA," he says.

"The O-club?"

His look is puzzled for a second. "Right," he says. "I forgot I told you about that." He taps his watch with a resigned smile. "Can't be late."

Christmas music, Pink Martini–style, fills the air as I browse through my e-mail in my favorite eggplant settee. Mike sits next to me, drinking coffee (he has coffee in his veins) and reading an ER board review book. No e-mail from Detective Adams yet. Googling "Eliza Sapierski," I gather a few hits. Instagram photos of a woman making pierogis and one Vine of a thirteen-year-old doing an impressive skateboarding trick. It was from a month ago, so that can't be my girl. I add "adopted" to the search, but nothing comes up.

A young couple with matching laptops and facial rings comes in through the door. They sit at the table across from each other, unfold their laptops, then proceed to ignore each other completely. Mike coughs and turns a page while I search for New Promises next, pulling up some rehab facility in New Haven as well as the Toronto adoption agency. I plug her name in the agency's search box.

Sorry. Your search did not reveal an answer.

The website is a hodgepodge of photos, pretty much what you'd expect—happy youngsters and babies, with every race equally represented. They also have a staff page of headshots with "fun facts" about each person below.

Clarence Adams
Social Worker
Fun Fact: Loves Pop-Tarts!

Raymond Donner
Social Worker
Fun Fact: Dresses up as Santa at local malls!

His picture reveals an overweight man with a gray-white beard and some poorly treated rosacea, so I can see how this would fit. He's even got the right name for the job. Donner, and Dancer, and Prancer, and Blitzen. I flip through a few more pictures from the website. Mike stretches and puts the book down. He sits down on the edge of the settee.

"So I've made a decision," he says.

I look up from the computer. "Okay."

"I'm taking a couple weeks' vacation and going to stay with my mom for Thanksgiving."

"Oh." I'm not sure how to take this, but my stomach churns. "When are you leaving?"

"Tomorrow, actually. Sort of a last-minute thing; I got a cheap flight. Sort of."

"Well, that's nice of you. To go see her." I'm hoping I sound supportive and not nervous.

"My brother will be there, too, and Samantha. And my mom's been bugging me."

"Good. Definitely. You should go."

He takes another sip and puts his cup down with a clink. "So, while I'm there, I'm probably going to meet with the urgent-care people. Get in an interview."

I nod and notice he's looking away from me.

"You have one set up already, you mean?"

"Yes." He meets my eyes this time.

"Okay?"

"Just to keep our options open," he adds, "until we've come to a decision."

"Right." I stifle a twinge of anger that I know is misplaced. As he said, sometimes doing nothing is the same thing as doing something.

"Anyway, we'll see," he says, standing up and leaning over my computer. "What are you looking at?"

"That adoption agency I was telling you about. New Promises." I go back to the home page, to the montage of baby and kid pictures. "Success Stories."

"Hey," he says over my shoulder, pointing at the screen.

"What?"

"The blond girl. She kind of looks like that picture you showed me…"

"Oh my God, you're right." I widen the screen to a picture of a young girl with blond, shoulder-length hair and blue eyes. Pulling up the photo Dr. Koneru texted me, I see the same smattering of freckles on her nose and the same cool blue eyes staring up at me from the dead face of Eliza Sapierski. I stand right up. "I've got to call Detective Adams."

I'm already dialing when Mike points to his watch with a rapid head shake.

"Hello?" The detective's voice is gravelly and tired. "Zoe?"

I figure out Mike's miming then and realize it's nearly eleven. After the last texting fiasco, I did promise not to call him after nine p.m. Oops. "Hi. I got some news." I head to the back vestibule so I don't bother the other patrons. "I just thought I should share it."

"Okay," he says with a groan and yawn combined. "What is it?"

"Remember Eliza Sapierski?"

He pauses so long I wonder if he's fallen back to sleep. "Hello?"

"Yeah, yeah. The girl with the scar. The adopted girl."

"Yes. Well, she's on the New Promises website." The laptop couple walk by me, laughing, on their way out the door.

"Really?"

"Yeah."

He clears his throat. "How sure are you that it's her, this girl?"

"I don't know—ninety percent? It's a good likeness. Plus

242

what are the chances that they have the same scar, both ended up in Buffalo, and both were adopted? It's got to be her."

"Yeah," he admits. "Pretty solid reasoning." A car idles outside with its hazards on, blinking a yellow rhythm into the rain. "I'll look into it tomorrow, okay?"

Chapter Twenty-Eight

I'm not good at reading EEGs but it looks slow to me. "What do you think?" I ask the tech.

"No seizures," she says, her eyes wrinkled from years of smoking. "Kind of slow, not too exciting." We sit a minute, watching Candy stare out, electrodes spouting out of her head like she's Frankenstein and we're experimenting.

"Lots of sweat artifact," the tech comments, wiping Candy's forehead off with a paper towel. She does this clinically, not like a mother dabbing her child but like a tech who's annoyed with all the artifact. "Does she always sweat like this?"

"Yeah, lately." Serotonin syndrome, but my attending doesn't agree. But then again, he's the "wunderkind" from New Orleans and I'm a lowly resident, on probation.

"Well, the doc will be reading it today. We'll let you know what we find," she says by way of dismissal.

"I'll check in later."

The tech doesn't respond, frowning and wiping at one of the electrodes. As I walk out, I nearly slam into Detective Adams.

"Hello there," he says, peeking into the room. "What's going on in there?"

"EEG," I answer. "She's still out of it. Catatonic. Encephalopathic. Whatever."

He stares at me like I'm speaking a foreign language. And I guess I am. I remember wondering how on earth I would ever learn all the Latin, all the -opathies, the medications. And one day, without warning, I was fluent.

"So I guess it wouldn't help to show her some pictures," he says.

"Pictures?"

He rattles the bulky manila envelope under his arm. "We have twenty cars with that partial in New York."

"Any limos?"

"No. But a couple of black town cars."

"Maybe it's worth a try." She was just this side of coherent when she picked out the license plate numbers after all. We walk in, and he takes out a close-up black-and-white glossy of a skinny white guy in a tracksuit. Candy's eyes drift down, and she does her mechanical moaning sound.

"Maybe that means something?" he asks, his eyes brightening.

"I doubt it. She does that all day."

"Been doing that for twenty minutes now," the tech adds. "And sweating. Did I mention sweating?" She reaches up to give her another wipe.

"Try another one," I say.

He picks a mid-twenties Asian woman, the picture an enlargement of her driver's license, with a soft smile and a bob haircut.

Same glance, same moan.

"Huh," he says.

"Yeah. That's what I mean."

His shoulders droop a bit as he stacks the photos up in a tight pile and fits them back in the envelope. "I don't like any of them for kidnapping anyway," he says. "No one's got a decent prior to speak of." We walk side by side out of the room, the detective's knees cracking.

"Did you find out if that was Eliza Sapierski?"

"No. The staff person I talked to last time supposedly up and quit, and the agency clammed up. Said it wasn't her place to talk to us anyway, and they won't release patient information without a warrant."

"Can you get one?"

"I'm trying. But we have no jurisdiction in Canada, and so far the authorities have been less than helpful." He pops a piece of gum into his mouth, filling the air with mint.

We walk toward the nurses' station. "But it looks like her, don't you think?"

He shrugs and throws the silver gum wrapper away. "I think so, but it's hard to know. I mean, that's a stark before-and-after photo. Smiling in one and a corpse in the other."

I tap my pen on Candy's chart. "So what do we do then? We can't just do nothing. Maybe I should try calling New Promises."

He puts up a hand to slow me down. "The Canadians are looking over all these photos right now, seeing if anyone matches up on their side. Frequent border crossers or whatever. That'll help us focus a bit more."

I nod, staring at the brown floor.

"I want to find her, too. But it won't help to send ten agents out on a wild-goose chase and miss our perp, will it?"

Perp, vic. Cop talk. A language *he* woke up speaking one day. "I guess not."

He looks me in the eye. "You get Candy better. Let me take care of Janita. Deal?"

"Deal," I answer, hoping to hell I can live up to my end of the bargain. As the detective walks out, I get to the nurses' station and start writing my progress note, when my phone rings. Dr. Berringer's name pops up.

"Hi, Zoe?"

"Hi."

"I'm down in the cafeteria. Do you have a few minutes to meet? Maybe discuss the case?"

I glance at my stack of waiting charts. "Um, sure. That's fine."

"I mean, if you don't have time or something..."

"No, no. I have time. It's no problem." Of course Probation Girl has time. "Be down in five."

Dr. Berringer waves to me from one of the alcoves in the cafeteria. These are the rooms they dress up on the holidays—

candles and wreaths on Christmas, hearts and chocolates on Valentine's Day—an effort to soften the blow of spending your holidays in the hospital. Though I've always found this fabricated cheer even more depressing. I pay for some coffee, grab some mini-creamers, and meet him at the table.

"Thanks for coming," he says as if this is his living room. "Just wanted to get some updates on Candy and stuff." He lifts his coffee mug to his mouth with two hands, like a kid drinking hot chocolate on a cold day.

"Oh yeah, sure." I dump in one creamer and take a test sip. Needs more creamer.

"Did Detective Adams have any more to say?"

"Yes, actually. I was going to tell you at rounds. I showed Candy's scar to Dr. Koneru, when she first was admitted. You know, the one on her ankle?"

He nods.

"And she looked into it and ended up finding the same scar on another girl from one of her old cases. And," I continue, "it turns out they were both from the same adoption agency. In Toronto, called New Promises."

He sits upright as if the revelation troubles him. "Maybe they were abusing them over there."

"Maybe. She could have run away or something. Though it wouldn't be so easy to cross the border like that." I take another sip of my coffee, which is now too creamy. "Did you think any more about the serotonin syndrome?"

"Yeah, it's not a bad thought. But everyone I talk to still thinks catatonia." He clears his throat. "We'll see what the EEG says."

"Right, that makes sense."

He taps his long fingers on the table. "This case is a bitch. Hardest one I've ever covered. I'm not afraid to admit it."

"For sure." We pause then as a group of residents sits down at the back table by the window, running through their patient list. It's a favored spot for this; visitors and patients don't usually venture into the alcove rooms. For a few minutes, we sip at our coffees, having seemingly run out of things to say about Candy.

"Zoe, I wanted to talk to you about something." He fidgets in his seat. "You probably figured out that I didn't just want to talk about work."

The residents at the back table start laughing. "I was kind of wondering."

"Yes, I needed to tell you something." He takes a deep breath, staring down at his coffee, and lowers his voice. "I lied to you before, that night on the twelfth floor. When I said I wasn't cheating. I was."

I lean back in the chair. "Okay."

"That was the main reason for the divorce."

I nod, crinkling the empty creamer.

"It's over now. It was stupid. She was a lot younger than me, and I guess I was just, I don't know, flattered."

Perhaps this explains the tense silence at the coffeehouse when he and his wife came that one time. "It happens," I say.

"Yeah, but not to me. Well, not before this time anyway. We had our problems even before all that, but this was the last straw."

I take off my glasses and start cleaning them, not sure

what I'm supposed to say. "I don't mean to be rude, Dr. Berringer, but why are you telling me all this?"

He pauses, flicking his mug with his index finger in a tinny rhythm.

"You know, Zoe, I don't have many friends," he says. "Good friends, I mean."

"Okay?"

"And I feel like we connect. You're going to be an attending soon, a colleague, not just a resident."

"This is true."

"I guess what I mean to say is, I think"—he looks in my eyes—"we could be friends, you know. You and me. I hope we can, anyway." He looks in his coffee again. "And I don't want to be lying to you. I want you to hear it from me before you hear it from someone else. I'm not a bad guy, Zoe. I did something stupid, but I'm trying. With everything, I'm trying."

The residents at the back table get up to leave, carrying their trays. "I don't think you're a bad guy. We all make mistakes."

"Well"—Dr. Berringer takes another sip of coffee—"thanks for saying that, anyway." He puts the mug down. "And how are you doing with everything? With the ADHD and all that."

"Good, I guess. Better anyway. I can focus for more than, like, three consecutive seconds."

He throws his head back with a laugh, and the overhead light shows a smattering of blond-gray stubble on his cheeks. A nascent fall beard? A three o'clock shadow? His eyes glitter gray blue in the light. "You're damn smart, Zoe. One of the smartest residents I've ever taught."

"Oh, you don't have to say that." I feel myself blushing.

"I know I don't. I mean it, though. You keep me on my toes." He touches my wool sleeve, delivering a static shock. "Sorry." He retracts his hand.

"That's okay. I'm not easily shocked," I say, a lame attempt at humor, and he gives me a sheepish smile and stands up. "Be right back."

As he walks off to the bathroom, I fight the buoyant smile about to take over my face. The telltale, stupid, budding-crush smile. Which is ridiculous, considering Dr. Berringer may be wunderkind smart and, yes, somewhat attractive even. But he's also married, for now anyway. And an alco-holic. And my attending.

Not to mention that I'm already dating someone.

Taking a sip of my cooling, syrupy coffee, I wonder about this. Is this why I haven't made a decision about next year with Mike? Just to keep my options open? The notion does not paint a pretty picture of me, and offers yet another reason for Mike to flee to North Carolina. The sound of a text interrupts my unhappy musings, and I search in my pocket. But then I realize it's Tad's phone, which he left faceup on the table. I shouldn't look, I know that, but I do anyway.

Sign the papers or I will tell them everything.

It's from his wife.

Chapter Twenty-Nine

I can make..." I say, mentally perusing my minuscule cata-
log of recipes, "cheese and crackers?"

Scotty openly guffaws. "You mean, you know how to open
up cheese and crackers and put them on a plate?"

"Yes," I say. "I'm very talented at that."

"Congratulations. Bring cheese and crackers. We're
thinking, like, four p.m."

"Four p.m.? What is this, the early bird special?"

"No," he says. "But Kristy has to work that night, so we're
starting early."

Kristy again. They've been going out over a month now,
which is like four dog years for Scotty. "Right. Red or white?"

"Both. Oh, and tell Mike to bring that crostini thing."

"Oh, Mike's not coming."

"He's not?"

"No. Last-minute decision. He's going to North Carolina
to be with his mom."

"Oh, okay, fine. Four p.m. Don't forget the wine."

Just as we're hanging up, Dr. Berringer dashes in the room waving an EEG report. "Hot off the press."

I grab it from him. The fax is blurry, but the bottom line is clear: *Normal. No slowing or epileptiform activity noted.*

"So we should be thinking ECT. Maybe as soon as next week." He raps his fingers on the counter in a staccato rhythm, thinking. "Yeah, next week. That'll give me time to line up anesthesia."

I scan the EEG report. "No mention of sweat artifact, huh?"

Dr. Berringer peers over my shoulder, and I catch the scent of lime shaving cream. Stealing a glance at the smooth skin of his jawline, I am struck with the sudden, bizarre urge to kiss him. I lower my head away from his, pretending to scrutinize the EEG report more closely. Jesus, I really must be missing Mike.

"You're right. No sweat artifact," Dr. Berringer says, step-ping back again. "Hey, Jason, I've got a couple things to wrap up in the office. Let's round in an hour?"

Jason looks up from a journal article. "Sounds good."

When he leaves, I start putting the EEG report in the chart. "So what do you think?"

"About what?" Jason asks.

"ECT. It just seems so... I don't know."

Jason keeps reading, moving his index finger across the page. "She isn't getting better. What other options are there?"

"I guess."

He looks up from his book. "So how did your hospital cafeteria date go?"

"I told you it wasn't a date. We just went over the case."

"Right," Jason says, smirking.

"He did mention a couple things." I debate how much to reveal. "And he said he wants us to be friends."

He laughs. "Oh my God, that is the oldest line in the book."

"I think he meant it." I pause. "Like he's just lonely or something. Going through some stuff."

"Whatever. I just hope we're done on time today."

"Why? And please tell me it doesn't start with a *D*."

He flips another page. "In more ways than one."

I file Candy's EEG in her chart. "Again, too much information."

"Dominic wants to meet for coffee," he clarifies.

"How civilized."

"Apparently he wants to do a debrief of his entire family before Thanksgiving. He's got something like a million cousins. You know these Catholic families." Jason stands up with a yawn. "Going to hit the library. See you later."

"Later." A whole hour of dead time looms before me. So I call Detective Adams. "It's your daily phone call."

"Yeah," he grunts. "I wish I had some news for you. A bunch of damn dead ends. Anybody stand out in the photos I sent you?"

"Not really." After much pleading, he'd finally e-mailed me the driver's license photos. "The guy you pointed out looked kind of familiar for some reason, but no one really stood out."

"The guy from Ontario? With the black sedan?"

"Right," I answer. "How'd you get those, anyway? I thought Canada wasn't playing."

"Yeah, well, let's just say I have a buddy from border patrol who owed me a favor." He yawns into the phone. "Anyway, he was the only one with any kind of prior. Taking a piss in his Santa costume."

I pause. A Santa costume? "Wait a second, let me take a look at him again." I pull up his picture on the computer. A pudgy guy with a white beard and a childish smile. His nose laced with the finest rosacea. "What the hell was his name again?" I ask myself out loud.

"Donner," he answers. "Raymond Donner."

"Holy shit!"

"What?"

"He's the guy!" I yell out.

"What guy?"

"Are you near a computer?" I ask. "Pull up the New Promises website."

I hear keyboard tapping. "Okay, yes, I'm on it."

"Go to the staff page."

It takes him a click. "Wow."

"The Santa guy. That's the same Donner, isn't it?"

"Yeah, that's him." He lets out a long breath. "Okay, we've got to get the Canadians working with us," he says. "I don't like where this is going."

⌐

Arthur gives Jason's knee an investigatory sniff, then decides to go full monty. Jason evaluates the humping form attached to his leg. "Your dog has issues."

"Don't we all."

"No, really. I think he's questioning his sexuality."

"Oh no, he's fully aware of his sexuality. I've caught him humping stuffed animals. He might have Klüver-Bucy syndrome."

"Klüver-Bucy syndrome," he snorts. "You're a total nerd, you know that?" He pushes Arthur off, and the dog dry-humps the air a few times, then skitters off to the kitchen to cause who knows what kind of chaos. Last week, he shredded an entire bag of frozen bagels, and I'm still finding remnants. Jason sits next to me on the couch, leafing through my *Us* magazine. "This magazine sucks."

"It's not high literature," I agree. Arthur trots back into the family room and noses me with his faceless monkey. A regular Hannibal Lecter, my dog. I toss the monkey as far as I can, and he is back in a second, thrusting the soggy monkey at me again. He could play Fetch until my arm falls off. I turn to another page in my review book.

"Any other magazines?"

"I think I have an *O* magazine in the bathroom."

Jason wrinkles his nose. "I'm not *that* gay."

"Listen, I'm trying to study. Why don't you pick up

Kaplan and Sadock?" I ask, pointing over to the tome of a textbook on my desk.

"Somehow that doesn't sound appealing."

"Well, amuse yourself. Play with Arthur. I told you I was going to study. There's a beer in the fridge." I take a cold sip of mine.

Jason heaves a sigh and stands up. He comes back from the kitchen uncapping his beer, takes a swig, then pulls out his phone to check his e-mail. He showed up tonight on my doorstep. It turns out the coffee date was not a briefing session after all, but a hundredth dumping. Jason didn't want to talk about it, so I'm cheering him up in the best way possible, studying while he sulks. And I needed a distraction from ruminating over Raymond Donner anyway. Detective Adams promised me he'd work on a warrant for him. *This might just break the case*, he said.

"So what's up with Berringer?" he says. "You think he's an alkie or what?"

My antennae elevate. "Probably." I flip another page, trying for nonchalance.

"I think the guy's kind of weird," he says, scrolling through his phone.

"Weird how? All psychiatrists are weird."

"Yeah, but he's, like, more weird. I don't know. I can't put my finger on it." He takes another sip. "Probably just because he's hungover all the time."

I hold the corner of my page. "Do you think it's impairing his judgment?" It's a question, I realize just then, that's been hovering in the back of my mind.

"Who knows?" He lets out a belch.

"I mean with ECT, for instance. That's a huge deal, and I just feel like we're rushing into it."

"Maybe," Jason says. "Maybe not. All his decisions are vetted at this point anyway."

I stare at him. "What do you mean by that?"

"He's on probation. The guy can't wipe his ass without conferring with a committee first."

"Explain further."

Jason leans back in the couch. "You know how he got transferred from Tulane for drinking."

"Yeah."

"So, as part of the agreement, he's got to report all his cases to a committee." He flicks off the fireplace with the re-mote.

"How do you know that?"

"He told me."

"He did?"

"Yes. I'm chief. He tells me everything. He reports on all his cases. It's part of the probation agreement." He takes an-other sip of beer. "Maybe the committee is the one pushing for ECT. Who the fuck knows?" Arthur has wandered over, and Jason pets his head. "Anyway, he said it's driving him nuts."

I nod, thinking. "It would drive me nuts, too." We sit in silence a moment, staring at the unlit logs. "Do you think I should call the Chair? About his drinking?"

He sets his beer on a Sabres coaster (a leftover from when Scotty lived here) and looks at the ceiling, thinking. "I'm not sure about ECT. It's probably the right move at this point. And would I call the Chair? No, I wouldn't call the Chair. She's a total witch." He puts his feet on the coffee table, and Arthur starts sniffing his socks. "Probation Girl might get booted."

Chapter Thirty

So I have some news," the detective starts, "but it's not necessarily good news."

"Okay." I'm on the phone, walking through Delaware Park by the zoo, and a pair of giraffes goggle at me over the fence. Like maybe I'm the one in the zoo and they're in this nice, grassy place where people keep feeding them freshly killed prey and the one lion in there just paces behind a fence without trying to eat them once.

"We got the scoop on Raymond Donner. A little bit at least."

"Did you find him yet?" A Rollerblader whizzes by me in a red fleece jacket.

"No, we're looking. He left New Promises two months ago, and they haven't updated the website."

"Huh."

"But the Canadians are finally on board, and we got some more info on this New Promises place."

"Yeah?" I quicken my pace.

"So you know Raymond Donner was a social worker there. Turns out he's got the best placement record out there, especially for girls. Ninety-nine percent of his girls and forty-three percent of his boys get adopted within a year. He's a real outlier, so we looked into it."

"And?" A golfer smacks the ball off the tee, and I jump.

"And all his kids seem to get lost."

"Lost? What do you mean, lost?"

"They all get adopted, and that's that. Then they just fall off the radar. Most of these kids didn't have anyone looking for them anyway. Their parents were in jail or on drugs, et cetera."

"Like Heaven."

"Exactly, like Heaven. Janita and Candy were both in his caseload. So was Eliza Sapierski."

"And no one can find the people that adopted them?"

"Every name listed is either wrong or disconnected."

"Which means?"

"Which means, number one, they're probably fake names. And number two, they're probably not even getting adopted."

"What's happening to them then?"

"We don't know for sure. But we think they're being sold. They figure twenty-eight of his kids have gone missing in the last five years."

"Sold? But why would he sell them?"

There is a pause. Up ahead, a brother and sister are laughing on the swings, their dirt-streaked sneakers reaching higher and higher into the sky. The swings croak out a rhythm as one swoops up and the other sails down.

"When kids get sold, Zoe, it's not usually for a very happy reason."

Bile rises in my throat. Of course. *These white dudes trying to rape me and nobody believes me.* "Human trafficking?"

"Yes, human trafficking. Pedophilia. Sick fucking stuff that nobody likes to believe is happening. Least of all in their own backyard."

I stand there, watching the kids swing up and down, up and down.

"Easy trade route from Toronto to Buffalo and then to God knows where," he adds.

"New York City," I say.

He pauses. "What makes you say that?"

"I don't know. It might not be. It's just, that's where Candy thought she was when she first woke up."

"It's plausible," he says. "We can certainly look into it."

The kids are laughing now. Up swing, down swing. Up swing, down swing. "Jesus Christ. We have to find Janita." There is panic in my voice.

"We will, Zoe. I promise we will."

I don't know if I believe him. The parents by the swing are watching me watching their children, and I decide to move on. A woman jogs by me in black spandex, her cheeks ruddy, and I wish I were her. Running, not talking about men who sell children.

"There is a silver lining here, you know," he says.

"Oh yeah? What could that possibly be?"

"She's got a value to them. Pimps don't usually like to kill their product."

"How's Candy doing?" Sam asks. "Any more appearances by Daneesha?"

"No, just Candy. She's not doing great, actually."

"Still catatonic?"

"I'm not sure, to be honest. But I don't think so. She just sits there and moans. And she's stiff as a board, sweating..."

"Doesn't really sound like catatonia." He clears his throat. "But I don't know," he adds, like he may have overstepped his bounds. "It's hard to say when you're not the one treating the patient."

"Sounds like serotonin syndrome, though, doesn't it?" I ply him.

He sits up archly in his chair. "Hard to say. Any more nightmares?" he asks, changing the subject.

"No. Thank God. Actually, work's been so busy, I haven't had time to worry about insomnia."

"What's your call?"

"Every fourth."

He leans back with a smile and looks out the window. A dusting of snow lines the windowpane. "Back in my day..." he starts.

"When you walked ten miles uphill both ways?"

"That's right." He nods. "We were on call every other. Not sleeping was just part of the training."

I finger the brass knobs on the chair. "You think that was better or worse?"

He ponders this one. "I don't know. Better in some ways, worse in others. I learned a ton. Things became second nature just from sheer volume. But we made mistakes. We all did." He takes off his glasses and starts cleaning them with his coat sleeve. "That's how the Bell Commission came into being, you know." He is referring to regulations that monitor resident work hours. "Some ER resident made a mistake, gave a girl Demerol when he shouldn't have. And she died. Serotonin syndrome, probably."

"Demerol?" I ask.

"Yeah. Do you know the case?"

"Sort of." My head is whirling. *Did any of you guys write a Demerol order yesterday? Someone took it from the Pyxis.* "I guess I never knew all the details."

He picks a white thread off his blazer. "I think she was on phenelzine back in the good ol' days of psychiatry. I still use it, time to time," he remarks, like he's talking to himself. "And she was on cocaine, too, so it's hard to know what did what, but the parents rightly sued and now we've got the Bell Commission, for better or worse."

"Demerol," I repeat.

"Yeah," he says, looking at me oddly.

"Wait a second." I start rummaging through my satchel.

"What? What are you looking for?"

"It's this guy...this priest..."

"A priest?"

I finally spot the tattered corner of the copy and yank it out. It's a blurry, shadowy picture but it's the same white beard, the same broad chest. I can't say for sure, but the priest looks a hell of a lot like Raymond Donner.

"Is he giving her Demerol?" I ask, aloud.

The psych ward is moribund tonight. As I emerge from the elevator, the unit is dimly lit, muted, and gloomy. Nancy, the head nurse, spies me heading down the hall.

"Are you on call? I have Dr. Chang listed here."

"Yeah. I switched with Jason."

"Oh." She looks puzzled. "I think he and Dr. B already rounded this morning."

"Yeah, I guess he forgot some things, so I'm tying up some loose ends." My face goes warm. I've never been a good liar.

"That's how men are, right? Always forgetting something," Nancy says.

I smile, grabbing some charts from the rack for show. They tremble in my arms, and I drop them down on the desk. "Hey, any more word on that missing Demerol?"

"Not really," she answers. "They did tox screens on all the night staff, but I haven't heard anyone turning up positive."

I flip through a chart. "What about that priest guy?"

She laughs and pulls the med drawer open with a squeak.

"No one's seen hide nor hair of him again." She steers her cart into the hallway. "Have a good one."

I nod in response and start reading through the patient notes, deciding on the next step. Candy is still listed as catatonic. But Dr. Berringer's wrong, no matter what he and his committee think. And if Raymond Donner's been slipping her Demerol, she's got serotonin syndrome. I could order a tox screen, but I would rather go under the radar in case Bad Santa is still out there somewhere. Who knows, he might even be going through her chart.

I fumble through a nurse's cart for a blood draw kit and have no idea if I'm supposed to use a red top or purple top, so I grab both. Of course, I haven't actually drawn blood since medical school, but I'm hoping it's like riding a bicycle—just with needles. As I step into Candy's room, the blinds throw stripes on the wall. Her IV pole whirs, the bag nearly bottomed out.

"Here goes nothing," I whisper to myself, girding my courage as I loop the rubber tourniquet around her arm and mumble an apology. Candy isn't feeling anything, though, which is a cold comfort at least. I push down for the rubbery feel of the vein and stick the needle in her arm and get nothing. Redirect, nothing. No blood return. I never was much good at drawing blood in the first place, and her arm looks like a pincushion. Bruises and needle marks everywhere, and with the IV running out, the veins are likely all collapsed. Slipping the tourniquet off, I hear footsteps coming down the hall. They pause a moment, while I hold my breath and invent a story about why on earth I'm drawing blood on a catatonic patient in the middle of the night, but they carry on again. A bead of sweat drips down my back.

Whipping the tourniquet on the other arm, I slap the skin a bit to get some blood moving, press down on where the vein should be, make a quick wish to God or whoever is listening, and stick the needle in.

God answers. The maroon color shoots into the test tube, and I fill one tube up halfway and shove the other one on. Then I rip off the tourniquet, toss my gloves in the garbage, and stash the tubes in my lab coat pocket. The hallway is empty, the head nurse bent over a cart at the other end. In the elevator, I tear a crumpled script off my pad, scribble down *tox screen*, and walk to the lab.

If the psych ward is moribund, the lab is way past dead. "Proud Mary" is playing from a dusty boom box in the corner, the bass jangling through a crappy amplifier.

"Hello?" I call out to the cavernous room filled with centrifuges, rows of test tubes, and petri dishes growing all sorts of nefarious things.

"Yup?" a guy calls out from the other side of the room. He takes his time coming over. He's over fifty with faded, bled-out tattoos covering his arms under his scrubs. I can make out a skull that somehow morphs into a mermaid. "Can I help you?"

"I have a tox screen to run," I say, pulling the tubes out of my pocket.

"Personal delivery?" he asks skeptically.

I don't answer.

He takes the script and tubes and reads them, again with

open suspicion. "So which is it then? The purple top or the red top?"

I debate an instant and decide stupid medical student would be the best play right now. "I—I don't know. We got called in on an emergency tonight. The attending told me to get this done stat. The resident told me to bring it down to the lab. It took me thirty minutes to find the lab, and I'm afraid if the blood needs to be cooled or anything. And they are seeing the other patients without me." I let my voice grow to a fevered pitch.

"Here," he says, taking pity on the gangly, clueless medical student and relishing the role as the savior, no doubt. "It's a red top," he chides me. "Red top for your tox screen. Purple top for CBC." He points to the striped tubes from a rack. "Tiger top for chem. That's your basics. If you know that as a medical student, you're good to go."

I nod as supplicantly as possible.

"Hell," he adds, "if you know that as a *doctor*, you're good to go." He tosses the purple top into a hazards-only bin and places the red top into his rack with a squeak. "You got a label?"

A label. Shit. My face registers unmanufactured dismay.

"Don't worry," he says, like he could be my big brother now. "Write down the patient's name on the script. I'll get one."

I write down the name and room number with care, planning to drop off a label later to be on the safe side. "Okay, I better go," I say, peering at my watch for effect.

"Off you go, chickadee," he says.

A name I've never been called in my life. Stork, dodo. Emu once, by a boy even nerdier than I. Tall birds mostly. I've never brought to mind a chickadee.

"Thanks," I yell out in my best thankful-med-student voice, without laying it on too thick, and tear out of there before he can think to ask any more questions.

Chapter Thirty-One

I don't know, Zoe. It would take some doing."

I drive past a row of cinnamon birch trees, the bark peeling in scrolls. "I'm worried about her, though."

"I understand," Detective Adams says. "But unless I have hard evidence she's in danger, it won't be easy to get uniforms in the room."

"Doesn't he look like Donner, though? The priest guy?"

"Sort of. The picture's rotten, though. He could just be a fat, white guy with a beard."

"Yeah, but he could be giving her Demerol."

"Who's to say he's giving her Demerol? You said he *might* be because of some serotonin thing."

A convertible races by me with a cold-looking teenager inside. A convertible in Buffalo is just an act of denial. "The tox screen should be back this morning anyway."

"Good. I've notified security at the hospital just in case."

I curve into the hospital parking lot, swiping my badge. "Any word on Janita?"

"No. We're following some leads in New York City just in case." There's a pause. "We'll find her," he says with a confidence that sounds forced.

After hanging up, I walk over to the hospital, the chalk-gray sky looming above me. As soon as I hit the floor, I call the lab.

"What's the name again?" the lab technician asks.

"Candy Jones. J-O-N-E-S. MR 00098764."

"One sec." The phone goes on hold, spouting a Muzak version of "Spirits in the Material World." They're midway through crucifying the keyboard solo when the voice breaks back in.

"Okay, we did find a label with her name lying around, but no blood sample. So it must have gotten thrown out."

I try to control my voice. "It got thrown out?"

"Listen, you can't just toss a label on some desk down here and think the test will get done," she shoots back, taking the offensive. "You'll just have to send another one."

"Yeah, I guess I will." I hang up, holding back every four-letter word I know, when Jason walks in.

"What's up?"

"Nothing." I sigh. "How's your floridly psychotic patient?"

"Connors? I would say he's gone down from florid to euphuistic."

"What the hell does that even mean?"

"Google it," he yawns, starting his note. "Hey, are you heading down to EEG by any chance?"

"I wasn't, why?"

"I have a ton of charts to catch up on, and I need to grab Connors's report. Fax is messed up for some reason."

"Sure, I can do it," I say, happy to stretch my legs and ponder my tox screen fiasco. When I get to the EEG office, the secretary comes out with overdone facial powder as if she just came offstage from *Rashomon*. "Bet you're here for Jeremy Connors," she says.

"You got it." Mr. Euphuistically Psychotic.

"Here it is," she says, handing it to me. "Normal as usual."

"What does that mean?" I ask. "Don't you get any abnormal ones?"

"Not from psych," she says so matter-of-factly that I choose not to take her insinuation that we only order bullshit EEGs as an insult.

"Oh, while I'm here. Could I see if you have one more from the floor. A Candy Jones?"

She opens up the file cabinet and peers in. "Okay." She ruffles through papers. "We have a million Joneses. Ah!" She grabs one, glances at it unsurely. "Candy with a Y?"

"Yes, that's it."

"We have two under her MR number. One is Jane Doe. The other is Candy Jones."

"That's right." The Jane Doe one is from when she first was admitted.

"Here." She hands me both.

I glance over them. Jane Doe, normal, awake and asleep. When she was catatonic. And Candy Jones.

Abnormal, slowing, excessive sweat artifact. Most likely consistent with encephalopathy.

I read it one more time. "Is it possible they got switched? Like the Jane Doe report got sent up to the floor instead of the newest one?"

She shrugs. "It's possible. Stranger things have happened."

"Can I have a copy?"

"No problemo."

I pocket the copy, along with Jason's EEG, and make my way back to the psych floor. Encephalopathic, not catatonic. Candy may have just dodged a bullet. "Here." I hand Jason his EEG.

"Danke."

I grab Candy's chart to replace the wrong EEG with the correct one and flip through to the report section. It is indeed the wrong, "normal" report. The one from when she first got admitted.

"What's up there, Zoe?" Dr. Berringer asks, walking into the room with his long, white coat swaying like a wizard's robe.

"I have some good news, I think."

"Oh yeah? What is it?"

"The EEG on Candy. It turns out they faxed down the wrong one, from when she first was admitted with catatonia." I show him the newest report. "This is the correct one, consistent with encephalopathy."

"Huh," he says, looking it over. "You're right." He looks

straight ahead, thinking. "Doesn't change the overall picture, though," he says, though he sounds undecided. "You can get slowing with catatonia, too."

"True." He has a point; that is reported in the literature. "But then again, maybe it's serotonin syndrome after all." I feel like a broken record.

"Maybe," he says, but I can tell he's appeasing me. "Let's round."

"It's just, if it's serotonin syndrome," I go on, "then ECT would be the wrong move, could be dangerous."

He nods. "I note your concern, Zoe. But if it is catatonia, and we wait any longer, we're taking a chance. Overcaution can be just as bad as undercaution sometimes." He drops the chart on the cart and starts to walk.

"And I had one other thought," I add, racing to keep up with him.

"Yes."

"You remember that guy they thought was stealing Demerol?"

He crinkles his eyes. "The priest?"

"Yeah. I talked with the detective, and that guy may be connected to this case. He looks an awful lot like the social worker at Candy's adoption agency. And if he's giving her Demerol, that could be causing serotonin syndrome."

Once verbalized, I'll admit it does sound a bit delusional.

"Um," Dr. Berringer says, then closes his mouth. I have actually rendered him speechless. He and Jason are staring at me like I should consider a quick admission to our unit.

"Okay." I laugh. "I know it sounds a little crazy but can we just do a urine tox to make me feel better?"

"By all means," Dr. Berringer says, walking ahead with the cart. "Whatever we can do to make Dr. Goldman feel better."

Hey, it's Mike here. Leave a message and I'll call you back.

I hang up, brooding, while Arthur slurps away at his water bowl. I left Mike two messages already today, as well as a casual what's up? text, and still haven't heard back, which isn't like him. He doesn't play games, so I don't think he's purposefully ignoring me. But then again, he's also a classic conflict avoider. I told him this once, and he didn't disagree with my assessment. I postulated it was the product of his parents' divorce; he postulated it was just him. But part of me wonders, is this the way a conflict avoider breaks up?

I call again but hang up before it goes to voice mail. I don't want to come off as a stalker, but the truth is, I desperately want his advice on calling the Chair. I know what he said before, but things are different now. We've got a sick girl and an attending who, wunderkind or not, might be impaired. It's a gray line, but...I text Jason, a distant second choice.

should I call the Chair about Berringer or not?

The answer comes right back. NOT!!!

So I decide to call the Chair. It could throw me right off probation and into the unemployment line (in which case,

275

Scotty's magical bonds would come in handy), but I've never been one for self-preservation. And Candy's worth the risk.

We finished rounding early, and it's 4:30 p.m., leaving me some time to call before the offices close. As I dial, my mouth feels papery. The secretary answers after two rings. "Hello, Dr. Connor's office."

"Yes, hi. It's Dr. Goldman. I'm just trying to get a word with Dr. Connor."

"Oh, hi, Zoe." Dawn, the secretary, is a motherly type, always bringing in peanut butter cookies and talking about her Zumba class. "She's out right now, but she'll be in tomorrow. Would you like to set up a meeting?"

"Oh, well, sure. Okay."

"Nine o'clock all right?"

If the Chair says nine o'clock, it's nine o'clock. "Sounds good to me."

I hear the keyboard tapping away. "Can I tell her what it's about?"

"Um... it's probably easier if I just explain it to her directly."

The keyboard pauses. "She usually likes to have at least some idea of what it's about, if that's okay."

Arthur knees me with his slobbery red rubber ball. I yank it out of his teeth and throw it. "Just tell her it's a concern about Dr. Berringer and my patient. Candy Jones."

"Perfect. Will do."

That settled, Arthur reappears at my knee with his ball, when my phone quacks.

nervous about wedding

Jesus, just what I need right now. My ex voicing doubts about his stupid fucking wedding. Though I don't blame him. I would be terrified to marry that monster.

that's natural, right? I text.

I guess

I pause, wondering how much further to go with this. He's obviously worried, but it doesn't really seem like an appropriate text conversation.

call me sometime if u want. Or talk w melanie abt it

My cheapo grandfather clock gongs five times, then my phone quacks again.

prob just having bad day. ttyl.

"Whatever," I say to no one, and Arthur runs back to me, perhaps thinking his name is Whatever. I scroll through some gossip sites to kill time before dinner. Not that I have any great dinner plans. Mighty Taco maybe. Checking my e-mail, I see no word from Mike. No Facebook posts from him either.

hellooooo out there?

I text to Mike, pausing right after I hit send as I think better of it. But it's too late; the text is already hurtling out to a satellite and landing on his phone. No app to retract second-thought texts. I sit for a while staring outside, hungry but too lazy to go anywhere. My RITE review book sits on the coffee table with my phone next to it, sullen and silent, as Arthur plops his faceless monkey on my lap.

My mood hovers around 1.7, in case anyone's keeping track.

Chapter Thirty-Two

Negative," the woman from the lab says.

"Negative?"

"Yes, negative. Nothing came up on the urine screen."

"And the blood tox? Did anyone ever find that one?"

"No, sorry," she says. "But you probably have your answer anyway."

"Yeah, I guess so. Thanks," I say, hanging up the phone.

Negative. Which means no Demerol. Which means it's either out of her system or Raymond Donner hasn't actually been running around trying to poison Candy after all. If it's even him in the picture. Maybe Dr. Berringer's right and this is catatonia. I close down her labs on the computer and check my phone again. Five minutes until my meeting with Dr. Connor, the Chair.

My phone rings and I silence it, and see it's Mike calling. I'd love to answer but don't want to be on the phone if the Chair opens the door early. A text pops up.

sorry, left phone at movie theater. Just got it back. Call me later? XO

I'm smiling at the XO—which you probably wouldn't text if you were about to break up with someone, even if you were a conflict avoider—when I realize it's already been the full five minutes and knock on the door. Dr. Connor opens it right away, like she was just standing there waiting.

"Hi, Zoe."

"Hi," I answer, out of breath all of a sudden.

She motions to a chair across the desk for me to sit. The chair has dark-gray fabric with odd purple swirls, which doesn't match the room at all. I sit.

"So how can I help you, Zoe?" She tilts her head, and a headful of gray ringlets moves en masse. Her pressed navy suit fits her to within an inch of her life, her matching heels polished to the perfect degree of shine. The woman is wound so tight she probably tracks her calories down to the decimal. I didn't like her even before she put me on probation.

"It's about Dr. Berringer." My heart flutters.

"Yes."

"Well, I'm a little concerned about him."

"Okay." She pauses. "Can you tell me more about that?"

I nod, scratching at my knee. My other knee itches next but I ignore it. I get itchy when I'm nervous. "It's just about this case we're on together." I'm still not sure if I'm going to tell her about his drinking. I have to assume she already knows.

"I see. Did you address your concerns with him?" she asks.

"I did. Yes, I did. But I don't think he's really hearing me, and I was hoping to get another perspective."

"Okay."

"It's about Candice Jones, our patient. She's only thirteen, and he's thinking about ECT to treat catatonia. But I think he's basing it on the wrong diagnosis. I don't think she's catatonic at all."

She smooths out a wrinkle in her sleeve. "You think it's serotonin syndrome."

I can't hide my shock. "So you already know about it?"

"Yes, actually. We've been in very close contact about this case."

"Oh." There is an irresistible itch on my scalp.

"And I'm actually glad you called me, because I was planning to speak with you anyway."

"Oh," I repeat dumbly.

"Frankly, Zoe, I'm concerned about you." Her voice oozes warmth, faker than the fireplace in my family room. As she leans over her desk, I catch a whiff of mothball.

"Okay." I brace myself.

"You understand that I ask the attending doctors to do monthly reports on all residents on probation, right?"

A queasiness creeps into my guts. "No, I wasn't aware of that."

"Well, it was discussed when you were first on probation."

That's quite possible. Given my mom just died and I couldn't focus for shit, paired with the utter shock of failing the RITE and discovering your dream of being a doctor may be dwindling fast, I may have missed a few sentences in her lecture.

"I'll admit, you score quite high on most portions of the evaluation, but not so on the PBL."

"The PBL?"

"Yes, the Practice-Based Learning initiative. Do you know what that's about?"

"Not exactly," I admit. But I have a strong feeling she's going to tell me.

"Basically, what that refers to is the ability to self-reflect, to realize our limitations."

"Uh-huh."

"In short, Dr. Goldman, to admit when we're wrong." She furrows her eyebrows, looking vaguely like a Muppet. "When I asked Dr. Berringer about your score on this part, he mentioned this case as an example. That you were convinced that this is serotonin syndrome to the exclusion of the more likely diagnosis of catatonia."

"Not to the *exclusion* of catatonia. But there's more going on here—"

"Zoe, I must tell you, there are multiple physicians involved in this case who agree with the catatonia diagnosis."

"Okay, but I also just wanted to—"

"And he mentioned you were worried about someone from the outside poisoning your patient? A priest?"

I take a breath. "Yes, I realize that sounds kind of weird, but the individual may be under investigation—"

"Listen, Dr. Goldman, I don't need to get into all the nitty-gritty details."

I wonder if she ever actually lets her patients speak. It's kind of a big thing in psychiatry, letting your patients speak.

"I know you're just trying to do what you think is right. But I must say, nothing you've just displayed so far in our conversation dissuades me from my apprehension about your PBL skills. I mean, here I am, telling you what several of your attendings think about the case, and yet you're still arguing with me."

I open my mouth and shut it. There is no way to win an argument that can't be argued.

"Right now, what I really need to hear from you is this: Yes, I understand that I may be wrong. That we are all on the same page here, all on the same team." She pauses and smiles, revealing a dot of spinach in her left bicuspid. Which seems odd, for breakfast. A frittata maybe? After a minute, her smile grows tense, and I realize I'm supposed to speak.

"Yes, yes. Of course," I assure her. "We're all on the same team, of course." I will even lead a cheer to prove it if she wants.

"Good." She leans back from her desk again. "And just so you're aware, no one is talking about dismissal here. Actually, Tad didn't even want me to bring it up with you. He was really underplaying it, but I felt it was important."

"Uh-huh."

"This is not about punishment, truly. We're just concerned about you. Knowing what happened with your patient in the past...and with the ADHD issues."

The room goes silent then, the buzz from her computer suddenly roaring. I feel my throat tighten, a telltale sign that tears aren't far off.

He told her? He actually told her?

"I appreciate your concern," I say, and clamp my jaw down tight as a latch. I will not cry in front of this woman.

I can't believe he fucking told her.

"All right. I think we're all done here, then." She straightens some papers on her desk. I have never seen such an organized desk. "Or was there anything else you want to address?"

There's no way I'm talking about his drinking now. "No, no, I think that's about it." I stand, my legs loose as jelly.

"Okay then." Dr. Connor stands up, too. "Thank you for coming, Zoe." She reaches out her hand for a shake, her pseudo-warmth ratcheting up a notch. "Let's keep in touch."

We exchange fake smiles, and I'm almost out the door when I turn around. "Just out of curiosity, did you ever examine the patient? Candy Jones?"

Dr. Connor pauses, a shot of animosity piercing through her warm, calorie-counted facade. "No," she says, "I did not." Her tone doesn't concede an inch.

"Okay. Thanks," I say, and walk out, giddy with this littlest of triumphs.

I avoid Dr. Berringer all day, which isn't easy considering he's my attending and I do have to round with him. Jason had a dentist appointment, so he's not even there to defuse the situation.

"Chloe first?" Dr. Berringer asks, piling up charts.

"Sure."

He glances at me, hearing something in my tone, but then keeps stacking charts, probably figuring I'm just premenstrual. "She's still gaining?"

"Yup."

He gives me another off look, but I ignore it and walk right into Chloe's room. "So I guess congratulations are in order?" I say.

Chloe does her signature eye roll. If there were an eye-roll competition, she would score straight tens.

"Five more pounds?"

"Looks like it," she mutters, flipping through a magazine. It's a fashion mag with dangerously skinny models pouting on every page. She whips her overgrown, strawberry-red bangs out of her face, but they slide back again by the next page. Chloe is a pretty girl when she is not skeletal. I never noticed. She creases a corner of a page, and I sneak a look to see a runway model in long, purple military garb. Something no one would actually wear. But maybe it signals something. A life ahead where she might wear a long, purple something. Something pretty and tangible that could be hers, in a life where she eats breakfast, lunch, and dinner, and maybe a snack, and doesn't think much about it. Maybe not today but someday. We exit toward Candy's room.

"Candy's the same?" he asks.

"Yeah," I answer. No change, staring, moaning. Even stiffer today, though. I tried to move her elbow, and it was lead.

"I actually got someone lined up to do ECT tomorrow. It's a Saturday, but I convinced him it was an emergency."

"Hmm."

"Do you want to come in? I know it's the weekend, but you don't get much exposure to ECT. Have you ever seen it done before?"

I shake my head.

"May be your only chance," he says, leaning over to grab an orange hard candy from the bowl. "It's four p.m. Only time Dr. Munroe was available." The candy clicks in his teeth.

"Hmm."

"Zoe." He lowers his voice and leans in toward me, his breath exuding tangerine. "Something wrong?"

I stare straight ahead. "Had a little chat with Dr. Connor today."

"Oh yeah? What about?" He looks nervous, like I might have said something about him.

"Something about problem-based learning?" My throat tightens again, and I feel tears threatening.

"Zoe, come on." He tugs my elbow, steering me toward the nurses' station, and I allow myself to be led. "Tell me what's going on," he says softly, once we've gotten to the room.

"Did you tell her about my ADHD?" I ask him, getting right to the matter.

He swallows. "Listen—"

"I told you that in confidence!"

"Zoe." He shushes me. "I didn't mean it, honestly. She sort of trapped me with this stupid resident competency form and—"

"So you felt you should tell her about it?"

His jaw tightens. "I thought it might help your case, actually. So yes, I did."

"Oh yeah?" I say, then lower my voice, too. "Well, what about *your* case?"

"My case?"

"Yeah, your case. Me driving you home drunk at three a.m. Ring a bell? You leaving early because you're too damn hungover to see your damn patients?"

He doesn't say anything but scratches at his collar. "I'm working on that, Zoe," he says, his voice injured.

"I'm sure you are. But in the meantime, Candy is the one suffering."

"No!" he yells out. Some nurses turn their heads toward the room, and he moves closer to me. "No," he repeats in a fierce whisper. "You've gone too far there, Zoe." He stabs a pointer finger on the table. "You're wrong. You might not like that, but you're wrong. Candy is catatonic. And no one is poisoning her. And it's not serotonin syndrome. She's catatonic. Catatonic." He enunciates every syllable. "And I'm sick and tired of being second-guessed on my every move. Sick of it. I'm not taking it anymore. Not from the Impaired Committee, not from the Chair, and definitely not from you."

I suck my breath in.

He leans away from me now, his cheeks splotched with red. "Let's just say she is encephalopathic. For the sake of argument. Why? What's the etiology? The tox screen is negative so we can rule out the priest. What else were you planning to look for? Tell me."

"Well," my voice wobbles, "infection."

"Done. CBC normal, CMP normal. Blood cultures sent. Negative. CSF negative. Goddammit, we even checked her for TB."

"Yes, that's true." I remember suggesting this.

"So there's one abnormal EEG. Which I missed, because somebody in EEG faxed us the wrong goddamn report. It doesn't change the basic picture, which is catatonia. And the longer we leave her this way, the less likely she is to come out. Is that what you want?" His voice swells again.

"No," I answer, shaken.

"All right then," he says, his voice calming. He exhales, settling himself. "I've given you a lot of leeway, Zoe. Because you're still learning, and because of your...issues and because, goddammit, I like you." A smile flits onto his face and falls. "But it's enough now. It's enough. We're doing ECT tomorrow. And you can come or not, that's up to you."

"Yes," I say immediately. "I'll come."

Probation Girl is skating on ice a millimeter thick.

The drink burns in my throat.

I stare at the glass, and the coppery liquid stares right back at me. My plan to relax just a little bit has turned into three fingers of Scotch. I don't usually drink Scotch, though it was my dad's favorite. He wasn't a big drinker, but every year on Father's Day and his birthday, he'd indulge. I still remember all four of us in a fancy restaurant, me in a dress despite my tomboy pleading, Scotty spilling chocolate milk on the tablecloth, and my dad cradling his glass with reverence. The unadulterated relief of his twice-yearly Scotch.

Detective Adams gave me this Scotch my first year of residency, when I got stabbed by my patient. An odd get-well present, but nonetheless being put to good use now. Sitting at my mom's old rolltop desk, I endure another burning sip, when my phone rings.

It's Mike, requesting FaceTime.

I push the FaceTime button. "Hello," I answer. The "o" in the hello seems to trail on forever.

"Hello to you." He grins and leans back. I can see the front spikes of his brush cut. I love touching his brush cut. I told him he should charge people for the "sensory joy" this provides. He told me he's keeping his day job.

"How was the interview?"

"Fine," he answers, nonchalant, perhaps too nonchalant. "What are you up to? You sound funny."

I hold my drink up to the camera. "I am drinking myself into oblivion," I say grandly.

"Sounds like fun. Any reason for such revelry?"

"Yes. I had a shit day."

"You, too?"

"Yes, a shit week, actually. And I am giving this mother-fucker a send-off with my finest bottle of Scotch." I lift up the bottle now, an adult show-and-tell. "My only bottle of Scotch, I should add."

"Yeah." He yawns. "I'm doing the same with a beer." He

lifts up a green beer bottle with a red label. I don't recognize the brand. "It appears you're further along."

"So what's the cause of your shit day?" I ask.

"Oh, this and this. You know."

"Meaning you're not going to tell me."

He chuckles and takes another sip. "Family stuff. It's a long, boring story which doesn't require analysis. How about yours?"

"A long, thrilling story which does require analysis. But if you don't share, I won't share."

He nods, hunching forward. His face freezes in the screen, then starts moving again. "I'm coming back soon enough, so it'll be fine."

"I can't wait to see you." I take another fiery sip. "We are totally going to kiss each other."

He smirks, a happy smirk. "How many drinks did you say you had?"

"Three. Possibly four. I got confused about the finger thing."

"Okay, got it. Well, I have an idea. Why don't you call me back tomorrow when you're sober?"

"I *like* that idea," I say with enthusiasm.

"*All right*," he returns with mock enthusiasm. There's the teeniest scratch on his forehead. Probably from bumping into something. We tall people are always bumping into things. He lifts his beer bottle. "Cheers, Zoe."

"*L'chaim*," I answer back. We hang up, and I wonder if I should have said "I love you." Cogitating over this one, I manage to spill my nearly empty Scotch on some papers.

Arthur jogs over and proceeds to lick every drop that made it to the floor. This strikes me as a good idea. He might be self-medicating. Grabbing a paper towel, I start wiping off the wood grain desk and open up one of the drawers to make sure nothing seeped through. But when I go to close it again, it sticks.

"Damn." I push harder but it's blocked somewhere, so I pull the whole drawer out and peer in, my head spinning with the motion. There seems to be a wooden slat in there—a false drawer maybe? I get down on my knees and shove my hand in, pushing the wooden piece down and reaching into the tiny space.

My fingers grasp some sort of paper, an envelope perhaps, and I retract my arm slowly so as not to tear it. Lifting it up to view, I see it is indeed an envelope, an oversized envelope folded in half and sealed shut. When I tear it open, two stiff papers come into view.

Mint-green papers, each with a picture of Uncle Sam, and each for one hundred thousand dollars. The magical Treasury bonds.

Well, I'll be damned.

Chapter Thirty-Three

When I walk in, the sound of the coffee grinder bores a hole right into my skull. I wander over to my usual settee and sit down, immediately fishing in my purse for some Motrin.

"Hey, what's up?" Scotty says, wandering over, then takes a closer look at me. "You look like shit. What, do you have the flu?" He backs up a step. "Don't come near me if you've got the fucking flu, man, because I seriously don't need that shit right now."

"Calm down, I don't have the flu. I'm just hungover."

"Oh," he answers, surprised. "Okay then. Hope it was worth it."

"Not really. Scotty, listen, I need to tell you something." I point to the chair next to me. "Can you sit down?"

"Um, no, I can't sit down. Because if you didn't notice, I'm actually at work and—"

"Scotty." I shush him, reaching into my purse again. I pull out the unsealed envelope. "Look inside."

He takes the envelope with some hesitation, pulling out the paper like it might bite him. His face transforms then, from a look of wary apprehension to one of shock. Shock and glee. "No fucking way," he says, almost in a whisper.

"Yes," I answer with a smile. "Yes fucking way."

"This is…" He searches for a word and doesn't find it. "I can't fucking believe this. Where did you find it?"

"In Mom's rolltop. It had a false drawer."

"I can't… it's just… I knew it. I just knew it."

"Yeah, I know. You were right all along. There were two of them in there. One for you, one for me."

"And you thought I was crazy," he says, half to himself.

I shrug. "Well, that is my training bias."

"I can't even…" He sits down, speechless, the paper trembling in his hand.

"Hey, you all right?" I put a hand on his arm.

"Yeah." But when he looks up at me, his eyes are wet. He brushes his tears off with some impatience. "This is crazy. I should be happy. I *am* happy. It's just… I don't know."

"It's a lot to take in," I say, shifting from sister to psychiatrist mode. Or maybe I'm just being both.

"Yeah," he answers, taking in a deep breath. "It sure is." He folds his arms across his chest, his lightning-bolt tattoo peeking out from under his shirt. "It's, like, her last words to me or something. It's hard to explain, but I knew she was trying to tell me something. I knew it was important to her."

The grinder starts up again, and my head throbs, though the Motrin is slowly kicking in. "Maybe she wanted to know we'd be taken care of, when she couldn't be there anymore."

Scotty nods, then smooths out the bond, staring at it again.

"Any ideas what you'll do with yours?" I ask.

"No," he says, still dazed. "No clue at all."

"Quit this place?"

"I don't know. Maybe."

"Well, we have time to think about it, for sure."

He turns to me. "What about you? Have you thought of anything?"

"Oh, definitely." All morning I've been smiling at the thought. Even with a massive hangover, still smiling. "Dr. Goldman," I say in an announcer's voice, "is going to pay off her loans and go for a fellowship."

"Third person, huh?"

I laugh.

"No, that's good." He fiddles with the paper. "A fellowship in what?"

"Yeah," I falter, "that's the question."

Scotty stands up, then sighs. "Anyway, from the sublime to the ridiculous, got to get back to work." He looks at the Treasury bond in his hand, not sure what to do with it.

"I can take it if you want," I offer. "I was going to put it in the safety deposit box."

"You have a safety deposit box?" he asks, skeptical. And since I'm not ultra-organized, I can see why he might be.

"Yeah. Well, it's Mike's, actually," I admit. "But when he gets back..."

"I'll keep it," he says, then lowers his voice. "I'll put it back in the safe for now." Then he gives me a smile, the

293

brightest smile I've seen on him in quite some time, and walks off. I lie back gingerly on the settee and open my RITE review book. I'm not due in the hospital until four p.m. for Candy's ECT, so I have plenty of hours to kill.

And I am, to put it mildly, dreading it.

"I still can't fucking believe it!" Scotty shouts into the phone.

My head pounds with his voice, and I turn the Bluetooth volume down. My hangover is still lingering despite another handful of Motrin and more than my fair share of coffee. This is the third time Scotty called with an idea about how he's going to spend his first million, or first hundred thousand in any case. I pull into an empty corner of the parking lot. The whole resident lot is dotted with just a handful of cars, for all of us unlucky on-call residents. The afternoon is cold, the sky fading to a lavender before nightfall.

"I was thinking about a start-up, maybe."

"In what?"

"Well, I've been kicking around a bunch of ideas," he answers vaguely. "Kristy's going to help me put together a business plan."

"Oh, that's good." A business plan for a bunch of ideas.

We hang up, and I make my way over to the lobby and then up to the eleventh floor after what feels like a day's hike. When I get to the room, my head still hurts and my stomach is queasy. Dr. Berringer, on the other hand, looks fresh as a flower, an irony that's not lost on me. The procedure room is a cold, pale-yellow box of a room with a border of lemon-yellow diamonds meant to cheer up the place, but the tattered corners only lend to the gloom.

Candy is stationed on the bed, stiff and foreign in this new room like a piece of moved furniture, her navy blanket lying across her like a shroud. Out of the bottom of the blanket, her foot pokes through, toes dotted with stubble. I can just hear Daneesha now. "Girl, you got to get me a razor. This shit is *nasty*."

We all stand around the room waiting for the anesthesiologist, who is late as usual. My legs are tired from standing. A peek at my watch says it's five p.m. So we've been waiting over an hour.

"You follow football, Zoe?" His voice is excruciatingly cheerful.

"Not really."

He grins, cracking his knuckles. "The Saints are a-marching. This is the year."

Nobody comments on this, and the pale-yellow silence grows. Candy is still as stone and as silent. She's stopped moaning for now.

"When was the last ETA?" Dr. Berringer asks.

"Dr. Munroe said fifteen minutes," Nancy answers. "But that was fifteen minutes ago."

"Oh," Dr. Berringer says, reaching into his pocket. "Just got a text." He throws his head back. "Stuck in traffic. He guesses an hour and a half longer."

"An hour and a half?" Nancy groans.

"He's coming in from Dunkirk," he explains.

"Oh, yeah," Nancy says. "I heard it's snowing pretty bad out there."

"Well, what do you think?" he asks me. "Break for now?"

"I'll help wheel her back," I offer. Nancy and I stash the ECT machine away and steer Candy back to her room. The wheels squeak rhythmically against the newly washed floor. Her room feels like home. Though it's no home really, she looks more comfortable here at least. Her scarecrow figurine, her self-portraits, and Gulliver's Travels, with its wrinkled, cracked spine, sits like a relic on the table. When I adjust her blanket, the tang of old sweat whiffs out.

Dr. Berringer walks into the room then. He's out of his lab coat now and puts his arm into his leather jacket sleeve. "I'm going to grab some dinner. You want to come?"

"No, I'm fine, thanks."

He stands there, staring at Candy with me a moment. The wind wails outside, making the window casing creak. "Zoe, I'm sorry about yesterday. I shouldn't have yelled at you like that. I've just been under a huge amount of stress."

I keep my eyes on Candy. "That's okay. I know I'm not exactly the easiest resident."

"No, never think that, Zoe. You should never just listen to what anyone says. You stick up for your patients. That's what you're supposed to do." He smiles at me. "You're going to be an excellent psychiatrist. I mean it."

I fight a smile. I've always been a sucker for praise—a fact I'm not proud of.

"This case," he mutters, like that explains it all, and in a way, it does. "Come with me to dinner. Let me make it up to you. My treat."

"Oh, all right." I have no energy left to argue. We walk to the nurses' station, and I hang up my lab coat next to Dr. Berringer's and grab my coat. The nurses are changing shift, all colors of scrubs milling around, rubber clogs and white sneakers. The buzz of activity cheers me up a mite.

"So where are we going for dinner?" I ask.

I didn't realize how hungry I was. We sit in a little blue booth by the window, me scarfing down fried noodles like I've just been rescued from a month in the woods.

Dr. Berringer assesses me with clinical interest. "You sure aren't one of those salad gals, are you?" The waitress hands him his soup, and he rubs his hands together with anticipation. The wind keeps up a steady howl outside, the pines swaying in the distance.

"So," he says, "how's your last year going?"

"Good."

"You doing a fellowship? You're a natural in peds."

I know this is untrue. "I'm not sure. I was thinking addiction maybe."

"Addiction?" he asks, surprised.

"Yeah," I answer. "Why? Do you think that's a bad idea?"

"No, no. It's just, most of the people I know that went into that fellowship were kind of...different..."

And no doubt he's had more than a passing acquaintance with many of them. "'Different' is something I've been called once or twice before."

"Hear, hear," he says. "To different." He raises his mini-teacup in a toast. I can envision many a bleary "hear, hear" in his past. The waitress comes by with the tray, and he digs right into his lo mein, using chopsticks expertly. I slather some plum sauce on my moo shoo pancake.

"I hope this doesn't go on too long," I say. "My dog is probably going crazy."

"Oh yeah? What kind of dog?" He wipes his mouth.

"A labradoodle."

He swallows another large bite. "Champ?"

"Good memory. But no, that was years ago. His name is Arthur." I shrug. "I don't know, my brother named him. Thought it sounded refined."

He laughs.

"It's better than Sizzle. That was my last dog. Black cocker spaniel."

"Sizzle?" he asks.

"Yeah, my mom named her. Said she was like a fire-cracker." We got her after my dad was killed in the car accident. With everything else she had to deal with, Lord knows what my mom was thinking, but it helped, as much as anything can help two kids who lose their father in high school. Little Sizzle, gazing at the gangly, sad-eyed girl that was me, and giving my cheek a sandpapery lick. The memory attacks me without warning, and my eyes fill up. I take a breath to steady myself. I really don't need to break down right now, over a moo shoo pancake.

"Zoe?" he asks, his eyes the color of denim in the shadow of the restaurant lighting. "You okay?"

I nod but don't speak. A yes might morph into a sob. I backhand my tears, but more are coming. I blow into the scratchy cloth napkin.

"It's okay, Zoe," he says quietly. Like a friend, not a psychiatrist. "It's about your mom?"

I nod again.

He doesn't say anything for a second, then clears this throat. "I know." He looks down at the table. "When my mom passed, it was…"—he pauses, resting both elbows on the table—"really hard. That's all I can say. I think she was the only one who ever really understood me." He shifts his hand to my arm. The touch is solid, warm.

"Thanks," I say.

We eat the rest of the meal in a semi-comfortable silence, until we finish our last little cups of tea and he glances at his watch. He sighs, almost ruefully. "It's about that time."

As we leave the restaurant, we are plunged straight into a wall of cold wind. The kind of wind that makes you gulp for breath and bury your face into your coat. Dr. Berringer reaches for his phone and has to scream above the howling wind.

"Yeah?" It comes out muffled. A napkin leaps up from the parking lot, twirls around and falls, and then gets swept up again. As we climb up into his black Jeep, I have to yank the door against the wind to shut it. Once in the car, we both sit a minute, assembling ourselves in the sudden silence. The car doors rattle.

"Wow," I say.

"Fifty-mile-an-hour winds, the news said." He pulls the car into reverse. "The case is back on. Dr. Munroe finally got in. It's up to you if you want to stay or not. I know it's getting late."

"Oh, no, I'll stay," I answer, though I feel bad for Arthur, who has probably eaten through the crate by now. I'll call Scotty to let him out. My phone quacks, and I don't recognize the number, so I answer.

"Hello, is this Zoe?"

"Yes?"

"Hi, this is Andy."

I pause, trying to place the voice. Andy?

"Andy, from the lab," he says, miffed that I possibly didn't remember him. It comes back to me now. Tattoo sleeve. "Proud Mary." "Oh, right!" I aim for medical student contrite. "Sorry, it's been a crazy day."

"Listen, I got that blood tox that you brought to me."

"Oh, really? I thought they said that was lost."

"You just didn't speak to the right person," he says with braggadocio. "You got a pen?"

"Sure," I lie.

"Okay, here goes. Negative for benzos. Negative for THC. Negative for alcohol. Opioids negative."

Jesus, he's going to go through the whole laundry list.

"Negative for cocaine—"

"Wait, sorry, I'm just in a little bit of a hurry." I make a "jabber jabber" motion with my hand, and Dr. Berringer grins. "Was it positive for anything?"

"Do you want me to fax it up to you?"

"No, that's okay. If you could just tell me, that would be great."

"Okay, one second." I hear pages flipping. "Here it is. Positive for meperidine."

Meperidine, also known as Demerol. "Wait, I thought you said opioids was negative."

"Actually," he boasts, "it *did* come up negative for opioids, but I ran a different assay that's more sensitive for the ol' demmies. And sure enough, it came up positive."

"Positive," I confirm.

"You got it."

I tap my fingers against my lips. "I don't get it, though. I just did a urine tox, which was negative."

"When was that?"

"Day before yesterday."

"Yeah, maybe it was out of her system by then. Also urine's not as sensitive."

"So you're absolutely sure it's positive."

"On my mother's grave," he says. "Naughty, naughty Candy, right?" He laughs.

I laugh back, but it comes out a nervous bark. "Thanks. Could you fax it to the floor, too?"

"Will do. Good luck out there, chickadee," he says, and the phone clicks off.

"Anything important?" Dr. Berringer asks.

"No," I lie, my head spinning. I can't exactly explain that I'd run a secret blood tox on Candy to prove a priest imposter was poisoning her when Dr. Berringer had already sicced the Chair on me for suggesting it.

So we ride off to the hospital in the silence of the warm car while I try to determine my next move.

What I come up with is this: I have no next move. All I know is somehow I have to stop this freight train, without being either fired or thrown off the case.

Candy is in the room when we get there, and Dr. Munroe is setting up, laying out swaths of gauze, various sizes of IV needles, rectangles of tape, a large syringe with white liquid that looks like glue. Propofol. The good stuff. His setup is the workbench of a mad but very organized scientist.

"I am sorry to be late," Dr. Munroe says formally. He looks up at us briefly, then back down to continue his arrangement. The bald top of his head shines in the light, the rest of his hair tight corkscrews on a monk's pate.

"Not a problem," Dr. Berringer returns, leaning back with his hands in his pockets, as loose and cheerful as Dr. Munroe is boxed and tight.

"It will probably be"—he looks up at the clock—"eight more minutes here."

"That's fine." Dr. Berringer and Nancy trade smiles. Not seven or nine minutes, but eight.

My stomach is twisting. The words are on my lips to tell him about the Demerol, when I get a better idea. The fact is, it has to come from someone else, not me. Somehow (by no fault of mine, I might add), I've shot all my credibility on this one. But I know he'll listen to Detective Adams. He has to.

"Sorry, I've just got to…" I motion to the hallway in a way that's meant to suggest the bathroom.

"Oh, yeah. Sure, sure," Dr. Berringer says.

I run to the nurses' station and call the detective. It rings six times and then goes to voice mail, which is odd. He always answers his phone.

"The Demerol came back positive. They ran a different sample. Listen, Donner's been giving it to her, I know it." I breathe in deep, collecting my thoughts. "I need you to call Dr. Berringer to stop the ECT. He won't listen to me right now; it's kind of hard to explain… so just please, please, please call me back as soon as you get this. Or better yet, call Dr. Berringer and order him to stop it. Okay? Just tell him he's got to and that's it. Okay? I'll try to stall him as long as I can. Thanks."

I'm hanging up when I see Nancy striding down the hall. "We're just about ready to go in there. Dr. B wanted me to let you know."

"Sorry. I just had to check one thing. I'll be right down."

"I'll let him know," she says, her tone a warning that I should hurry the hell up if I know what's good for me, then hurries back down the hall.

303

A phone rings then, "The Saints Go Marching In" ring-tone. Glancing around, I see a phone lighting up the pocket of Dr. Berringer's lab coat hanging on the rack. He must have left it in there. I pull it out, hoping it's Detective Adams, but it's not. It's a long-distance number I don't recognize, which has gone to voice mail. Then a text pops up on the screen.

Is it done?

The name on the text is Raymond Donner.

My scalp goes hot, like it's been seared. I touch the num-ber on the screen, my hand trembling against my ear.

"Yeah, it's Donner. What's the status?"

I don't answer, holding my breath.

A frustrated sigh comes out over the other end. "We went over this, Berringer. Either kill the girl or do that brain-fry thing you talked about. I don't care either way. But it needs to get done."

My heart drops a beat, and I tear down the hall, skidding down the tile floor, and whip open the door to the procedure room, smacking the knob against the wall. Everyone turns to look at me as Dr. Berringer adjusts the dial on the machine.

"Did you start yet?" I ask, breathless.

"No, as a matter of fact," Dr. Berringer says, annoyed at me for showing up late. "We're just about to. Come on over."

"Don't," I say as strongly as I can. "Don't do it. Please."

Dr. Munroe takes his hand off the IV. Silence steals over the room, except for the bleating of the heart monitor. "What did you say?" Dr. Berringer asks.

"I know everything, Dr. Berringer. I know you're involved with Raymond Donner. I know you don't want to kill her, and maybe this is the best you could come up with, but please don't. Don't do it."

His face goes ghost white; his shoulders tremble.

"What's she talking about, Tad?" Dr. Munroe asks.

"Nothing," he answers curtly. He puts his hand on the dial again but doesn't move it, just clings to it like a lifeline.

"I know you're trying to do the right thing. But they found her sister. Dr. Berringer, they found Janita," I say, hoping my lie sounds convincing. "It's over now. Don't do this. Don't do this to Candy."

Dr. Munroe clears his throat. "I'm not comfortable with this, Tad. I need some answers, or I'm afraid I'm going to have to reverse the anesthesia. I won't be party to something unethical."

"It's not," he barks out, "unethical. Jesus Christ." But his voice loses steam. He takes his hand off the dial and stares right at me. Nancy watches us both. "It's not what you think. I never wanted to—"

"I know." I take a step toward him.

Dr. Munroe is fumbling with another syringe. "I'm reversing," he announces.

"I never meant…" Dr. Berringer says, his voice strained. The wind roars out against the window like a train. "I loved her."

"I know," I say again, but he is walking away from the dial, away from the bed.

"I have to…" he mumbles, looking around the room in a daze. "I…I have to—" he repeats, then runs out of the room.

"Nancy, can you take her back to the room? Once Dr.

Munroe is finished here?" I ask, at once feeling like the attending I will be in six months' time. "And call security. See if they can stop him from leaving."

"On it," she says, heading into the hallway.

I step out into the subdued light of the psych ward and call Detective Adams. Again, it goes to voice mail. The operator's strident voice is calling security overhead. I get inside the elevator and stand there. The elevator feels unnaturally still, waiting for me to push the button, to make my decision. And for some reason, I don't push the smudged button to the lobby.

I push the button to the twelfth floor instead.

"I knew you'd come," he says.

Dr. Berringer is collapsed in the pink chair. I sit down beside him. He doesn't say anything for the longest time. We just sit side by side, watching the window like we're watching waves at the beach. The wind is wreaking havoc on the little world below us. Buffeted trees, overturned garbage cans, traffic signs jerking. A utility truck pulses a yellow light up to the sky as it tends to a downed power line.

"Zoe." His voice is hoarse, a plea.

I don't answer.

"I know I don't deserve it, but I need to explain something to you."

I still don't answer.

He sighs and shifts in the chair. "I was raped, when I was thirteen." Pausing, he scratches under his neck, his expression invisible in the dark. "Family friend. We were all on a camping trip, and we were off looking for wood." His voice is flat, without emotion, retelling someone else's tale. "I could have handled him now, but at that age, I was skin and bones, and..." He takes a deep, pained breath. "You know how these things go. I don't have to spell it out."

I nod.

"After that, I just wasn't the same. I don't know how else to explain it. There was the before me and the after me." His hands are gripping the wood arms of the chair. "For a while, I was just angry. At everyone, for not guessing what happened. At the asshole who did it and still had a round with my dad at the bar." He looks down at his hands, like he's looking for something, a drink maybe. "I got over it in time, as much as you get over these things. Drank too much, of course. You know all about that." He lets out a harsh laugh.

I want to mirror him and offer him a laugh back, but I can't bring myself to do it.

"It changed me, Zoe. I wish I could go back and make it never happen, but I can't do that. And I can't change who it made me."

I pause. "A pedophile?" There is an edge to my voice.

"Sounds like an excuse?"

"Yeah, a bit."

He tattoos a rhythm with his fingers on his thigh. "Maybe it is. Maybe so... but then again, I don't know. I can't help it."

307

I turn to look at him. "So you're saying being raped made you want to rape these girls?"

"No, no!" he breaks in, focusing his gaze on me. "I'm not saying that at all. I've only been with her, Zoe. With Candy. I know it sounds crazy, but I love her. I want to marry her."

Goose bumps crawl on my arms. "But she's a child."

He scratches the edge of one blond sideburn, sprinkled with gray. "Not really. You never really knew her."

"It's rape, plain and simple."

"No, Zoe," he insists. "I'm gentle with her. I would never hurt her. Never, never, never. Not in a million years. That's what I'm trying to explain to you. I'm good to her. Not like some asshole out there would be."

I stare at him in dismay.

"Someone who'd take her into the woods, hold her down in some dirty ferns until she can't even breathe. I would never do that to her. Never."

"It's rape." I say it softly. "You may not be brutal or vicious about it maybe. But these are young girls."

He stares out the window.

"And maybe you were only with Candy, but she's not the only one caught up in this. What about Janita? What about Eliza Sapierski? And the others? Young girls, Dr. Berringer."

"Tad," he corrects me.

"They don't want to have sex with you."

"No, you don't see it, Zoe. We relax them first. I make sure of that."

My stomach sinks. "You mean you drug them?"

A long silence follows before he answers. "Nobody hurts them, Zoe."

I can't hear another word. My ears can't take it. My brain can't take it. My heart can't take it. "I can't—"

"I know," he interrupts me, his face glum, guilty. "My wife didn't understand it either. No one understands. I don't expect them to."

We sit another minute, the wind whipping against the window. The utility truck crawls away. He stands and stretches his arms up high, like he just finished a long nap. He walks over toward the window, steps as graceful and measured as a cat, and leans his palm against the glass. Peering down at the wind-strewn chaos of the hospital grounds, he reaches down for something. Only when the window is lifted with the wind barreling through, the sudden noise like a plane taking off, do I realize he's opened it. I leap to my feet as he sticks his head into the howling wind, dipping down like he's trying to get a better view, before he turns back to me.

"I'm sorry, Zoe," he says. "There is a crack in everything." And then he jumps.

I try to stop him. I do. I lean out the window and grab some fabric—a shirt maybe or his khakis—that slips through my fingers, and he falls. It doesn't take long for a body to fall. Gravity is quick. There is a ghastly thud, some yelling outside, and then silence.

I never understood that cliché, deafening silence. Now I do. I stand there, awash in it, with no idea of what to do next, when my phone rings.

"Zoe, we found her!"

"Who?" I say. My voice echoes in my ears. Who, who, who, who? The word goes on forever. Maybe this is what it's like to lose your mind.

"Janita! We got a hit off Donner's phone, and we got him, Zoe. He wasn't in New York City after all. Though it appears that was his next stop. He was in Niagara Falls, and we nailed him. And more importantly, we got Janita." His voice is humming with victory.

"How…how is she?"

"She's fine. Shaken up, but fine, all things considered. Are you okay? You sound kind of funny."

"Yeah." I look out the window again. Police cars are racing down the street toward the hospital.

"Hey, I got your message. And I need to warn you, Zoe. Dr. Berringer may be involved in this. That's who Donner was calling. I don't know all the facts yet, but you need to be very, very careful here. I'll get the ECT stopped, but don't say anything. Just stay away from him."

"Um, well…" I pace around the room. "He actually just jumped out the window."

The phone goes silent for a second. "Excuse me?"

Two hours later, we're in the family therapy room with its dusty blinds and metal-framed baby animal posters. The twelfth floor is a crime scene now, so the therapy room has become an ersatz incident room.

"I still don't get what you were doing there," Detective Adams says.

I rub my skin, which feels weird, rubbery. The feeling I have right before the flu. "I just knew he'd be there."

"And isn't it possible," the other detective asks (Detective Gonzalez, she said her name was; I can't figure out if Detective Adams is her boss or vice versa), "that you got so upset about the news that you pushed him out the window?" She leans in toward me, her lanyard banging against the desk. Hot-pink lace from her bra peeks through her button-down when she leans back. "I mean, I know that's what I would have done. Is it possible that's what happened?" Detective Gonzalez appears to be playing bad cop, a role more suited for Detective Adams. But I know he's a good cop, so that wouldn't work. Or maybe I've just seen too many cop shows.

"No, it isn't possible." I think for a second. "I guess it's possible, but I'd have to somehow lure him over to an open window, then overpower him and throw him out. He's pretty tall, actually. Taller than me."

"You could have used the element of surprise."

I shrug. I think even she realizes this sounds improbable. "Maybe, but I didn't. He jumped. I tried to stop him. I couldn't." I'd already been through this with them ten times. I already mimed exactly how he did it. I don't have it in me to do it again.

"How long did you know about the O-club?"

"The O-club? I don't know. Dr. Berringer mentioned it a couple months ago."

"He did?" Detective Adams breaks in with obvious shock.

"Yeah. That's what he called Alcoholics Anonymous. For Omar, Oscar, and Ozzie."

Detective Gonzalez looks at me like I'm loony tunes. "The O-club?"

"Yeah. That's all he said. It was like his pet name for AA. I didn't ask him much about it, figuring it's anonymous and all."

They both stare at me a second.

"What?" I ask to their stares.

"The O-club is what they called their group, Zoe," Detective Adams says gently. "The pedophilia ring."

My mouth falls open.

"And you didn't know about any of it? About his relationship to the girls? To Donner?" When Detective Gonzalez leans over again, a strong scent of perfume wafts up. "Because I would understand if you did. If you knew about it, but you wanted to protect him. He is your boss after all."

"No. I didn't know anything about it. Not until I saw the text. I only knew what Detective Adams knew—"

"Were you in a relationship with Dr. Berringer?" she breaks in.

I pause. "I guess. He was my attending."

"Yes, I know. But anything more than that?" She gives me a knowing smile. "I heard he was all kinds of handsome."

"Yeah, and he was also all kinds of married. At least for a while. And he was all kinds of my boss. So no, we weren't…"—I struggle for the word—"intimate."

"So if we look through his diary, we're not going to find out that you two were more than that?" she asks.

312

Detective Adams shuffles through some paperwork.

"I don't know what the hell you'll find if you look through his diary," I answer. "But in any case, I wasn't sleeping with him."

She moves in uncomfortably toward me, encroaching on my space. I have to think this is straight out of the detective's handbook. "The nurses said you two were rather close."

I shrug. "We were friends, sort of. But close, I don't know about that. There's close and there's close." Suddenly a thought strikes, and I turn to Detective Adams. "Why the O-club? Like the *Story of O?*"

"What's that?" he asks.

"It's erotica. Well, sort of. More like S and M and misogyny dressed up as erotica. You could Google it, probably. But don't do it at work."

"You seem to know a lot about this," Detective Gonzalez observes.

"Not really. I took a feminist course in college. Sort of an easy course, actually, but I was taking Chem at the time, which was kicking my ass, so..." I trail off, and Detective Adams looks down at the floor and rubs his knee. Obviously I'm getting off topic here, but any trace of Adderall is long gone from my bloodstream at this point.

"Dr. Goldman, I'm wondering about something else. The phone call from Donner. The phone just *happened* to be in Dr. Berringer's lab coat for you to discover? Seems very coincidental, doesn't it?"

"I would say lucky more than coincidental."

Detective Gonzalez leans back and cracks her knuckles

with great verve, a move that looks practiced, the brash confidence of which is offset by her pink bra peeking through again. "Let's talk about something else."

"Okay."

"The Demerol."

"Right."

"You seem pretty well versed in how that would work. The Demerol making her sick."

"Yeah?"

"How do we know, for instance, that it wasn't you that gave her the Demerol? You had the access. You had the knowledge of—"

"That's it!" I yell out.

Both seasoned detectives jump. "What?" Detective Adams asks.

"The scar. It's not a zero; it's an O."

Detective Adams scrunches his eyes half closed, the way he does when he's thinking. "For the O-club?"

"Yes. They branded them in the story, too." I run my hands through my hair, dry and limp at this point. "He fucking branded them." My hands are trembling. There is silence in the room then, an ugly, angry silence.

"Dr. Goldman," she says, "we were talking about the Demerol."

"I didn't give her Demerol," I say, losing patience. "I mean, why would I give her Demerol, then go tell everybody I thought someone was giving her Demerol, which almost got me fired by the way, then get a lab to prove it? Two labs, actually."

She pauses here and rests her elbow on the table too close to mine. A white piece of thread makes an S on her sleeve. It takes all my will not to pick it off.

"Sometimes it's hard to understand why we do the things we do."

"Yeah, but that's sort of my job description," I grumble. I'm not generally so grouchy, but I'm hungry and this woman is just plain being ridiculous in her pink lace bra. I have no idea what she's driving at, and I suspect she doesn't either. I yawn. I feel like someone unplugged me and I'm losing charge fast. "Could we maybe talk more tomorrow? I'm really tired."

"Yeah," Detective Adams breaks in. "I think we're done here, Angela. Dr. Goldman would have had to be one hell of an actor or just a goddamned idiot to have masterminded this whole thing, all the while keeping me informed with regular updates." Detective Gonzalez shoots him a look. Bad cop turns into pissed-off cop. "And I mean annoyingly regular updates," he adds.

I sneak him a smile.

Detective Gonzalez stands up, visibly irritated. "I'm just doing my job, Frank."

"I know, I know." His voice is appeasing.

"Hey," I say, standing up, too, as the debriefing appears to be over. "Can I see her real quick before I go?"

He glances at Detective Gonzalez, who shrugs her approval.

"Sure," he says. "I'll come with you."

We walk down the hall to her room. It's just past midnight, and it feels like my legs are a hundred pounds each. Detective Adams knocks, and the policeman guarding the room looks up from his reading, a three-month-old *People* magazine, covered with reality stars that have been married and divorced by now.

"How's she doing?" Detective Adams whispers.

"All good here," he whispers back. "The girl really wanted to sleep with her sister. So I figured it was okay. We probably won't get much out of her right now anyway."

"Yeah, that's okay," Detective Adams agrees.

The dim, tawny-yellow light suffuses the bed, Candy stiff on her back, eyes fluttering, and Janita asleep and clinging to her sister with one leg thrown over her in protection, the O-shaped scar just visible on her ankle.

And for the first time in the case, I think things might just turn out all right.

Chapter Thirty-Four

I know he was your patient." I didn't plan to say it, but the words just come out. Two weeks later and I'm sitting on Sam's couch.

He takes off his glasses (new, modern, square, black ones; I like them, but I miss the old tortoiseshells). "I can't talk about that. You understand that."

I nod. "Yes. I do."

He slides his glasses back on. "And if I were his doctor, confidentiality stands, even after death."

I build a tower out of the magnet bits on the shiny black block, pinching it up high until it shrivels over. A new toy. The Zen sandbox has been stashed away somewhere. "Did you know about it, though? What he was doing?"

He lets out a sigh. "Listen, Zoe, I can't talk about Dr. Berringer. Just as I wouldn't reveal any details about you to someone who asked." He smooths his goatee. "But I will tell you this. I have a responsibility for the well-being of others.

So if my patient revealed his intention to hurt someone—his wife, for instance, or children—I would have to tell someone. I would be *obligated* to tell the authorities." Putting his palms together, he stares right at me. "Do you understand what I'm saying?"

"Yes," I say. "I think I do." Lightness fills my chest then, a surge of relief. I didn't realize how much the question had been weighing on me. "You know, I need to tell you something."

"Okay." He leans back from his desk, opening his posture.

"I liked him."

He spins his fake Montblanc on his yellow notepad. "Dr. Berringer?"

"Yes."

"I'm not surprised. He's a likable guy."

"No, I mean *like*, like. Not that I would have ever told him. I barely even admitted it to myself."

"And that makes you feel...?" he asks, letting me provide the word.

"Guilty."

He nods.

"Stupid, bad judge of character, shallow—you pick the adjective. That's how it makes me feel."

He shrugs. "People like that can be very charming."

"Charming...as in narcissistic?" We both know the psychiatric code word for *charming*.

"Maybe. Mind you, I'm not saying anything about *this* patient," he reminds me. "But people like this can be very attractive. They're the favorite priest, the coolest football coach."

The one who scores all tens on his evaluations, I think. Who has the nurses wrapped around his pinkie. Who makes all the mothers swoon.

"It's the person no one suspects," he goes on. "They leave a lot of damage in their wake. A lot of guilt for a lot of people who think, 'How didn't I know?'" He taps his pen on the pad. "But how could you know?"

"I should have known."

"It's a tragedy, Zoe. But it's still his fault. You can't take any blame for not figuring it out sooner. Nobody did."

"Yeah, but—"

"And," he continues, uncharacteristically interrupting me, "you saved that girl's life. You told me how high he had the ECT jacked up. Who knows what would have happened?" His voice is furious. "And just so you know, ECT can be a very helpful tool for the right patients, in the right hands. I've seen it save lives. But he misused it. That's all there is to it."

"And you know," I say, getting angry myself, "she wasn't even catatonic. I was right. As soon as the new attending came on, he checked her CPKs, and they were sky-high. It was serotonin syndrome and a neuroleptic malignant syndrome wrapped into one. And her kidneys were starting to fail."

He shakes his head. "How is she now?"

"Better. Much better. We got her off all her meds except benzos as needed." I grin then. "I think the best therapy has really been her sister."

"Janita?"

"She's been practically living there," I say, scrunching up more magnet pieces. "You know, I'm wondering, in your professional psychiatric opinion..."

"Yes?" he replies with some amusement.

"Why did she pick Daneesha to turn into? How does that make any sense?"

He pauses, thinking about it. "It does make sense in a way. It brought her younger sister back. And maybe, in her confused mind, that allowed her to bring back Janita."

"Maybe."

"And it protected her. Who knows what Daneesha would have been like as a thirteen-year-old. But Candy envisioned her as strong, powerful, ready to stand her ground. And that's what she needed. Protection. She couldn't do it herself, so she got someone to help her."

I nod, thinking it through. "That's not half bad." I play with more shredded magnets. "You should do this for a living."

He laughs. "And how are you doing with all this?"

I search for an honest answer. "I'm not sure."

Someone pulls into the parking lot, and I realize for a second that I was looking for Dr. Berringer's black Jeep, worried he might see me here. But he won't be coming here anymore. The psychiatrist who swan-dived will be a tall tale in Buffalo for years to come. A warning maybe. Or just a punchline.

After checking out, I get into my car, when the phone rings.

"Hey, it's me," Mike says, "just checking in." Mike flew back right after Thanksgiving when he heard what happened. He and Scotty have been "checking in" a lot.

"How's work?" I ask.

"Crazy. Tons of dumps."

Dumps, meaning families are dumping their decrepit or Alzheimer-addled loved ones just in time for the holidays. Sad, but a reality of ER life. "Any word on the job front?" I ask.

"Yeah, I was going to tell you later." A doctor's name is paged on the overhead. "Got an offer from North Carolina. The urgent-care one."

"Hmm."

"Haven't said yes or no yet."

"Uh-huh."

"It pays more than Buffalo, though."

My heart falls an inch. "I see."

"How about you? Fellowship thoughts?"

I sigh, turning on the engine. "I'm not much further than yesterday, actually. Not pediatrics—too depressing. Not geriatrics—too depressing. Not addiction—"

"Let me guess," he interrupts. "Too depressing."

I put the Styrofoam cup down on the wood-paneled desk. My lipstick has left a half-moon on the rim. It's my third cup today.

"It's dead around here," I observe.

"Yeah. Saturday." Then Detective Adams harrumphs. "Did I mention I wanted to retire?"

"Once or twice."

He flips through some more sheets in the case file, and I sign innumerable papers. "You sure do kill a lot of trees around here."

"Don't I know it." He slides over another form for me to sign. "How was your Thanksgiving, by the way?"

"Oh, fine." And it wasn't bad, all things considered. Other than I missed Mike. And Arthur spent the entire time hiding under the table with a turkey leg he somehow pawed off the island (Scotty giving me a look like, "Why'd you bring your dog to my house?" and me giving him a look like, "He was supposed to be your dog in the first place"). Kristy turned out to be a welcome change from his usual type. She has both breasts and brains. She was actually advising him on investing his Treasury bond, and he was listening. "How about you?"

"Good. Lots of family, huge dinner, beckoning me faster to the inevitable heart attack." He searches through some more of the file, and I drop the pen on the table, where it rolls halfway to the other side.

"So do you know what's going to happen with them?" I ask.

"Who, the girls?"

"Yeah." I stamp my foot, which has gone numb from sitting on this uncomfortable metal chair so long.

"Not sure. It really has to do with international issues at this point. But I think they'll get back to Toronto eventually."

"Hopefully we can get them back with Heaven. It's what they want."

He shrugs. "Who knows? That's up to Social Services at this point. Not really my jurisdiction."

"Not mine either," I say. Once they're discharged, they're gone. I usually never see them again. Except for Tiffany, who I saw over and over until I didn't see her anymore.

"Listen. I'm a happy man. Didn't you hear?" His smile is hearty. "We shut down an international pedophile ring. Toronto to New York City. Closed for business, folks."

I smile at his justified jubilation, signing another paper. "Did you find out any more about the Demerol?"

He pushes smudged silver reading glasses back onto his nose. "Yeah, we tracked it down to a nurse. Department of Health took over the case."

"Did you get to interview her at least?"

"She lawyered up pretty quick," he says. "But it looks like Dr. Berringer was paying her to get it for him, and she assumed it was for him. She didn't know he was giving it to Candy."

I made sure they were comfortable.

Snow starts to fall outside the window. Tentative, thirty-degree flakes that could just as easily go back to rain. "Snain," as my dad used to call it. The detective skims through the bulky green folder one last time, then pats it with his paw of a hand. "I think that's it. We're finally done with all the signing."

"So I'm free to go?"

He laughs. "It's not like you were arrested." Standing up, he grabs his gray-black heather tweed hat, a hat I would picture a policeman wearing. We walk out of the deserted building. The afternoon is cold. Christmas lights hang over the ledge of the Irish bar across the street, snow reflecting the blocks of colors.

"Where did you park?"

"Just down the street," I say, motioning up ahead.

We walk in silence for a bit, the soft snow falling around us. "Did you have any idea?" I ask.

"About what?"

"Dr. Berringer?"

Detective Adams shakes his head without hesitation. "Not a clue."

"Nothing from New Orleans then?"

"We looked into that, but no. All we knew about was his drinking." Thick snowflakes stick to his gray wool coat. "But he was all over the O-club files. He was with quite a few of these girls. A good customer, I guess."

So he lied about that, too.

"There's e-mails between him and Donner that date back to Tulane. Buffalo's probably been on his radar for quite a while."

Which is perhaps what enticed the wunderkind to Children's Hospital in the first place. We keep walking, the sound of our footsteps swallowed up by the snow. "You know, I don't think he actually wanted to kill Candy. He wanted her to forget him. And he wanted to get away with it. But in his heart of hearts, he didn't want to kill her."

We get to my car. The sky above us is eggshell white. "You know, Zoe, I've stopped trying to figure out what goes on in the hearts of criminals."

As he says this, it strikes me. He put it perfectly, exactly what I *do* want to do: Figure out what goes on in the hearts of criminals. Not child psych, not addiction.

Forensic psychiatry, of course. Now I've just got to tell Mike.

When my phone quacks me awake, I have no idea where I am.

I am of course in bed, where I should be at three a.m. I pat the space next to my bed and remember Mike's on call tonight. Arthur sniffles, then falls back to sleep.

I don't recognize the caller ID. "Hello. This is Dr. Goldman."

"Zoe?" The voice has a foreign quality to it. French. It takes a few more seconds to attach a name to the disembodied voice.

"Jean Luc?" I start to sit up.

"It is so good to hear you," he says, which sounds heartfelt. His words are slurred and hoarse, and there's banging music behind him.

"Are you okay?"

"Oh," he says, like he just realized it might be odd to be calling someone in the middle of the night. "Yeah, I'm okay."

"Where are you?" I ask.

"DC."

"Not Paris?"

"No, wait a second," he yells above the noise. I hear footsteps, a door creak closed, and then the music falls to a soft throb. "That is better."

"Yes, I can hear you at least." I glance at the clock, realizing I have to be up in three hours to see patients. Dr. Grant likes to round early. "Are you in a bar?" This would be very un–Jean Luc. Jean Luc doesn't like bars. (*Very loud and drunk people, how is this pleasant?* he asked me once.)

"Yes, well," he explains, "it's my bachelor party."

"Really? I thought your wedding wasn't until April."

"This was the only weekend it would work in DC."

"Oh," I say again. Arthur knocks his tail against my knee, woofing in a dream.

"Zoe, I think I made a terrible mistake." There is a pause as the song changes in the bar. He sighs into the phone, a long theatrical sigh. Again, very un–Jean Luc, which means he must be pretty drunk. "A terrible mistake."

"What do you mean?" I ask. Though I know I shouldn't ask. I should cut him off right here and now. But the bait is dangling before me, plump and shiny, and it's so damn hard not to bite.

"With Melanie," he explains.

"Right."

We both pause here, treading into dangerous territory. My heart is thumping in my pajama top.

"Sometimes she is so difficult, so demanding. Not like you. Things were so easy with you."

Too easy, I think. But I don't say anything.

"I think I've made a terrible, terrible mistake." He sounds like he's about to cry.

"You know, Jean Luc, things didn't go so well with us either, if you remember."

There is silence on his end, waiting. He doesn't agree, but he doesn't argue either.

"You missed Melanie, remember? When you came to visit? You got sick of me after, like, four hours."

I laugh, though I don't feel like laughing, and he laughs, though it sounds like he could also be crying. "I was an idiot."

I lie there a minute, warm in my bed, a glow floating in me. He *does* want me. He does want me after all. And maybe this is what I've been waiting for all this time. My reward pellet. "It's natural to be nervous, Jean Luc. This is a big life change. But it doesn't mean you don't love Melanie." Though I myself don't know how anyone could love that ghastly creature.

"Maybe," he says, like maybe not. But then again, Jean Luc was never of a strong backbone. My halfhearted speech could be all it takes to convince him.

"Take some time. Think about it. Don't rush into a decision either way. You know what they say about fools rushing in where angels fear to tread."

He pauses, and a rubbing noise muffles the phone. "I don't understand. What is this about the angels?"

"Never mind, it's a saying." I suppress a yawn, not well.

"I should let you go. Do you have...the hospital in the morning?"

The hospital. My job was always faintly mysterious—and perhaps a bit distasteful, truth be told—to Jean Luc. "Yes, I do."

"Well, okay." He pauses, not quite ready to let go of the phone. "Zoe." He swallows. "*Je t'aime*."

And before I know it, I answer "*Je t'aime*" back.

We hang up then, and I lie for a while, listening to the creaks, the lone cars passing, the noises of the night. I start crying, though I couldn't say why, warm tears soaking into my pillow. Maybe because it's been a tough month. Maybe because it's been a tough year. Maybe because it's three a.m., I have to round in three hours, and I don't even love him anymore, in French or English. And the only person I really want to talk to right now is Mike, and he'll probably end up in North Carolina.

The bed shakes as Arthur shifts his body, and suddenly I find a warm tongue licking my face. I pet his goofy, puffy, labradoodle permed head and fall back to sleep.

Chapter Thirty-Five

I n the light of day, it seems ridiculous to us both. I know this as I drive half awake into the hospital in the rose gray of the morning and get his text.

sry abt last nite. All good w melanie now

I allow myself a bitter laugh. glad 2 hear

do u mind not telling anyone abt our talk?

I turn the radio on and write mum = word. Let him puzzle over that one.

still hope u will come to wedding

I don't bother to text back. *Hope you'll come to my wedding?* Ha fucking ha. Not until there's a life-form on Saturn. Stepping onto the hospital floor with the familiar beeps and overhead pages, I feel better already. Exhausted and in need of a nap, but better. Jean Luc impairs my judgment, like a too-strong cosmo. And now that he's safely in the arms of maleficent Melanie, I can stop pulling that damn lever. *C'est fini*, and I mean it this time.

I stop by Chloe's room first, since she needs her discharge orders today. "You all set?" I ask her.

"Damn straight." She scoops her bright red bangs out of her eyes.

"Great." I scan through her meds. "No change in anything then. You're staying on the Luvox, a hundred twice daily. Sound right?"

"Whatever. Write me the pills, and I'll take them. I just want to get the hell out of here."

"Okay. I'll still have to see you once more with my attending, but then you'll be good to go."

Her eyebrows lower, darkening her face. "Which attending?"

"Dr. Grant? You've met him a few times now."

Her face relaxes. "Oh yeah, right. Geeky little dude."

"Right," I affirm. This is the most succinct description of the man I have ever heard. I tap my pen on the chart. "You never did like Dr. Berringer, did you?"

She shakes her head, picking at her nails, which are chewed to nubs.

"Was there a reason for that?"

She shrugs. "I'm not shedding any tears over his leap from a tall building, I'll tell you that much." She examines another nail. "And I don't care if it makes me sound like a bitch."

I nod. "It doesn't, really. But what makes you say that about him?" I ask, trying to sound nonjudgmental.

"Nothing," she mutters, chewing on her fingers again. "Just...nothing."

I have a bad feeling, a sick-gut feeling. I wait a long

minute until she's looking up at me again. "You can tell me, you know. You're safe now. You can tell me anything."

She bites her lower lip, which is trembling.

"Did he hurt you, Chloe? Is that what you were trying to tell me before? That no one believed you?"

Chloe looks down at the bedsheets and straightens out a wrinkle.

"He hurt some other girls, Chloe. If he hurt you, too, if he made you do something you didn't want to do…you can tell me about it, you know. I can help you."

But she keeps looking down at the sheets and doesn't answer.

Candy is herself again.

Herself being someone between the old Candy and Daneesha. Janita is in foster care for now, spending her time between therapists, tutors, and visiting her sister. A cobbled-together life that approaches normal. A semblance of normal, which will have to do for now. Candy is back to beaming smiles, drawing purple pictures as well as complaining about the food, and rolling her eyes at me. Acting more like a teenager, I guess. A normal teenager. Or an almost-normal teenager. Better than the girl I've seen recently anyway, swimming in serotonin and dopamine, her brain deep-fried and making no connections to the world around her.

Dr. Grant follows her every blood lab like a hound.

"Sodium today?" he asks, more of a command than a question.

"One forty," I answer, not even glancing at my sheet. The man's been so annoying about her labs that I've been memorizing them unintentionally.

"Glucose?"

"Eighty-three. Normal."

"CPK?"

"Trending down still. One seventeen today."

"Okay," he nods, satisfied. "Oh, wait. Tox screen."

"Still pending," I say. "But it was normal yesterday." He's been getting them every day. He's more paranoid than I am, though not enough to merit a diagnosis yet.

"Let's see her then," he says, shoving her chart in my hands and taking off down the hallway for me to run and catch up. He greets the sisters in his usual manner. Stiff, but not unfriendly. He doesn't have the Dr. Berringer "charm," as Sam called it, which is obviously a good thing. "Candy, Janita." He nods to each of them. "And how are we today?"

They give each other a private grin. "Good," says Candy, and Janita follows with a "good," too.

"Excellent," he returns.

"Hey, that Tina lady said I'm gonna be out of here soon. Maybe next week?" Candy asks.

"Did she?" he says, noncommittal.

"You think that's so?" she asks, pushing him.

"I hope so," he says, which is as good as she'll get. "As long as your labs remain stable and you've got a stable place to go." "Stable" is one of Dr. Grant's favorite words.

"I'm going to live with Janita," Candy announces.

"Uh-huh, that's right," Janita agrees, going for the double-team. "Mrs. J's got a nice place set up with a bunk bed. So Candy can sleep on top. And that'll help with the night-mares, too."

"The Tina lady said so," Candy backs her up.

They look at us like they're talking to their parents, trying to convince them to get a puppy. *I'll walk her and feed her every day. I promise!*

"How have your stools been?"

They glance at each other.

"Bowel movements?" I say, in translation.

"Oh. They fine." Candy's face turns crimson. "No prob-lem there."

"And your physical therapy? How is that going?" he asks.

"With Jeremy? That's okay."

"Yeah. Jeremy. He's fine, too," Janita jokes, and they give each other a rapid, complex handshake that they were trying to teach me the other day.

"Muscle aches?" he asks.

She rubs her arms, involuntarily remembering them. "Better."

"Okay." He approaches her and runs through the exam. Muscle tone, listens to her heart and lungs. She sits up at attention and relents, like a good patient, eye-rolling and grinning to her sister all the way. Dr. Grant backs up from the bed. "You check out nicely today. I don't see a reason you can't go home very soon."

This gets a bright smile from them both. "And she can

stay with me, right?" Janita says, her voice more entreating than challenging now. "You tell that discharge lady? We can use the same tutor. And Mrs. J's got it set up real nice. Until we go back home with Heaven."

Heaven. I wonder when they stopped calling her Mom.

"We'll see," he says, turning to leave, and I smile a good-bye to them on the way out. Their laughter rings out as we hit the hallway. Maybe at us or maybe not. Who knows? It's the best defense they've got right now, laughing at all this. And they're going to need their defenses intact for a long while yet.

He writes his note, squeaking and wiggling the cart with every pen stroke. A sheen of dandruff rims his shoulders.

"So do you think that'll happen?" I ask.

"What?" He doesn't look up from the note.

"That they'll get to stay together?"

He shrugs. "Maybe, probably. Depends if the foster mom agrees to it. Knowing Mrs. J, she probably will."

"You know the foster mom?"

He smiles at me, lifting his head from the chart. "I am just full of surprises, Dr. Goldman."

The fire warms my numb, tingling toes. It's rude to have my shoes off, especially with my rather loud, purple argyle socks. But my feet are cold and I forgot my meds this morning, so I don't actually care. Eddie wanders over with a latte and a muffin for the couple at the next table and gives me a wave.

"Scotty coming in today?" I ask.

"Later," he answers. "Like four, I think?" Someone comes over to the register then, and he goes to greet them. I circle the last question on the last pretest in the last chapter of my RITE book. The exam is in two weeks. If I don't know it by now, I should probably hang up a different shingle. Folk singing maybe, if I could carry a tune and had made it past my first and last guitar lesson in eighth grade. I check the answer and do an invisible fist pump. Yes! Bring that bitch on! I am tempted to write a Facebook post about it, when the door opens, carrying a chill in its wake.

"Nice socks," he says, and I look up to see Mike.

"Hey, stranger," I say with a smile. "How was call?"

"Not terrible." He pulls off his coat and sits down next to me at an awkward angle on the settee. When he leans over to pick up my RITE book, the scent of warm pine follows him. "How are you doing on this?"

"Two weeks, baby. Ready or not, here I come."

Mike drops it on the table with an unceremonious thud, attracting some stares, and gives an apologetic grin. "You're going to kill it."

I put my feet back in my shoes, since my socks are burning now.

"So are you still decided on the forensic psych thing? Or did you decide that was too depressing after a few more seconds of thought?"

"Nope." I sip my coffee. "It's decided. One-year fellowship, doing it at the County. Signed, sealed, and delivered."

He gives me a dubious look. "You sure now?"

"One thousand percent. I already spoke with Dr. Grant."

"Then I'll accept the job in Buffalo," he says with equal finality.

We look at each other with matching, idiotic smiles. "So that's that then," I say.

"That's that." He looks up at the register to figure out his order. "How's Candy doing, by the way?"

"Pretty good. Better anyway." I spin my coffee mug around. "So do you have any plans for April?"

"April?" He leans back in the settee. "I don't know, why?"

"You want to go to Paris with me?"

"Paris?" He looks suspicious. "It wouldn't have anything to do with a certain annoying what's-his-name, would it?"

"Yes. I want you to go to the wedding with me."

"And why would I want to do that?"

"Because you're my boyfriend, of course. It said Dr. Goldman and Guest."

He raises his eyebrows, staring at me in amiable disbelief.

"Come on, it'll be fun! We can eat some croissants, see the Louvre... Hey, didn't you hear? I came into some money. So the trip's on me. Consider it a cultural experience."

He crosses his arms, his biceps bulging against his sweater. "So you're saying you want me to travel thousands of miles to make your ex-boyfriend jealous?"

I pause a moment. "Yes, that is precisely what I'm saying."

He considers it. "Well, okay then. I guess we're going to Paris."

Chapter Thirty-Six

Christmas lights twinkle down Elmwood as we drive off to the temple.

It's cold, colder than it was last year when my mother died. At that time, it still felt like fall, like the weather was holding out until the official winter solstice. So the snow at her funeral surprised us. Even in Buffalo, we weren't ready for it yet.

Scotty greets us as soon as we walk in. He and Mike shake hands with warmth, genuinely pleased to see each other. Scotty and Jean Luc tolerated each other. There's a difference.

"We're not late, are we?" I ask, walking past the rows of royal-blue seats (which look more comfortable than they feel, especially after you've been fasting all day, which is when I usually sit in them).

"No, no," Scotty says, sitting back down. "The cantor's here, and the rabbi's around somewhere." We sit in silence while the congregants, mostly elderly, file in, leaning on canes and walkers, hair silver and mussed from wool hats, their bulky coats half unzipped. They smile at us, the young people, then find their seat. Mike (who told me he hasn't been in a temple since seventh grade, for a Bar Mitzvah) appears completely at ease waiting in the pew, his dark-gray suit coat a touch snug in the shoulders. The soft plinging of guitar strings emerges from the pulpit. The rabbi leans toward his guitar like he's listening to a secret. Finally he stops tuning, walks up to the bimah, and we begin.

The service flies by. The prayers fall in an easy order: praying, davening, greeting the Sabbath bride. We sing, Mike in a deep baritone. The deep blue of the stained glass darkens with the night; the yellow glass sun mellows to a burnt orange. Scotty goes up to recite a prayer for Mom and then walks back down the center aisle to stares, his face flushed. When he reaches our seat, he puts the prayer book down, his hand trembling. It takes me back to his Bar Mitzvah all those years ago, his face young and nervous but triumphant—a real man.

"Good job," I whisper, and he raises his eyebrows with relief.

I can't believe it's been a year already. A year spinning by in the blink of an eye, all blending together: the spooky Halloween decorations (formally approved or not), Thanksgiving with Arthur gnawing his purloined turkey leg under the table, Christmas lights twinkling down the street. Signposts of our lives that go by, year after year, until we don't notice them anymore. But we are only offered so many of these, these first days of spring, birthday candles, Halloweens. Seventy or eighty harvest pumpkins in our lifetime if we are lucky. Or fifty-five, like my mother, if we are not lucky.

A year ago, we were driving to the gravesite in a limousine that smelled like old cigarettes, past fields dotted with new snow. We stood in the graveyard on an unaccountably pretty day. The sky was bright blue, snow clumped on the junipers, a flock of geese honking above us, reminding me that the earth doesn't stop being beautiful just because you're burying your mother in it. The rabbi chanted a prayer, and with hoarse voices and pale faces, we sang along with him.

Yisgadal, v'yiskadash, sh'may, rabah . . .

We chant together as a congregation now, as we did that day. A prayer of thanks to God. To say that in the midst of our sadness, we still acknowledge God, we still acknowledge that the world is beautiful. I pray for my mother and my father. And my birth mother, who died so many years ago. I pray for Candy, Janita. I pray for Tiffany. And yes, even for Dr. Berringer.

Standing there with my brother and with Mike, I am praying for us all. And for the cracks nobody can fix. The cracks that let the light in. The cracks so big we could fall right through them.

READING GROUP GUIDE

Dear Reader,

"We call her Jane, because she can't tell us her name."

The idea behind *The Girl Without a Name* came to me as a first line. Then Jane Doe sprang to life—a young African American girl, lying in a hospital bed with no idea of who she was or how she got there. She appeared to be a girl no one cared about. A girl someone had thrown away.

This central question looms throughout the book: Who is Jane Doe?

The search for the answer pitches us into a maze of smoke and mirrors. The closer we inch toward her identity, the further away we actually are. She may be a girl named Candy, a girl named Daneesha, or neither. Jane Doe is part and parcel of this topsy-turvy world, riddled with cracks, detours, and dead ends. A world peopled with a drug-dealing priest, a boy who fears the number six, and "clanging" patients. A labyrinth of art projects with hidden meanings, erroneous EEG reports, and the search for imaginary money.

Cracks run through every facade, and no one is exactly as

341

they seem. Dr. Berringer appears to be a handsome, happily married wunderkind from New Orleans. But scratch the surface and we see a recovering alcoholic in the throes of divorce. Zoe herself is a psychiatrist and Yale graduate who finds herself suddenly on probation and struggling just to control her own thoughts.

The world is veined with cracks, but these aren't always bad. As Leonard Cohen points out, "That's how the light gets in." These rifts are a natural part of life, like basic plate tectonics from seventh-grade geology. The earth is continually breaking open at fault lines in order to renew itself. But sometimes, the gap can swallow you whole.

In Judaism (Zoe's religion), there is a concept called *tikkun olam*, or literally "repairing the world." Zoe is doing her part by healing her patients and by striving to find out who this lost little girl is, even if she loses her job doing it.

But Zoe ultimately learns that not everyone can be saved. Not all cracks can be mended. And the world remains beautiful despite them, or perhaps because of them.

I hope you enjoy reading the story as much as I enjoyed writing it.

All my best,

SANDRA BLOCK

Discussion Questions

1. Can you relate to Zoe and her sometimes offbeat perspective on life? She often seems to use humor as a defense mechanism. Do you ever do this or know anyone who does?

2. Indentity is a central theme of the book, with Daneesha and Candy being an extreme example. In some ways, every person is made up of different personalities. Do you ever feel this way? Do you see this tendency in other chararcters?

3. "Cracks" are referenced throughout the book. Can you recall some points where these are mentioned and where it resonated with you?

4. Many of the characters in the book are cracked or broken somehow. Which characters do you see in this way?

5. Do you think cracks are always a bad thing? When can cracks be a positive part of life?

6. Did you suspect the ultimate villain in the book? What are the clues that lead us there?

7. How does Judaism play a role in Zoe's quest to find Jane

Doe's identity and in her journey to navigate the world after her mother's death?

8. *Tikkun olam*—literally "repairing the world"—is an important concept in Judaism. How do you think Zoe is doing this?

9. Do you empathize with Dr. Berringer at all? Do you understand Zoe's attraction to him?

10. Do you think Zoe belongs with Mike? Do you see him as a stabilizing influence in her life? Does she accept this or fight this?

11. Do you think Zoe and Mike will stay together? Should they get married?

12. Do you know anyone with ADHD? Did Zoe's struggle with this condition seem realistic?

13. Have you lost a parent or someone close to you? Do you understand what Zoe is going through?

14. Scotty has his own way of coping with his mother's death, different from Zoe's. Have you ever experienced this in your own family?

15. What do you think Scotty should do with his windfall of money?

When Zoe becomes obsessed with questions about her own mother's death, the truth remains tauntingly out of reach, locked away within her nightmares of an uncontrollable fire. She has no choice but to face what terrifies her the most. Because what she can't remember just might kill her.

Please see the next page for an excerpt from *Little Black Lies*.

Chapter One

She picks an invisible bug off her face.

A pink sore swells up, adding to the constellation of scabs dotting her skin, remnants of previous invisible bugs. Tiffany is a "frequent flyer" as they say, in and out of the psychiatric ward. She's been my patient twice already, both times delusional and coming off crystal meth. She does the usual circuit: emergency room, psych ward, rehab, streets, and repeat. A cycle destined to continue until interrupted by jail, death, or less likely, sobriety. Tiffany sits on her hospital bed staring off into space, the skimpy blue blanket over her knees. She is emaciated, her spine jutting out of the back of her hospital gown. A penny-sized patch of scalp gleams through her bleach-blond, stringy roots, due to her penchant for yanking out clumps of hair (otherwise known as *trichotillomania*, in case Dr. Grant asks me, which he will).

"I've got to go now, Tiffany. Anything else I can do for you?"

She doesn't answer or even look at me. Either she's psychotic or ignoring me or both, but I don't have time to figure out which because we're rounding in five minutes, and I still haven't finished my charts. I run down the hall to the nurses' station, which is in chaos. Jason and Dr. A, the other two psychiatry residents, are elbow to elbow in the tiny room, mint-green charts in precarious towers around them. The nurses jog around us, saying "Excuse me" too loudly, as they sort out meds and record vitals, ready to sign out, punch out, and get the hell out of Dodge as the seven o'clock shift drifts in.

Dr. A grabs an order sheet from the stack. "Did anyone discontinue the IV on Mr. Wisnoski?"

"Mr. who?" one of the nurses calls back.

"Bed nine. Mr. Wisnoski. This should be done expediently."

"Whatever you say," the nurse answers, putting on latex gloves and heading to the room. Dr. A's real name is Dr. Adoonyaddayt, and his first name is just as unpronounceable. So everybody calls him Dr. A. He has a strong Thai accent and obsessively studies an online dictionary to improve his vocabulary. He is, as he told me, "building a *compendium* of knowledge." Dr. A appointed Jason to be his "idiom tutor," to better connect with American patients. He used to be a neurosurgeon in Thailand but is slumming with us in psychiatry now because it's impossible for foreign medical graduates to get into neurosurgery here. Dr. A is easily the smartest of our threesome.

"I thought Wisnoski was mine," Jason says. "He's yours?"

"Mine," Dr. A answers, taking the chart from his hand. Jason is dressed to the nines as usual, with his trademark bow tie (he has more colors than I thought existed, a *compendium* of bow ties in his closet), bangs gelled up and bleached just so. Jason is gay to the point of cliché, which I pointed out to him over beer one night, though he disagreed. "I'm Chinese American. Cliché would be me tutoring you in math."

The new medical student (Tom?) hasn't picked up a chart yet. He watches us running around like beheaded chickens and yawns. I like to play a little game, figuring out which fields the medical students are headed into, which I can usually guess in the first five minutes. This one, surgeon for sure.

"Zoe," Jason calls out to me. "You got the new one?"

"Which one, Tiffany?"

"No," he says. "The transfer. Vallano."

"Oh, the one from Syracuse. Yup, I got her," I answer, grabbing her enormous chart, which tumbles open. "Dr. Grant's special present for me."

Jason guffaws, cracking open his own charts. "He sure does love you."

"Ah yes, such is my lot," I answer, flipping through her chart. It's obvious Dr. Grant doesn't like me, though I can't figure out why. It could be the Yale thing. But then again, maybe not. Could be a lot of things. Could be that I don't like him, and being a psychiatrist extraordinaire, he senses this.

Footsteps thump down the hall as Dr. Grant appears in the doorway. Beads of sweat mix into the curly hair at his temples from walking up ten flights of stairs. In my opinion, anyone who walks up ten flights of stairs on a daily basis needs a psychiatrist. Dr. Grant is wearing gray pants with a thin pinstripe and a checkered blue shirt, a combination that suggests his closet light burned out. He is a small, slight man. I could crush him in a thumbsie war.

"Ready to round?" he asks.

We file out of the cramped nurses' station, and the medical student strides over to shake his hand. "Kevin," he says.

Kevin, Tom, same thing. We stack the charts into the metal rolling cart and then Jason pushes it, clattering down the hallway. We pass by gray-blue walls, sometimes more blue than gray, sometimes more gray than blue, depending on the soot. The floor tiles are an atrocious teal blue (the approval committee was either color-blind or on mushrooms), dented and scraped from years of residents and food carts rattling down the hall.

"All right, first victim," Dr. Grant says, stopping just outside the room. Dr. Grant always calls the patients "victims" when we round. I haven't taken the time to analyze this, but it does seem peculiar. To his credit, he says it quietly at least, so the already paranoid patients don't get any ideas. "Mr. Wisnoski. Who's got this one?"

"This is my patient, sir," answers Dr. A. He calls everyone "sir."

"Okay. Go ahead and present."

"Mr. Wisnoski is a forty-nine-year-old Caucasian gentleman with a long-standing history of depression. He was found unresponsive by his wife after overdosing on Ambien."

"How many pills?"

"Thirty pills, sir. He took one month's dose. He was taken

by the EMT to the ER, where he underwent gastric lavage and quickly recovered."

"Meds?" Dr. Grant asks.

"Prozac, forty milligrams qd. He's been on multiple SSRIs before without success but had reportedly been feeling better on Prozac."

"So why did he try to kill himself?" Dr. Grant glances around and zeroes in on me, as usual. "Dr. Goldman?"

I'm still not used to the "doctor" thing, telling nurses "Just call me Zoe." "The problem is," I answer, "Prozac actually was effective."

Kevin is chewing a large piece of pink gum, which smells of strawberry. I can tell Dr. Grant is feeling the stress of ignoring this.

"Tell us what you mean by that, Dr. Goldman."

"Oftentimes a patient is most at risk for suicide when there is some improvement in functionality," I explain. "They finally have the wherewithal to commit suicide."

"That's right," he admits, though it pains him. We all head into the room, but it is empty, the patient's disheveled blue blanket crumpled on the bed. The room reeks of charcoal, which stains the sheets from last night's stomach pump. After some consternation, we discover from a nurse that Mr. Wisnoski is off getting an EEG.

So we move on down the list to the next room. The name is drawn in fat black marker into the doorplate. "Vallano." This is my add-on, the transfer.

"Dr. Goldman?"

"Okay," I say, ready to launch. "Ms. Sofia Vallano is a

thirty-six-year-old Caucasian female with a history of narcissism and possibly sociopathy on her Axis II. She has been in Upstate Mental Community Hospital since age fourteen for the murder of her mother."

"Holy shit" escapes from Jason, to a glare from Dr. Grant. Still, you can't blame him; she did kill her mother.

"Any other family members?" Dr. Grant asks.

"One brother, listed as a lost contact, one sister the same. The brother was reportedly injured in the incident."

"Go on," Dr. Grant says.

"After the closure of UMCH, she was transferred here for further treatment and evaluation," I continue.

"And," Dr. Grant announces, "possibly for discharge, pending our recommendations."

"Discharge, really?" I ask.

"Yes, really."

I slide her chart back into the cart. "Based on what findings? Has her diagnosis changed?"

"Well now, Dr. Goldman, that's our job to find out. She's been a ward of the state for over twenty years now. If she's truly a sociopath, I grant you, we may not be able to release her to society. If she's narcissistic, however, maybe we can." He skims through her old discharge summary. "From what I can see, UMCH has been kicking the can down the road on this one for a while now."

"She never went to prison?" the medical student asks, still chewing gum.

"Not fit to stand trial. Okay, let's see how she's doing." Dr. Grant knocks on the door in a quick series.

And there is Sofia Vallano, perched on the bed, reading a magazine. I'm not sure what I expected. Some baleful creature with blood dripping from her eyeteeth maybe. But this is not what I see. Sofia Vallano is a stunning mix of colors: shiny black hair, royal blue eyes, and opera red lips. Something like Elizabeth Taylor in her middle years, curvaceous and unapologetically sexual. They say the devil comes well dressed.

"Hello," she says with a smile. A knowing smile, as if she's laughing at a joke we aren't in on. She does not put down the magazine.

"Hello," says Dr. Grant.

"I'm Dr. Goldman," I say, extending my hand. My skin is damp in hers. "I'll be the main resident taking care of you, along with Dr. Grant, who's in charge. Just saying hello for now, but I'll be back to see you later."

"Okay," she answers and looks back down at her magazine. Obviously she's been through the likes of us before. A cloying scent rises off the magazine perfume ad on her lap. Redolent and musky.

We say our good-byes and all head back to see Mr. Wisnoski, who still isn't back from EEG.

"Who's next?" Dr. Grant asks. "Dr. Chang? Do you have anyone?"

"Yes, I have Mrs. Greene," Jason answers.

"Would you like to present?"

"Fifty-six-year-old African American female with a history of bipolar II. She came in today after a manic episode, now apparently consistent with bipolar I."

"And how was that determined?"

"Last night, she climbed onstage at *Les Misérables* to sing during one of the solos."

"Which one?" I ask, immediately regretting the question, which is not terribly relevant to the diagnosis and also tells me my Adderall hasn't kicked in yet.

"'I Dreamed a Dream,' I think," he answers.

"Ah, the Susan Boyle one," says Dr. A in appreciation. "I find that song most gratifying."

Dr. Grant surveys us all with incredulity. "Doctors, could you at least *pretend* to be professional here?" Dr. A drops his gaze shamefully, and Jason twirls his bangs. Kevin chews on. "Meds?" Dr. Grant asks.

"She was on Trileptal," Jason says. "Three hundred BID but stopped it due to nausea three weeks ago. The history is all from her sister because the patient is not giving a reliable history. Her speech is extremely pressured."

"Ah yes," Dr. A says. "In bouts of mania, actually,"—he pronounces this *act-tually*, with a hard *t*—"the speech is quite rapid, and one cannot get the word in edgily."

"He means 'edgewise,'" Jason explains.

"Ah, edgewise, so it is." Dr. A pulls the little black notebook out of his lab-coat pocket, where he jots down all his ill-begotten idioms.

Dr. Grant crosses his arms. One summer when I was in high school, my mom enrolled me in ADHD camp (sold to me as a drama camp) to boost the self-esteem of her ever-slouching, moody giant of a daughter. We played this game called Name That Emotion, where one group would act out an emotion and the other group would call out what it was. If I had to name that emotion for Dr. Grant assessing his crop of psychiatry residents, it would be disgust. We head to the next victim, our Broadway hopeful, but alas, she is getting a CAT scan, so we head back to see Mr. Wisnoski, who is *still* in EEG.

Dr. Grant looks supremely frustrated. "Anyone else to see?"

"I have Tiffany," I say.

"Oh, Tiffany, I know her. She can wait." He chews on the inside of his lip, thinking. "All right. I guess we'll finish rounds this afternoon. Just make sure you see all your patients and write your notes in the meantime."

So we split up to see our respective patients. The nurses' station has slowed to a hum now. I settle down to Sofia's chart, which is massive, not to mention the three bursting manila envelopes from UMCH, but at least I can feel my focus turning on. As I open the chart, the perfume card from the magazine falls out, the heady smell of perfume rising up from the page like an olfactory hallucination.

Acknowledgments

Rachel Ekstrom, my super-agent, who is there whenever I need her.

Alex Logan, who gave Zoe and me a two-book chance. I will always be grateful.

Julie Paulauski, who put her heart and soul into spreading the good word about my books.

Wunderkind (Tanya and Elena—wonder-twins activate!—and the whole team), who were both savvy and sweet in promoting Zoe in *Little Black Lies* and beyond.

All the folks at Grand Central, who made a newbie author feel like a best seller!

All my agent sibs (yes, that's you Sarah Henning, Amy Reichert, and Sarah [Br and Ju]) and all the other writer-reader-Twitter peeps who supported me.

All my friends (FB, roommate, and other!) who shared their kind words about my book and badgered their bookstores to carry Zoe.

My parents, who traveled in minus-nine-degree weather

to my book launch and gave me another warmer one in Florida. Who have my back, always.

Margie Long, for loving my kids and helping us always.

Charlotte and Owen, for being my sun, moon, and stars.

And finally, Pat, for hanging out with me on this crazy and wonderful journey.

ABOUT THE AUTHOR

Sandra Block graduated from college at Harvard, then returned to her native land of Buffalo, New York, for medical training and never left. She is a practicing neurologist and proud Sabres fan and lives at home with her family and Delilah, her impetuous yellow Lab. She has been published in both medical and poetry journals. *The Girl Without a Name* is her second novel.